THE WAYWARD COURSE OF TRUE LOVE

Miss Sarah Baxter was deeply, wonderfully in love. But the object of her ardent affection—the dashing Lieutenant Grenfell—was across the Channel, fighting England's enemies.

Thus Sarah was left alone to fight her own war: her father was determined to trade her hand in marriage for a title worthy of her dazzling beauty and bountiful fortune.

Sarah knew she would have to use her every wile and weapon and sly stratagem to defeat her father's design and deny the notorious Earl of Drakefield the dowry he desperately needed to save himself from ruin.

If only Sarah's own true love were not so far away . . . and her infuriatingly engaging enemy so temptingly near. . . .

THE
DANGEROUS
DANDY

by

Carol Proctor

A SIGNET BOOK

SIGNET
Published by the Penguin Group
Penguin Books USA Inc., 375 Hudson Street,
New York, New York 10014, U.S.A.
Penguin Books Ltd, 27 Wrights Lane,
London W8 5TZ, England
Penguin Books Australia Ltd, Ringwood,
Victoria, Australia
Penguin Books Canada Ltd, 10 Alcorn Avenue,
Toronto, Ontario, Canada M4V 3B2
Penguin Books (N.Z.) Ltd, 182–190 Wairau Road,
Auckland 10, New Zealand

Penguin Books Ltd, Registered Offices:
Harmondsworth, Middlesex, England

First published by Signet,
an imprint of New American Library,
a division of Penguin Books USA Inc.

First Printing, March, 1993
10 9 8 7 6 5 4 3 2 1

With love and deep gratitude to my family and friends for the generosity, the sacrifices, and the understanding that made this book possible. Special thanks go to Mom and Dad; Buddy; Mom and Dad Proctor; Gina McEuen; Barbara Tutone; Douglas Garrett; Margaret, Natalie, and Marla Dumont; Matthew Proctor; Laura and Michael Urbis; Alice, Wendell, Christopher, Grace, and Andrew Johnson; and of course, Drexel and Ed.

Deo optimo maximo

AUTHOR'S NOTE

To anyone familiar with the game of cricket, the discussions of it in this book will probably seem peculiar. Unfortunately, the language of cricket has changed dramatically in the past two hundred years. Most of the expressions we associate with the game date from the late nineteenth century. Therefore, they fall outside the time frame of this book. The colorful language of modern cricket was regretfully sacrificed to historical accuracy.

1

HE WAS QUITE possibly the handsomest man she had ever seen and she hated him. She hated him from the uppermost pinnacle of those carefully pomaded dark curls, marked with that one arresting streak of white down to the highly polished toes of his evening slippers. Dressed all in black, he might have been a silhouette except for the white ruffles about his neck and wrists, and for the pale face that stared arrogantly down at her. A jackstraw. A Bond Street beau. A fop. In short, a dandy!

"And of course, my lord, you have already met my daughter Sarah. A beauty, is she not?" Her father, rigged out in his finest flowered waistcoat and satin knee-smalls, was perspiring freely.

She lowered her eyes modestly and curtsied. After all, no one could see that she was gritting her teeth.

The Earl of Drakefield, although undoubtedly annoyed by his host's thrusting eagerness, bowed and murmured the requisite compliments. Well, at least *he* would not enjoy this evening either. She hoped that it might be the worst one of his life. Perhaps then he would go away and leave her alone.

Since their guest had been fashionably late, and her father was not one to delay his meals, they proceeded into dinner immediately. Had the occasion been different, she might have been amused by Drakefield's obvious irritation when her father urged dish after dish upon him. Didn't my lord wish to try the sweetbreads? Or the fricandeau of veal? Surely he was not about to refuse the lobster?

She was sorry that she had urged her mother to limit the

dinner to two courses. She had thought to shorten this painful evening for her own sake. Now she realized that Drakefield should have been made to endure a full and opulent three.

Once or twice she thought she saw him cast his glance about the room as if looking for help. *She* did not intend to give him any. She had kept her mouth firmly shut, and that was as far as she meant to go for amiability's sake. It would have been much easier if her parents had agreed to include other guests at this dinner, but her father had been firm on that point. Nothing was to interfere with the business at hand.

Her father, at least, seemed unperturbed by her silence. He was ready to supply all the conversation that dinner could require. Her mother, quite cowed by their guest's rank, tried meekly to put in a word or two, but earned herself only a ferocious scowl from her husband. He was sharing all the particulars of a recent transaction in which he had, by his foresight, profited mightily. Drakefield could not conceal his boredom.

Good! Let him be bored. As for herself, she found it hard to imagine just what other females saw in that arrogant, sneering countenance to attract them so prodigiously. The features were regular enough, if a little harsh, she supposed, but she could not like the deep-set, heavy-lidded gray eyes with their enigmatic expression. A manly, frank aspect was what she preferred. Who could love a man who so patently was already in love with himself?

Just then that unsettling gaze met hers, and she lowered her eyes modestly to her plate again. Wonderful! She undoubtedly had made him think that she, too, was swooning over his good looks.

"Your beauty, as ever, does not alter, your grace." He bent low over the aged beringed hand and kissed it before straightening gracefully.

"Hmph. You need not think to come over me with your bamboozling ways. You may save that for the strings of young misses who sigh over every one of your footfalls."

The regal chin lifted slightly and a pair of piercing gray eyes raked him from head to toe. "Still given to your affectation, I see."

He inclined his head slightly. "Some would call it my pursuit of an ideal."

"You are the picture of your father at that age. A handsome popinjay. I warned Celeste not to have anything to do with him, but even I could tell it would be of no use. Their elopement was the greatest scandal of its day."

"So you have often informed, me, Grandmother."

"The late duke warned her that she might not expect a penny from us if she wed the scoundrel. To do her credit, she never did ask," said the duchess with a trace of sadness.

She looked up at her grandson again, adding sharply, "And neither have you until now. Would do you no good— the money is all Wiltham's anyway. Under the hatches, are you? Following in your father's footsteps?"

"Your vocabulary never ceases to astonish me, Grandmother. I could hardly follow in my father's footsteps when the money had all vanished long before I inherited."

"You dress well for a pauper."

"One can always find some tailor to lend one credit . . . for a certain amount of time anyway."

"So you *have* come for money."

His face flushed slightly, but he remained calm. "Given that I've never asked you for a farthing, I should think that you would know better by now. However, since the fourth earl was my father, I understand and will forgive your suspicions. Actually, I have come to you about rather a different matter. I am in a fair way to repairing my fortune—but I would like your help." He glanced at the chair beside him. "May I?"

"Impossible! Yes, you may." For the moment curiosity had overcome suspicion. "How do you mean to do it?"

"Thank you." He drew up the chair and sat. "An heiress. Does that satisfy you?"

"A cit! I knew it would come to this—or worse. I am right, am I not? Do you expect me to launch her?"

His mouth tightened slightly, but he replied in an even

tone. "I expect you to do for her what you would do for any lady marrying into the family, yes."

"Who is she? Where did you meet her? Is she presentable?"

He sighed faintly. "Her name is Sarah Baxter. She is a school friend of Judith's youngest child—"

"I have always said that they should have had a governess for her instead—"

"It is rather more expensive, although I suppose that is a matter which you cannot appreciate. In any case, I met Miss Baxter at Eglantyne's coming-out ball." He tilted his head thoughtfully. "She is tall, fair, quite handsome, and will not embarrass you in any way."

"Who are her parents?"

"He made his fortune in shipping and they are quite what you'd expect, but your dealings will be with the daughter only."

She stared directly into his eyes. "Don't gloss over the matter. Do you expect me to spend months instructing her how to go on? I've no mind to take anyone by the leading-strings at my age."

He shrugged indifferently. "You may put your mind at rest. She does not smell of the shop. No, all I ask is that you countenance the match. There will be a court presentation undoubtedly, and I may need your help procuring vouchers for Almack's—"

"You should ask Wiltham. It is his approval that you require, not mine."

He said nothing but merely lifted an incredulous eyebrow.

She gave a short bark of laughter. "Well, I daresay that if I countenance the match, he will not oppose me. You may do your family credit yet, my boy. I promise you nothing. I must see the gel myself before I make a decision. There are those who cannot be taught, you know."

"Thank you, Grandmother." He rose and kissed her hand.

"Will I like this gel?" Again those shrewd gray eyes bored into his.

"I can hardly say—since I've only met her twice my-self."

To his surprise, she looked faintly alarmed. "Mind what you are about, then. Marriage is not a thing to be rushed into. You don't know enough about this gel to—"

"I know all I need to know about her. She does not re-pulse me, she will not mortify me, and she has a great for-tune." Meeting the duchess's look of outrage, he gave a bitter smile. "Marriage is a financial transaction, after all. My parents' own proved that."

"Drakefield—!"

He ignored the interruption. "I learned at an early age that it is unwise to close one's eyes to business when one enters into wedlock." He inclined his head to her again. "*Au revoir*, then, Grandmother."

She watched him go, her expression bleak. After the door closed behind him, she said softly, "Still wearing his heart on his sleeve for that other empty-pated little chit, after all this time."

Sarah paced the room busily and unthinkingly. Fashion-ably attired in a morning gown of white India muslin with an antique ruff collar and long, full sleeves, her tall, elegant figure seemed designed to command attention as she swished back and forth across the room. Its only other oc-cupant, however, was apparently preoccupied with her needlework. Every now and then a sudden idea would make Sarah pause for a few moments while she considered it. Each time it ended with a muttering and a vigorous shak-ing of her blond curls and the quick resumption of her pac-ing. Other than the sound of her tread upon the parquet floor, silence reigned.

Her companion, a petite brunette of deceptively fragile good looks, put down her sewing with a sigh. "Are you cer-tain that your parents will not relent? They have always seemed so kind to me. I cannot imagine that they would be so indifferent to your welfare."

Sarah shook her head again, with a certain weariness in it this time. "You do not understand. They are convinced that they are acting in my best interests. They are certain that I could not be as happy with a cornet as with a coronet." She did not smile at her own jest.

"But Sarah, they cannot force you to spend time in his company—nor can they compel you to accept him. What—do you think they would lock you in your room until you relented?" She giggled at the thought. "Confess it—this is simply a flight of fancy. We do not live in the Middle Ages, after all."

Sarah paused before replying. "How can I explain it to you? You cannot know what it is to be killed with kindness." She sighed. "First there would be the constant, reproachful looks and then the whispered comments. Something would serve to remind my mother of Lord Drakefield and she would burst into tears when in my company."

"But surely—"

"Despite all my resolve, it would begin to eat away at me. Within a matter of days I should feel like the most ungrateful worm that ever crawled upon the earth. My life would become unendurable until I weakened and changed my mind. It is inevitable," Sarah concluded with finality in her voice.

Her companion started to speak, then glancing at Sarah's face, hesitated and instead altered the direction of the conversation. "And there still has been no letter from Mr. Grenfell?"

"No, but I did not expect one. They undoubtedly are constantly on the move—and the mails are so unreliable . . ." She paused for a moment and continued, "I suppose that is the worst part of it—knowing that he might be lying wounded somewhere right now and that I should not hear of it for weeks or even months."

The other interrupted her hurriedly. "But Mr. Grenfell is of a good family, even if he is a younger son, and he may yet distinguish himself, given this terrible war. He may not possess a fortune, but neither does Cousin Everard. Your parents' objections seem so—"

"I have talked until I was blue in the face. It is entirely

useless. I am doomed to marry Drakefield, as long as he offers for me."

"I am sorry. I had no idea when I invited you . . . and of course, we had both looked forward to it for so long."

Sarah smiled sadly at her friend. "It is not your fault, Egg." Like most of the intimates of the Honorable Eglantyne Adstock, she addressed her friend by the preferred diminutive. "It is just that fate is against me."

"Cousin Everard is so whimsical. I did not at all rely upon his being here. And it was by the most unfortunate mischance that his eye happened to light upon you. Why, he has rejected scores of eligible females Mama has tried to bring to his attention, some with fortunes greater than yours. This one was too idiotish, this one was too vulgar, another was too loud—"

"I take it you think I should be flattered by his attentions," said Sarah dryly.

Eglantyne frowned. "You know very well that is not what I mean at all. However . . . I have often wondered if all Miss Draymore said of him was not somewhat colored by pique. You know how tales become exaggerated as they are passed around school. Mama has a fondness for him, after all, and I am sure that she could not if he were really so—"

Sarah shook her head. "I am sorry to say it, for he is your cousin—but I have found him to be everything he was reported. Conceited, arrogant—and concerned for no one but himself." Her eyes narrowed. "Insufferable! That is what he is. It is the worst muddle." Squeezing her eyes shut in anguish, she sank onto the green striped satin sofa. When she opened them again, her hopelessness was evident in her voice. "There is nothing I can do. If Drakefield offers for me, I shall be forced to accept. I suppose his affairs are so desperate by now that he will not hesitate."

Eglantyne decided to take the bright view. "Well, he hasn't offered for you yet," she said in a practical manner. "Moreover, though I do not say that Cousin Everard is agreeable, precisely, I do think that you may be doing him an injustice. When you come to know him better, you may find—"

"Wait!"

Eglantyne halted in the middle of her speech, surprised. Sarah's face bore a scowl of concentration. "There was something you said . . . "

Eglantyne waited patiently.

"He has not offered for me yet. Once he does, my fate is sealed. But what if something were to keep him from offering for me?"

"I do not understand."

Sarah's brow was clearing as the idea began to take form. "He does not know me well."

"But he knows you have a fortune—and you made a most favorable impression upon him."

"Exactly! It was but an impression. And you said that a great fortune was not enough to induce him to marry those he thought too vulgar, or too loud or too idiotish . . . and I mean to be all three!"

Eglantyne only narrowly avoided gaping at her. "But the matter is so near to being settled. He had dinner at your house last night, after all."

"Yes, and that means I must work quickly. Of course, if it comes to the worst, perhaps I might contrive to have him break the engagement—"

"But that would mean a scandal."

"Pooh!"

Eglantyne frowned with a sudden thought. "And besides, I hardly imagine that your parents would view such behavior with composure."

Despite herself, Sarah could not help blushing. "I believe that if I am careful, they will not suspect me." She smiled suddenly. "I do not know why it did not occur to me before. Drakefield's own fastidiousness will serve as my weapon against him."

"Sarah, it is the worst scheme I ever remember your contriving," said her companion quietly, folding up the neglected needlework. "How may I be of help?"

* * *

The difficulty with making plans lay in that Sarah could not know what Drakefield's next move would be. If he meant to ask her for her hand immediately, there would be no time to disillusion him and she must instead embark upon the more distasteful task of forcing him to break the engagement. It seemed unlikely that he meant to take the time to court her, and yet hope was possible, given that he had restrained himself at dinner the night before.

It was an impeccably groomed Drakefield who called at the Baxter residence early the following afternoon. Sarah glanced out her bedroom window to see a black phaeton drawn by a pair of black horses. Her mother had come upstairs herself to inform Sarah of her suitor's arrival.

"He wishes to take you driving in Hyde Park, my dear—imagine, for all the fashionable world to see!"

Particularly for his creditors to see, thought Sarah sourly, but she obediently rang for her maid and began to dress. At least he apparently meant to engage in some pretense of a courtship. She should be grateful for that, anyway. It would give her desperately needed time.

"And *such* a lovely carriage as he has—"

Which looks like an undertaker's hearse and for which he undoubtedly still owes a king's ransom.

"And his clothing—well, last night I thought I had never seen anyone finer but I must say, he just looks like a picture out of a magazine—"

And his tailor's bills, past, present, and future would probably consume the majority of our income.

"I am sure that I nearly swooned when he bowed to me—such a handsome gentleman—"

And well he knows it.

"My dear, you are such a fortunate young woman—" Surprise deprived her mother of speech for a moment. "But, Sarah, I thought you had disliked that bonnet!"

She had. An excessively high-crowned, wide-brimmed confection of lemon-colored chip, lined with satin, it had captivated her by the becoming way it framed her face. She had purchased it upon a whim, even though it contrasted with the prevailing modes. It wasn't until she saw it at home that she had realized that the five ostrich feathers upon it were certainly excessive and that instead of being ahead of the fashion, it could not be considered other than *outré*. Fortunately, her fond parents were not of the type to make their daughter wear her mistakes, and so the bonnet had simply reposed, neglected, in its box for some weeks. To suddenly wish to wear it now must seem rather odd.

"Do you know, I have changed my mind about it. I think it's really quite pretty," she said brightly.

"Well, I have always thought so myself," returned her mother uncertainly. "And no one can deny that it is most handsome on you."

And no one could deny that the effect was most striking, particularly when one considered that few would have been bold enough to accompany it with a pelisse in such a deep hue of lilac. But as Sarah cheerfully pulled on her lemon-colored gloves, her mother, trusting to her daughter's sense of fashion, saw nothing that might not be admired in the picture.

It was a small step, but it was a beginning. When she went downstairs, she had the satisfaction of seeing that Drakefield was not immune to the bonnet's effect. He recovered quickly, but not before Sarah had observed that momentary look of shock.

He, of course, was the pattern of fashion. Was there anyone else in London who had such gleaming top boots, such well-fitting inexpressibles, such high shirt points, or so snowy white a starcher? Of course, most gentlemen would have worn light-colored leather breeches, but as usual, Drakefield was clothed all in black. Another man similarly garbed might have looked ludicrous, but Drakefield looked elegant, if slightly ominous. If dress, like manners, made the man, then certainly she was in luck. Unfortunately, though far from indifferent to appearances herself, Sarah did not view it as the single most important quality in a future spouse. Even if she had no cause to resent him, the positive impression engendered by his appearance would have been blasted by the fact that he was all too clearly aware of his own perfection.

He bowed deeply. "Miss Baxter. I am honored that you consented to drive with me this afternoon."

She giggled. It had been part of Eglantyne's advice. "He has always said that he cannot abide giggling misses," she had told Sarah.

"Oh, la, my lord, it is poor *I* who am honored by your most affable invitation," she exclaimed between titters. Good. She sounded like a shopkeeper, and a particularly sycophantic and stupid one at that.

Her mother, gazing at her affectionately, perceived nothing amiss, but Sarah thought she detected a slight frown of consternation on Drakefield's face.

"Shall we go then?" he asked curtly. He did not add that Tavistock Square was a fair distance from the fashionable world of London and Hyde Park and that consequently, they had a long drive ahead of them.

One she was seated in the carriage, she could not help glancing longingly at the green fields that faced her home. Had she been with Alan, or anyone agreeable, she would have preferred a drive in the country. Of course, since she was with Drakefield, she would rather go to the Park. Anything was better than being alone with him, even with the groom behind them.

To her surprise, instead of turning in the direction of the Park immediately, he inclined his head toward hers, so that his shining black top hat nearly bumped her bonnet. "Would you care to see how they are progressing with Regent's Park? It is not much out of our way."

Startled, she assented, completely forgetting to giggle. It was the first time he had asked her a question as if he cared about the answer.

Accordingly, he turned the carriage to the north, and soon they were upon the New Road. She had her wish, after all. It was most interesting to see the developments, like Euston Square, which were springing up everywhere.

"It seems a shame," she breathed aloud without thinking.

"What seems a shame?"

"I mean, it seems such a shame to tear up these farms."

"I am certain that they are being handsomely rewarded

for their land. It is inevitable that London should grow, Miss Baxter. There is no way to stop it." He hesitated for a moment, then continued. "I suppose that we are fortunate at least to have a regent who, whatever his shortcomings, has the intelligence and taste to employ an architect of John Nash's ability."

Sarah, who was accustomed to hearing the regent vilified rather than praised, could only gape at him. Most appropriately, the truth of his words was now borne out, for they had reached the pleasing, pale stucco-clad buildings of the Park Crescent. He pulled the carriage to the side of the road for a minute and looked over his right shoulder at the far reaches of Regent's Park. "It looks as if they haven't accomplished much since I was here last. I suppose it is difficult to find anyone to invest in it. It will be a lovely place, though, if they hold to Nash's scheme."

The sun was out, the air was fresh and cool, and the notes of songbirds filled the air. With a shock she realized they had been enjoying a pleasurable drive so far. Drat it. He had caught her off her guard. She had not appreciated that under that sneering manner he must conceal a certain amount of charm—else why would silly girls always be falling in love with him? Well, she was too perspicacious to be taken in by it. She quickly must make up for lost time and hit upon a way to provoke him.

It took just a moment for the idea to occur. He himself had provided her opening. She giggled by way of prefacing her remarks.

"Yes, our dear prince must always be considered the arbiter of fashionable taste. His person is always so fine—I have been told that he never spends less than three hundred guineas on a coat." She fluttered her lashes at him. "I am sure that you must study everything he wears, as fashionable as you always are."

It was a slap in the face. No gentleman of fashion would seek to copy the prince, who was renowned more for the opulence of his clothing than his tastefulness, especially since his added years had inclined him to bulk. Now that he was no longer on speaking terms with Brummell, the regent had abandoned all pretense at restraint. It was even more insulting when one considered that Drakefield was universally acknowledged to be one of fashion's leaders.

Good, the sneer was quite pronounced now. "Shall we go on to Hyde Park?" he asked, giving the reins a shake, not bothering to wait for a reply.

Well, it was a start. As they began down Portland Place, she busied herself with thinking of other ways to antagonize him. By the time they reached the Park, she had thought of several. She giggled and simpered until she herself was becoming heartily sick of it. She called attention to her bonnet with little pats of her brightly gloved hand and was gratified to see a few open stares of curiosity. As they jostled among the other carriages for position, she wondered in carrying tones who the other occupants were. She was never to know whether he had intended to present her to any of his acquaintance, for whenever anyone seemed desirous of speaking to him, he merely gave a curt nod and whipped up his horses.

She had to admit a grudging admiration for his powers of self-restraint, for though he undoubtedly was embarrassed, he forbore criticizing her or even advising her as to proper behavior. She was enjoying herself so enormously that she was taken aback when his self-control finally broke. She had leaned out of the carriage to ogle a dashing young lady in a beautiful dark green barouche, surrounded by several admirers. "How pretty she is! And it is a lozenge carriage, of course! Do you happen to know her—"

She was not allowed to complete the sentence. "Be quiet! Do not gape that way. It isn't done." His face was pale with fury. He flicked his whip and guided the horses away from the Park.

What could have caused this outburst? Was it merely the straw that broke the camel's back? In any case, she should be glad. It had served her purpose.

They drove in silence back to Tavistock Square. Sarah could not help blushing a little at the thought of her behavior, but at least her escort was too preoccupied to notice. She congratulated herself on her scheme's succeeding so well. She thought it unlikely that Lord Drakefield would be troubling her any further. She was soon to discover she had been too optimistic.

Upon their arrival, as he handed her down from the carriage, he gave a low bow and said curtly, "Miss Baxter, might I hope that you are not engaged tomorrow? I should like to take you to meet my grandmother."

It was on the tip of her tongue to refuse, but her mother had seen their approach and was waiting fondly for her in the doorway. Well, at least it would give her another opportunity to be disgustingly effusive. "Oh, la, my lord, your grandmother—I am most honored. Oh, dear me—I shall look forward to it most *eagerly*, of course." She went on to thank him profusely for the drive and had the satisfaction of seeing the corner of his mouth curl down again.

Her mother, though she did not rush from the house to meet her, was fairly hopping up and down in her excitement. "Oh, my love! Did you have a nice drive? Tell me, whom did you see? Did I hear that Lord Drakefield wishes to take you to meet his grandmother tomorrow? Oh, there could be nothing more auspicious!"

"Drakefield! Is that who you said? Sally, don't tell me you've gotten your claws into the Black Dandy?"

A tall, gangly youth with a shock of unkempt red hair and bright blue eyes addressed her as he made his way hurriedly down the stairs.

She stared at him in frank amazement. "Bertie! What on earth are you doing here?"

2

"JUST A LITTLE trouble, don't you know." Her twin's gaze suddenly dropped so that he no longer quite met her eyes.

"What on earth have you been doing now?"

Mrs. Baxter, who might well have been justified in frowning, instead beamed fondly at both her children. "It is unfortunate, of course, but at least you will have a chance for a nice visit this way. I'll go talk to Cook and see if she couldn't fix you some tea. You two will have a great deal to say to each other, I am certain. Why don't you have a comfortable coze in the drawing room?"

With these words she departed, leaving her two children to trickle into the drawing room.

"The Black Dandy! What a stroke of luck. I must say I'm rather—"

She was the elder of the two by only forty-five minutes or so, but occasionally she found herself forced to stand upon her superiority in age. Now was such a time. After they both sank into chairs, she fixed her eyes coldly upon him and cut off his effusions.

"That's all very well, Bertie, but obviously we should be discussing your affairs instead of mine. What happened? Did you sound the fire alarum bell again?"

He gave a sniff of outrage. "The alarum bell! Why, that's schoolboy stuff! I'm not a runny-nosed lad of thirteen any-more—I'm at university now. Dash my wig, I should have thought you would have known better!"

"But you're not at university now," Sarah said pointedly.

He could not quite meet her eyes. "It was just a lark—just a bit of fun."

She waited in silence. His eyes still lowered, he added softly, "There was a pig, you see—"

"A pig?"

"Yes, and well . . . well, it somehow found its way into Dr. Wallis's chambers . . . "

"Bertie, no—you didn't—"

"And, we'd had a great deal of rain, so the animal was rather muddy—"

"Bertie—" In spite of herself, she was beginning to smile.

"And then you see, I suppose the poor pig was frightened, so it committed an indiscretion right in the middle of the doctor's Turkey carpet, of which he's so proud." He was smiling himself now at the memory.

She couldn't help laughing. "Oh, no!"

"Yes, and it bolted—pigs are amazingly fast, did you know?—and knocked over a table or two and smashed a few knickknacks."

She couldn't even venture a spoken response.

"And the worst of it was, I might never have been caught, except that it began squealing as soon as I set it down—didn't like the look of the room apparently—and who could blame it?—but I couldn't get the confounded animal to hush—and the more I chased it, the louder it became."

Completely forgetting her role as stern elder sister, Sarah remarked sympathetically, "You should have left."

"That occurred to me after I'd been pursuing the animal for a minute or so, but by then it was too late, I suppose. Everyone in college had heard the squeals and the crashes—"

"And the curses—"

He caught her eye now and a grin flashed across his face. "Yes, well, I won't deny it."

A sudden fear occurred to her, "Bertie, they didn't—that is, you still are—"

He smiled his relief. "Nothing like that, Sal, they just

sent me down for the rest of the term. Of course the doctor hauled me over the coals for a few hours along with Raspy and Sheepnose—" He interrupted himself to explain, "The farmer saw Sheepnose make off with the pig—was ready to lodge a complaint and all—we would have brought it back the next day."

Sarah shook her head. "You are fortunate they mean to allow you to return there—and I suppose it was all the result of some silly wager."

"It was not! Silly, that is—can't possibly expect a female to understand—and Wallis deserved it if anyone did." His eyes narrowed as a thought occurred to him. "And here, you're a fine one to talk. What about the time you wedged the headmistress's door shut and then blew smoke under the door?"

"That was different." Now she was the one who could not quite meet his eyes.

"And what about the time that you hid the chamber pot in—"

"I do not think there is any point in discussing the distant past in this way."

He gave a victorious laugh as the tea tray arrived. After it was properly settled and the servant had departed, he turned back to his sister, who was pouring the tea.

"Now, Sally, squeak!"

"What?"

"Tell your tale. Make your confession. You can have no secrets from me, you know. Quite a feather in your cap— the Black Dandy! Tell me, if he's to be my brother-in-law, d'you think he'll be willing to give me the name of his tailor?"

"Oh, do be quiet, Bertie," she said as she handed him his cup.

His surprise was evident. "What's this? I thought you'd be capering about, kicking your heels for joy! Why, there isn't a girl alive who wouldn't swoon at the thought of capturing such a prize. Lord knows enough of them have tried to snare the Black Dandy."

"Will you stop calling him that?"

He sipped his tea and, giving a satisfied sigh, leaned back in his chair. "I suppose you met him because of that snip of a girl you're such great friends with. I had given up hope on that prospect—though, of course, it is to your credit that he . . . "

His words faltered as he observed a tear running down Sarah's cheek. "What's this?" He extracted his handkerchief and handed it to her. She wiped her eyes fiercely.

"I do wish you could stop being such an idiot."

He waited silently. Blue eyes met blue eyes, though hers were reddened and still brimming over with tears. "He doesn't want to marry me, you buffle-headed clod! He needs money"—she gave a shaky laugh, —"And I am the least repulsive heiress he has happened to meet."

He gave his head an almost imperceptible shake. "There's more to it than this," he said softly, setting down his teacup.

She blew her nose in an unladylike manner.

"Tell me. That cornet you told me about at Christmas— the one you seemed so fond of—" His face suddenly darkened. "My god! Has he—"

She shook her head. "No. You are wrong. I am in love with Alan, that is all. And he is in Portugal, or Spain, or somewhere over there. And I do not know if he is wounded . . . or . . . " She gave a little sob and could not continue.

He leaped up and stepped over to give her a reassuring hug. "Here, now. All will be well, I'm certain of it." He patted her shoulder. "It can't be as bad as you seem to believe."

She sniffed and began wiping her eyes, making a brave attempt to recover.

He went over to pull his chair next to hers. "You'd better tell me about it from the beginning," he said.

He listened for over three-quarters of an hour to her sad, and occasionally disjointed, account. He nodded in all the right places and made encouraging noises just as he should, but Sarah had the feeling that his sympathies were not altogether with her, particularly when she shared her grand scheme with him. As soon as she had furnished him with the relevant details, she taxed him with it.

"Bertie, you know that you can never lie to me. You agree with Mother and Father, don't you? Even after all I've told you, you think I should marry Lord Drakefield, just so that I could have a title—"

He was shaking his head. "You're wrong, you know. When have I ever refused to take your part? It's simply that—"

"Well?"

His eyes met hers, pleading for understanding. "I've always helped you with anything you've asked me to do. At the same time, you are my only sister and I would not help you to throw yourself from the Tower if it occurred to you to—"

Her eyes flashed at him. "So, you think that my judgment is poor."

He shook his head again. "Not at all. It's simply that I cannot imagine our parents forcing you into a match against your wishes or best interests."

She tossed her head. "Oh, no, they would never force me to do anything, but you know how they can bully you with kindness."

"Well, confound it, Sally, they may have cause. You knew this Grenfell just a month before he was shipped over. Hardly seems long enough to become acquainted, let alone—"

It was time to stop this. "Bertie, have you ever been in love?" she asked sweetly.

"No."

"Then don't speak of things you know nothing about."

"Well, Miss High-and-Mighty, neither should you."

"What do you—"

"I mean that you judged and convicted Lord Drakefield even before you met him—and based it upon nothing but silly schoolgirl gossip."

Her color had risen alarmingly. "You forget I have met him, and found him every bit as insufferably conceited as he was reported to be."

He screwed up his forehead in a frown of concentration. "Well, it was hardly a fair trial, though, was it? And he might be the sort of fellow that improves upon acquaintance." He gazed squarely at her. "I don't mind telling you that his reputation is of the highest. Why, when I was in school, they were forever talking about the match against Eton where he scored over a hundred off his own bat in a single inning—"

"Cricket!" She sniffed contemptuously.

He darkened but continued doggedly, "And he's reputed to be a fine classical—"

She took him by the hand and gripped it tightly. "None of this matters to me, don't you see?"

He added despairingly. "And it means nothing to you that all the world observes and imitates him—"

"You don't understand." She drew a deep breath. "Were Lord Drakefield possessed of all the virtues in the world, it would not be enough to recommend him to me. There is only one man that I could ever consider marrying."

"I wish you could hear what you are saying," he said ruefully.

She abruptly rose, brushing against her teacup and knocking it off the table in her haste. Ignoring the sound of china shattering, she faced him, flushed with anger. "You have made your opinions plain. I will not trouble you further with my—"

"Sally. If your heart is truly set on this Grenfell, I'll do what I can to help."

She gave a delighted, tremulous smile. "Bertie! Oh, I knew I could count upon you."

"Well, don't cry at me. I've had enough of that for one day. We'd better go change for dinner, anyway. Wouldn't wish to keep *Pater* waiting. He's already bound to be a trifle mumpish about the pig."

As his sister hurried up the stairs ahead of him, he shook his head once more and muttered to himself, "And they say those of us with red hair have tempers."

The next day found Sarah more nervous than she would liked to admit. It would be the first time she had ever met a duchess, and the dowager duchess of Wiltham's reputation was formidable. Bertie had attempted consolation by assuring her that the duchess would probably be easy to offend, but unfortunately that was not what was worrying Sarah.

She hoped she had as much resolution as anyone else in the world, but she did not know if she could bring herself to be deliberately rude to an elderly lady, even though it might be a quick way to scotch the match. She was prepared to undergo all sorts of trials and sufferings for Alan's sake, she was prepared to face society's ostracism, but this seemed rather to break the pale.

At the same time, it might be possible that Drakefield was only waiting for his grandmother's approval to make an offer. If Sarah passed muster, it might ensure her speedy wedding.

An easy way to make a bad impression would be to wear the wrong sort of clothing. Sarah could don one of her satin evening gowns and explain to her mother that it was the usual sort of garb one wore to meet a duchess. If she were fortunate, Drakefield might not even notice the rich lace peeping from beneath her pelisse. If she added her diamond necklace and the matching bracelet also, she would need to do very little to convince the duchess of her vulgarity.

Knowing this, it defied logic that she should have worn instead a simple dress of fine india jaconet in white, ornamented by nothing more than a ruff of lace around the throat. She had chosen a bonnet of white chip ornamented by a single ostrich feather, edged with blue. Since the day was fair, she draped a blue silk scarf negligently about her shoulders. Blue slippers and blue kid gloves finished the ensemble. She wore no jewelry save for the gold locket which contained one of Alan's reddish-brown curls. Her mother might be disappointed, but Sarah knew that she looked the picture of elegance.

Bertie had intended to busy himself about the entry in hopes of catching a glimpse of Lord Drakefield, but his mother had vetoed this idea with a firmness unusual for her. Nothing was to interfere with Sarah's courtship.

Sarah herself was feeling heavyhearted, and her spirits sank further upon Drakefield's arrival. His surprise and approval of her appearance was evident, though he made her only the standard sort of compliment. Why on earth had she let vanity dictate to her? Now the only way left to alienate the duchess was through her conduct. It would be a painful afternoon.

It was a fair distance to Bruton Street, but Sarah hardly noticed the time, since she was full of her own thoughts instead. It was too difficult to giggle and simper, and fortunately Drakefield was not providing any openings. He seemed preoccupied, and ventured no more than a polite remark or two. Most of the drive was accomplished in silence.

The duchess's house was just as imposing as Sarah had feared it might be. From the arrow-headed iron railings about it to the statuary atop it, it proclaimed that this was the residence of a person of importance. But Sarah hardly had time to notice the fine Palladian facade of dressed stone before she stood in the magnificent arched entry and was ushered into the drawing room by the most majestic butler she had ever encountered.

In one corner sat a tiny woman, fine-boned, with classical features that must once have been beautiful. She looked frail until she raised her eyes to them and Sarah felt the force of her gaze.

"Good afternoon, your grace. May I present to you Miss Sarah Baxter? Miss Baxter, my grandmother, Her Grace, the dowager Duchess of Wiltham."

Without thinking, Sarah curtsied, murmuring the required pleasantries, then stepped forward to take the hand which the older woman extended. There was surprising strength in that bony hand. The gray eyes which blazed out at her held an unfathomable expression.

"Leave us, Drakefield."

Sarah was surprised to see that he quietly complied. She just managed to restrain a sigh of relief. With him gone, she need not take up the pretense. With luck she might offend the duchess without being deliberately vulgar.

"Please be seated, my dear. I am afraid that my neck will tire from looking up at you. Are all your family so tall?"

"Without exception, your grace, we *are* all so fortunate," she replied, taking the gilt-and-embroidered chair which the duchess indicated.

A smile rose to the duchess's lips, but she did not speak for another moment, instead using the time to study Sarah. Sarah chose to meet the other's gaze with some defiance, lifting her chin a fraction of an inch as she did so. Her cheeks pinkened with emotion, but she still held her tongue.

The duchess spoke abruptly. "My grandson tells me that you and he are to make a match of it."

Sarah's color deepened, but she still refused to drop her eyes. "He has not confided those plans to me, your grace."

To her surprise, the older woman let out a chuckle. "Do you know, I think Drakefield may have a surprise waiting for him. He told me that your father was a merchant. Who are your mother's family?" She paused, and added, "If you do not mind my asking."

Well, if she expected Sarah to be ashamed of her origins, she would learn differently. "My mother's family live in Uxbridge. They are engaged in the corn trade and are quite successful," she added defiantly, ready to pounce on the duchess's objections.

"Are they Quakers?"

Sarah was surprised by the question. The duchess must be extraordinarily well informed. "No, although I know that many of their associates are." Her mother still had many Quaker friends, some of whom had involved her in their various reform societies.

"Have you any brothers or sisters?"

"One brother. My twin." Did she mean to ask Sarah the size of her fortune next?

"How old are you?"

"Eighteen." She did not like the speculative look in the

duchess's eyes, so she felt impelled to remark, "I finished school last year."

"Seven years, then. It is a good gap." The duchess did not explain her remarks. There were a few moments of silence while the older woman ruminated. At last she lifted her gaze and seemed to notice Sarah's hostility, as if for the first time. She smiled and stretched out her hand to Sarah.

"Come now, pray do not be offended with me. I cannot plead age as an excuse, for I have always been plain spoken."

Sarah was unable to refuse this candid appeal. She put her hand out, and the duchess took it and patted it.

"You see, Drakefield has asked me for my help in one or two little matters, and I felt that I must make sure of you before I committed myself." The gray eyes met Sarah's directly, and again the latter was jolted by the power that radiated from this delicate-looking creature.

"I daresay that this match does not meet with the idea of romance, which all you young people seem to regard so highly nowadays." She paused to marshal her thoughts, then continued. "It is perhaps too early to tell anything, but in my opinion you and my grandson may have qualities that might complement the other. To my way of thinking, there may exist the possibility for a good marriage, given a basis of mutual respect and affection— "

Sarah could listen no more. She tried to interrupt, but was not permitted to do so.

"—Which must grow over time." She still retained Sarah's hand in her own and now she squeezed it forcefully. "I think that you could both benefit, so I ask you to consider well what you do. Above all, do not act hastily."

Tears had sprung up to Sarah's eyes. It was as if the duchess could read her very thoughts. The older woman released her hand, and Sarah fumbled in her reticule for a handkerchief. She could no longer meet those level gray eyes. Drat it! She had the duchess's approval.

She passed the rest of the afternoon as if she were an automaton. Indeed, her mind was so far away that she hardly noticed their farewells or the carriage ride back to

Tavistock Square. Again her companion did not seem to notice her omission. It wasn't until they had arrived back at her home that he ventured to comment that his grandmother had been most taken with her. Sarah awoke instantly to her danger, then realized that he was hardly likely to ask for her hand on a public street with his groom watching. She murmured some sort of response, and was aware that his eyes were regarding her keenly. "She said that she will endeavor to procure vouchers for Almack's next week, if you should wish it."

It was unprecedented for the duchess to introduce Sarah to society before she became Lady Drakefield; in fact, it was quite peculiar. Of course, it might mean that she expected the engagement to have become official by then.

Sarah's face flushed. To attend an assembly at Almack's was quite beyond anything she had imagined. The portals of that famous institution were held tightly shut against cits and the rest of the newly rich. Even high birth was no guarantee of admission. The seven patronesses bestowed their vouchers for the weekly balls upon the fortunate few with a whimsicality born of absolute power. It was thrilling to know that she might be among the select. It was also humiliating to realize that the invitation had nothing to do with her own virtues or abilities, but only because of this man whom she despised. She suddenly recalled her role.

"Oh, la, my lord! What a . . . what an honor! I declare, I may faint! Why, I don't know how I will contrive to sleep between now and then. My heart is pounding so that I can scarcely breathe!"

As she fluttered her eyelashes at him, she had the satisfaction of seeing his lip curl downward in a scarcely disguised sneer of contempt. Almack's, indeed! What could provide a better opportunity for her to offend and, if necessary, humiliate him? Eglantyne, who had attended balls there before, had told her of the strictness of the rules: no one was allowed to enter after half past eleven; no one was permitted inside without a ticket, even if they were on the list; and dress for the occasion was strictly prescribed.

Also, she had told Sarah how it felt to have the haughty eyes of the patronesses constantly upon the newcomer to see if there were any violations of convention. Why, it would be child's play to commit a gaucherie or two in such a situation.

With such an opportunity before her, it was easy to form an optimistic frame of mind. Even more fortunately, Bertie was not at home to give her conscience any further prods. She had a sense that despite the tragedy of having secured the duchess's approval, things now might very well fall into place. As if to confirm this happy thought, she found a letter from Alan waiting in her chamber. With a sigh of satisfaction, she closed her door and locked it and settled down to read the laboriously written words

                                                    15 January

          My dear Miss Baxter:

          Although I am alive to the impropriety of it, the memory of your sweet importunities has overcome my better judgment, and so I take pen in hand to write you this letter.

          The passage went well, lasting just ten days, although I suffered somewhat from *mal de mer*. The conditions here in camp are worse than I may describe to you, and the weather has been detestable. I am heartily tired of mud. Food is insufficient both for man and beast.

          The worst part is that we have yet to see any real action, and I find the waiting intolerable, as do the rest of the new arrivals. The seasoned campaigners only laugh at us and say that we will sing a different tune once we are in battle, but I cannot think so.

          I hope that this letter finds you and the rest of your family well.

                                                    Yours & c,

                                                    Alan Grenfell

Sarah turned it over in her hands. There was no extra sheet tucked in cunningly somewhere. The missive was disappointingly brief, and as a love letter it left a great deal to be desired.

As soon as the disloyal thought arose, she crushed it. His conscience was troubling him, after all. Why, he had mentioned it in his first sentence. And indeed, even her parents, whose notions of behavior were not at all strict, would be shocked to know that she was carrying on a clandestine correspondence with a single gentleman. If it had not been for her own ingenuity and the help of a willing maid, Sarah would have had no way to receive his letters. Doubtless he felt that he must exercise circumspection in case of discovery.

Obviously, he meant for her to read between the lines. He was unhappy—might that not be at least partly the result of having to forswear her company? There must be comfort, too, in knowing that at least of this date, he was still safe and well. Of course, the letter was over a month and a half old. Tears rose to her eyes at the thought. She hadn't even thought to notice how carefully he had hidden all his fears from her—there was no mention at all of them in this letter. You might think he was almost unaware of the dangers he faced. No, his feelings ran too deep for him to pour them glibly out onto paper. The very existence of this letter showed that his thoughts were very much with her, and that even at this distance he was trying to shield her from anxiety. She had to apply a handkerchief to her eyes at the thought. How noble he was, and how sensitive! Was it any wonder that he had captured her heart with such ease or that she could hardly bear to even look at another gentleman? She gave a little sob. A tap sounded at her door.

She thrust the letter quickly under a pillow. "Come in."

Bertie entered, a cheerful expression upon his face. "I say, I just saw the most bang-up pair of horses at Tatt's. I wonder if *Pater* would lend me enough of the ready to have a proper turn-out? Of course, I'll have to let him recover from this pig episode first." Belatedly he noticed her reddened eyes and nose. "Offended the duchess, did you? I thought that was what you wanted, Sal. Still, best to make a clean break of it, what?"

"Oh, Bertie." She shook her head. "The duchess liked me." She wiped her eyes again.

"Hm. This is a bit of a poser." His face brightened suddenly. "Well, no sense in worrying about it now. It's time to dress for dinner."

The room, although large, was dingy and badly lit. Tubes, pipes, beakers, and all sorts of unidentifiable apparatus littered the tables, chairs, and floors. The earnest young man with the serious expression busied himself with a set of bellows while he carefully studied the glass-enclosed flame.

"You see, I think that if I increased the air to the flame, it would keep the gas from igniting, but of course, more experiments are necessary, and I really have a great deal of work to do before I could possibly create a practical working model."

The exquisite in the corner, incongruous in his black evening dress, gave a slight yawn of weariness. His face was pale with fatigue, the lines under his eyes were deeply marked, and his hair was in an unwonted state of dishevelment. "Forgive me, Johnson. It has been a long day."

The other glanced at his pocket watch and exclaimed, "Why, it's well after four in the morning. You should have told me. I keep such odd hours myself that I scarcely notice—"

Drakefield waved a negligent hand at him. "It is of no importance. I have been most interested by everything you have had to say. I only wish that I had some capital to back you."

Johnson shook his head. "You've done more than enough. Why, I daresay I would have been forced to close my laboratory months ago if it hadn't been for your—"

"My motives are purely selfish, old fellow. I don't think there's a more capable fellow in England. The demand for coal will only increase as time goes on—with luck, we could both become wealthy men."

The other shut off the flame and turned to Drakefield, his face lowered. "I know that I could find the solution—with your help—if only I had the time."

Drakefield smiled at his friend. "Come, you must spend your time working upon that for which you are paid. I only regret that I don't have the blunt to—"

Johnson shook his head slowly. "None of this would have been possible without your help. I should not have had a laboratory now. When I think—if only you had explained your situation to me . . . "

Drakefield smiled again, but this time it was with bitterness. "Well, my situation is shortly to improve. I'm to become leg-shackled to an heiress."

Surprise was evident in Johnson's features. "Oh." Feeling that he must elaborate, he searched his mind for a moment, then added, "Congratulations."

Drakefield heaved an unexpected sigh. "You might offer condolences rather." He caught his friend's eye and grimaced. "I suppose I am ungrateful to feel this way. I should be glad I was able to find a passable-looking chit of eighteen with a large fortune who was interested in purchasing a title."

Johnson's honest face contracted into a frown. "I must say, it does not sound so terrible to me."

"Yes, but you have no estate to maintain, no tenants, no servants dependent upon you." One side of his mouth twisted wryly. "You cannot know what it is to be a prisoner of your birth."

"Well!" Johnson extinguished the lamp at the end of the table. "I may not be able to offer you lavish hospitality, but I can give you what you need, and that's a drop of good highland whisky. It will help steel your nerve. Come upstairs with me."

3

"MADEMOISELLE BAXTER! What a pleasure to see you and your friend!" Madame Vauban's eyes brightened as she hurried forward to meet one of her favorite clients and to usher her personally into her salon. The day was dismal and gray, and her salon had remained distressingly empty all morning. Miss Baxter might not be a leader of fashion and her taste in clothing might tend unfortunately toward the conservative, but she was not afraid to order in quantity, and more important, her bills were always paid on time. What was more, her tall and elegant figure displayed Madame Vauban's skill to a nicety. If she might only shine farther afield, she would prove a marvelous advertisement. Of course, if the gossip that had reached the modiste's ears was true, it was possible that Miss Baxter was upon the brink of just such an opportunity. Madame Vauban had learned in her fifteen years as a modiste that it was never wise to ignore rumor.

"Ah, I see that your delightful mother is not with you today. I hope that she is not ill?"

"No," replied Sarah unblushingly, "she is busy elsewhere and I needed some new dresses rather urgently, so Miss Adstock was kind enough to accompany me."

The young ladies were properly chaperoned by their maids, but the dressmaker's eyes narrowed thoughtfully for an instant. It seemed there was some mischief afoot. Ah, well, perhaps it was just a young girl's need to assert her independence. There was no fear that the bills would not be honored, after all.

"I am greatly relieved to hear it. Would you care for coffee?" As they shook their heads, she led them to red plush chairs and added, "And how may I help you today? There is a demi-toilette of the most *ravissante*—but of course, still in Miss Baxter's excellent style—"

Sarah interrupted her, and this time she could not help pinkening just a little. "I am afraid that I am looking for something out of my usual mode—something rather more . . . something rather more striking."

Madame Vauban could not help blinking as she digested these words. Suddenly it all became clear to her. Miss Baxter, having made such a notable conquest, now intended to cut a dash (and what could be more reasonable?). This would require many new gowns, and then there would be the trousseau . . . Madame had already begun adding up pleasing figures in her head.

"In fact," Sarah continued, "since I am to go to Almack's this week, I should like to look at any gowns you have already made up."

"*Merveilleuse*! Ah, mademoiselle, I have the most perfect frock—a gossamer silk in the very palest shade of yellow—very beautiful, and very *jeune fille*—"

Sarah cut her off ruthlessly. "I would prefer to see a gown in a bright color."

Eglantyne made a choking sound deep in her throat, and the dressmaker could not help looking at her with an appeal in her eyes. For a young unmarried lady to go to Almack's in a gown other than one of white or pale pastel was simply not done. The dressmaker cleared her throat and made a brave attempt. "Mademoiselle Baxter, I can understand your sentiments, and applaud them, and if it were a ball anywhere else—"

"I am quite certain," Sarah told her firmly. "Do you have anything in red perhaps?"

The dressmaker fairly reeled under the blow. "But Mademoiselle," she protested, "you must consider—"

"I have considered," said Sarah, "and I am very sure of what I want. Now, have you any dresses to fit my needs or not?"

The modiste was momentarily confounded. Could it be

that Miss Baxter was so unaware of convention? It would be like a dream come true to have one of her gowns appear at Almack's—but if it were totally unsuitable, it might well kill custom instead of increasing it. Looking at the set of the young lady's chin and the glint in her eyes, she realized, hopelessly, that all her protests would be useless. Moreover, she could not take the risk of offending one of her best customers.

"I will go and see, mademoiselle," she said heavily, and disappeared into the back of the showroom.

There were many lovely and suitable gowns, she thought, rummaging among her creations. What a pity! What odd idea could have taken possession of Miss Baxter? Surely any lady would wish to look her very best while on the arm of the Black Dandy!

As the thought entered her mind, she smote herself on the forehead. What an idiot she had been. Miss Baxter was far cleverer than she had previously imagined.

Was it not true that almost any young lady would pale into insipidity on the arm of such a partner? A young lady in a pastel dress would probably vanish next to such a striking gentleman, particularly with his insistence upon being garbed all in black always. Madame Vauban could almost laugh at her own stupidity.

How could Miss Baxter expect to hold her own except by wearing dresses in the most vivid hues? How many scores of pastel-clad girls had been led upon that infamous arm, only to vanish forever into obscurity? Miss Baxter meant to be set apart—as his future countess, she had the right. *She* would be noticed. She would make an impression upon society. In fact, given that she wore dresses so well, she might even set a fashion.

And though her curls were fair, those unusual dark brows and the vividness of those dark blue eyes meant that she could wear colors well. In fact, they fairly demanded it. Madame Vauban could not imagine why she had not seen it before. Living all these years among the English must have dulled her sense of fashion.

She pulled dresses from the rack and loaded them upon

her assistant until the poor woman fairly staggered from them. She surveyed the remainder to see that she had neglected nothing. A sudden thought occurred to her, and with a cry she reached to the back of the rack to extract a hitherto neglected creation. After executing it, she had feared that it was too daring, that it conflicted too greatly with the current modes. Now she realized that it had only been lacking the right opportunity. She carried it in triumph into the showroom.

She was rewarded by the simultaneous gasps which sprung from the lips of the two young ladies. Sarah added enthusiastically, "Exactly what I had in mind!"

The red silk net frock, edged with black and worn over a red satin slip, was pretty enough, though rather unremarkable except for the bold notion that had seized Madame Vauban of embroidering it with yellow roses about the neck and hem.

"Oh, Sarah, you cannot—" breathed Eglantyne.

"May I try it on?" asked Sarah.

After this had been accomplished, the modiste, fairly bubbling over in her enthusiasm, had other recommendations to make. She had another evening gown in mind. She would not recommend it for anyone except a lady of Miss Baxter's height and bearing and coloring. Also, if Mademoiselle Baxter cared to consider the purchase of a walking dress . . . In a few moments, fabrics and fashion plates were laid out before them, while Madame exhibited various sketches and discussed trimmings. Eglantyne, who had remained unwontedly silent during this whole escapade, looked apprehensive, but Sarah entered into all these ideas with enthusiasm.

It wasn't until they were in their carriage that Eglantyne broached the subject.

"Sarah, I know that your parents are most . . . most generous, but do you not think they will object to your purchasing so many new clothes when you really have no need of them?"

"Pooh! I shall tell them it is necessary since I am moving

in elevated circles now. It is their desire for me to do so, after all."

Another circumstance was troubling Eglantyne. She looked at her friend with surprising diffidence. "Forgive me, but if you succeed in driving away Cousin Everard, and so never wear these clothes again, will they not object?"

"It will not matter then," said Sarah dreamily, "for I shall be engaged to Alan and I shall not give a fig for dresses or anything else as trivial."

It was unfortunate that her shopping expedition had induced a state of complacency in Sarah. She awoke the next morning in a sunny mood, which was not affected in the slightest by the pouring rain outside. She was not even perturbed by the realization that Drakefield had promised to call upon her today. It was a pity that none of her new morning gowns would be ready for some time yet, but of course, her giggling and simpering alone might yet give him a distaste for her.

She was in a buoyantly optimistic mood which remained unmarred even though Bertie insisted upon peeping between the drawing room curtains to admire her beau.

"I say! What a coat! D'you think you could find out the name of his tailor? And I wonder what he calls that style of tying his cravat? You know, looking at him, you'd never suspect he hasn't a feather to fly with. He looks very fine— don't mean to go driving today, I suppose. Rather damp."

"My brother the rattle," commented Sarah, but she was feeling too cheerful today to exercise genuine sarcasm upon him.

"Since *Mater*'s not about, would you mind if I stayed? You needn't introduce me—it'll be enough to say that I was in the same room."

His worshipful attitude was a little irritating, but Sarah refused to let it bother her. "I do not mind. In fact, if you wished to remain for his entire visit, I should be glad."

He shook his head ruefully. "I daresay the parents would take it in dudgeon."

He was not permitted to elaborate, for at that moment

Drakefield was announced and shortly afterward entered the room. Sarah had to admit grudgingly that Bertie had some reason for his praise of the man—at least for his praise of Drakefield's dress. The rain was sheeting down outside, and yet Drakefield looked as if not a drop had touched him. He carefully furled his umbrella and handed it to the departing butler before crossing the room to kiss Sarah's hand.

"Oh, la, my lord. What an honor to see you today."

He looked up and caught Bertie's awe-struck gaze and cast a quizzical look at Sarah.

"My lord, may I beg to make known to you my brother, Bertram? Bertram, this is Lord Drakefield."

He looked surprised for a moment but quickly recovered. Without any obvious reluctance, his lordship extended his hand, which was caught heartily by Bertie's.

"By jove! What an honor, your lordship. It seems I've heard about you all my life. There was the time in the game against Eton where—"

Drakefield smiled slightly. "Are you a cricketer yourself?"

Bertie nearly blushed. "Not in your class, my lord, but I did play for Winchester."

"You must join me sometime, then. I play for the M.C.C. now."

Bertie, who was overwhelmed by this condescension, could only stammer a reply. Sarah, who had never seen Drakefield when he was exerting himself to charm, observed this interchange through narrowed eyes. Could it be that he did not know that she had a brother? If he had thought she was her parents' sole heiress, he was undoubtedly severely disappointed. He did not show it in the least. She might have expected him to be cold to Bertie, even under the best circumstances, and yet he was at his most affable. She could not comprehend it. Of course, Bertie held a high opinion of him also. Perhaps Drakefield was kinder to his own sex than to hers.

Bertie, still overcome, was bowing his way out, murmuring various disjointed phrases, and generally appearing to be an idiot. Drakefield turned and observed her scrutiny of her brother. Her opinion must have been too evident, for something flickered in his eyes and he gave a half smile of understanding. It startled her into the realization that she had been perilously close to abandoning her act, so she giggled and rushed forward to catch Bertie's arm as he exited.

"But, Bertram, you must tell my lord Drakefield of your other scheme." Her brother gazed blankly at her, as still clinging to his arm, she turned eyes upon Drakefield. "My brother is so timid, you see, he would not ask this for himself, but he means to select a pair of carriage horses at— where is it? Tatt's, did you say? And I am certain that he would be most grateful for your advice."

Bertie just managed to stifle an oath. His eyes were about to pop from his head at this blatant piece of manipulation. Drakefield's black brows had drawn together sharply. Good!

"I am not considered an expert in the matter of horseflesh, but I would be happy to accompany you to Tattersall's if you should wish it."

It was a magnanimous offer, and Bertie was too overwhelmed to manage more than a bow by way of response. He fled quickly, before Sarah might force him into an even more embarrassing position.

Abruptly she realized that she was in the room alone with Drakefield. He was regarding her with a serious expression. Her heart began to pound. Drat it! She hadn't realized the danger before. This was the result of overconfidence.

"Miss Baxter, I am glad we are alone, for I would like to speak to you about a matter which concerns both of us."

He had his grandmother's approval. There was nothing now to keep him from proposing, after all. Of course, as she had suspected, the trip to Almack's was dependent upon their being engaged. She must stop him, quickly, now!

"You see, Miss Baxter, I ask that you will do me the honor of—"

With a shrill giggle she rushed over to him, and taking him by the arm, squeezed it. "Oh, my lord, I too am glad we are alone, for I have something most important to ask you also!"

She saw with satisfaction that shock had silenced him. She simpered at him. "It is most urgent that I visit the milliner's today. I have ordered several new dresses, you see, and how oddly they must look with one of my shabby old bonnets!"

He was smiling slightly now. "Miss Baxter, I think that I may safely say that the matter concerning which I wish to speak to you may take precedence over a bonnet."

"La! Just like a man! You would not say so if you were female, I assure you!" She was already rushing from the room. "Let me call Mary and have her bring my cloak."

She was already in the hall. He could say nothing with the servants about them. He protested again, "But it is raining furiously outside. Would you not prefer to wait until—"

"Pooh! I am not afraid of a little water," she called as she fled up the stairs.

Once in her chamber, she felt like flinging herself down upon the bed in her relief, but it would hardly be consistent with the sense of urgency she had attempted to convey. She called for her cloak and a bonnet. She was safe for the moment, she thought, as her maid helped her on with them. The biggest danger had lain in her own complacency. She was vulnerable now, and would have to keep her wits about her.

He was unlikely to ask for her hand when his groom was seated behind them, and certainly not in the milliner's shop. She must make certain that he was so disgusted with her that he would not make another attempt after the shopping trip was over.

He conducted her into the carriage with perfect civility. She could only tell by a certain tightening of the lips that he was at all displeased. The rain was pouring down in earnest, and she resigned herself to getting wet. It was a small price to pay.

As he walked around the carriage to the right side, a crested barouche going by happened to hit a large puddle, and splashed a generous amount of muddy water upon him.

He just managed to contain an oath, and indeed, he paused for a moment beside the carriage. Sarah wondered if he meant to order her from it. In another few seconds he had stepped into it. His face was quite pale and wore the most forbidding expression. Sarah's nerve almost failed her. Had she been carrying things too far? No, it was her entire future happiness that was at stake. She steeled herself to make matters worse.

"La, my lord! I hope that you did not get too dreadfully wet!"

The corner of his mouth twitched, but he replied with awful civility, "Pray do not even mention it, my *dear* Miss Baxter." He gave the reins a shake and they were off.

Was he suspicious or did he simply think she would not recognize sarcasm if she met it? It must be the latter, she decided, and turned an innocent smile upon him.

"I cannot tell you how grateful I am to you for helping me in this way. Since Bertram does not have an equipage of his own, I had quite despaired of reaching the milliner's today."

"And I suppose that your mother had other uses for the carriage?"

"Yes." How fortunate it was the truth. Her mother had attended her usual meeting of the Ladies' Charitable Society today. Sarah fluttered her eyelashes at him, but his attention appeared to be concentrated on his driving. "Of course, I am most glad to have you with me, because your help will be invaluable. It is well-known that my lord Drakefield has the most exquisite taste of any gentleman in London. Why, what a feather it will be in my bonnet to be able to say that it was my lord Drakefield who helped me select it." Drat it! She had not meant to make a joke. He might think she was not a complete simpleton.

She had not time to worry over the matter, for at that moment the front left wheel of their carriage fell into a hole and splashed water up over her cloak and the hem of her dress. "Oh!"

"My dear Miss Baxter! I hope that *you* did not get too

dreadfully wet. Would you care to abandon this expedition?"

It was almost as if he had done it on purpose. Her kid boots were soaked through, she was shivering, and the hem of her gown was generously splattered with mud. She felt miserable and she knew that she must look a fright. Unconsciously she raised her chin a little. All the better! With luck they might pass an acquaintance of his on the way to the milliner's so that she might truly embarrass him.

"Pray, do not mention it," she replied, her teeth chattering only slightly.

She might look odd, but again such a reliable customer was always bound to meet with a warm reception. The establishment's proprietor, a Mrs. Green, bustled forward to greet Sarah enthusiastically, her eyes widening as she recognized the gentleman beside her. Her shop had never been so honored before, but she was wise enough not to comment upon it. His accompanying Miss Baxter here could only mean one thing. Her smile widened. Although she enjoyed the patronage of several noble ladies, they were mostly elderly. Here was the chance for her business to leap to the forefront of fashion.

Filled with the spirit of battle, Sarah decided to be as vulgar as she possibly could. "Mrs. Green, I am in need of several bonnets. Please show me your most expensive ones."

A lady at the other end of the room did cast a rather startled look at her, but Drakefield's face remained impassive. Sarah was nettled. Well, she could be even more obvious.

The milliner did not hesitate. "I have several new creations in the back which I hope may please you. If you will excuse me, I will fetch them."

As Sarah and Drakefield waited, the door to the shop swung open, and an excessively pretty girl entered. Modishly dressed, with dark curls and large dark eyes, she might have stepped from the pages of a fashion periodical. "But, Aunt, I am certain that I will not be able to find anything wearable in this—" Her eyes flickered in their direction, and she stopped as if frozen, her lips foolishly open. The tall gray-haired lady behind her nearly bumped into her. She would have exclaimed at the girl, but her eyes fell upon them also.

Sarah turned to look at Drakefield, to see what he made of this phenomenon, but he had paled, his visage wooden. The girl took a few steps toward them.

"Lord Drakefield. It has been a long time since we last met."

He bowed over her hand. "A very long time."

She rested her eyes upon Sarah, and the latter did not like their expression. The tousled curls, the wet cloak, the mud, had all been noted and taken into account. Sarah suddenly felt that perhaps it had not been the wisest course to make an absolute spectacle of herself.

The girl looked inquiringly at Drakefield, clearly demanding an introduction. "This is Miss Baxter," he said expressionlessly. "Miss Baxter, pray allow me to introduce Miss—or rather Lady Fernsbury."

The latter smiled and Sarah's hackles rose. There was no mistaking the arrogant amusement in her face. "Charmed, I am sure, Miss Baxter."

Though she hardly felt like it, Sarah murmured a civil response.

"My dear, I feel certain that you are right. Let us go elsewhere today." The elderly lady tugged at the younger's sleeve, having done no more than nodded at Drakefield.

"Whatever you say, Aunt." She smiled unpleasantly at them both and followed her aunt out the door. It was then that Sarah realized that, except for their own conversation, the room had remained deathly silent for the duration of the ladies' visit. She looked at Drakefield curiously, but his countenance was expressionless.

"Miss Baxter, I know that this bonnet will suit you admirably." The milliner, oblivious to the tension created by the little scene, came out of the back beaming with her prize in her hands. An elaborate confection of white chip, and much taller than current fashion dictated, it was trimmed with tufts of yellow satin, but most notably it boasted a profusion of cornflowers from brim to crown. Sarah's eyes sparkled. "Exactly the thing. Let me try it on."

Looking in the glass provided, she had to be satisfied with the effect. What was more, it would perfectly accompany the carriage dress she had ordered in an almost blindingly bright shade of blue. She turned to look for the familiar sneer upon Drakefield's face. Apparently, his state of preoccupation was too great to be penetrated by a mere bonnet. Sarah turned back to the milliner. "I shall also need something for evening, full dress."

She should have been grateful to the girl, she supposed. Although she did not get a chance to repulse him further, at least his mind was too full for him to think about proposing again. During their carriage ride home, she took advantage of his abstraction to peek at that classically perfect profile now and again. Really, he *was* handsome, even if he bore too much resemblance to one of the languid gentlemen etched upon the pages of *La Belle Assemble*. As he made his farewells to her at Tavistock Square, she could tell that he didn't even see her. Who was the girl and why did she affect him so? She would have to ask Egg about it at the earliest opportunity.

4

SARAH'S WISH was to be thwarted, for when she confronted Eglantyne, the latter could only protest her ignorance. She had done her best to speak to Sarah upon another matter, that of wearing the red dress to Almack's. To Sarah's surprise, the invitation there had proved not to be dependent upon her being affianced, but that had not shaken her determination. She had dismissed Eglantyne's arguments.

"Why, you were the one who told me only last month that Lady Dagonet had scandalized everyone by almost falling out of her dress during the—"

Eglantyne had shaken her head. "It is a different thing. She is a duke's daughter—"

"Which I am not."

"How can I explain it to you? They are apt to be critical of anyone. The fact that you are on the arm of Cousin Everard will be enough to make some ready to declare war at a trifle. If you offer them this provocation—"

Eglantyne had seen that she had made a mistake. Sarah's eyes sparkled with anger. "Let them. What do I care for their good opinion?"

She had tried once more. "But you are the one who will suffer. It is *your* reputation that will be harmed—"

Sarah had laughed. "I hardly think that would prevent my marrying Alan—and nothing else matters as far as I'm concerned."

"But you will be with the duchess," Eglantyne had added in a low voice, "and I do not know that she will look kindly upon it."

It was hard for Sarah to reply to this, for despite the duchess's blunt tongue, she had quite liked the elderly lady and did not wish to cause her pain. Still, she had her own future to consider. "Perhaps she will change her mind and disapprove of me, then, and it will put an end to this business once and for all."

Eglantyne had given up in disgust, seeing that her words made no impression whatever upon her friend.

Still, as Sarah dressed for the evening, Eglantyne's words continued to sound in her ears. Bertie, who observed her putting the finishing touches on her toilette, was no less critical than Eglantyne. He advised Sarah that she was making "a deuced fool" of herself, but since he also gave it as his opinion that she could not find an admirer superior to the Black Dandy, she ignored what he had to say. Seeing that his words were wasted, he consoled himself with the thought that his sister would put herself so far into her parent's black books that the pig would surely be forgotten. He offered to take her riding in the new carriage he would surely buy after she had disgraced the family name. "Of course," he added, "I'll have to take you after dark. Wouldn't want anyone giving *me* the cut direct." He thought for another moment, then added, "By the way, I'd keep from saying 'la' quite so much around Drakefield if I were you. He's likely to have you sent to Bedlam."

It was no wonder that Sarah's spirits were depressed as she waited for Lord Drakefield to arrive. She could not know how well the dress became her. Her maid had twisted her hair up simply with a gold comb in the back, allowing the curls to hang freely in front. She wore no other jewelry save for a gold necklace. In the candlelight, the bright yellow of the roses on the gown was muted to a shade which matched her hair. To a less critical eye than her own, she might have appeared ravishing, but all she could think of was how unsuitable the gown was for the occasion. She gave a little sigh as Lord Drakefield's name was announced.

She had thought for a cowardly moment to wear her evening mantle and so delay the inevitable moment of discovery. Steeling her nerves, she had chosen a fine Kashmir shawl instead. She took a deep breath and walked to the landing.

Drakefield was waiting below, and as she stood at the top of the stairs, he glanced up at her. For a moment his gaze was arrested. There was a curious expression in his eyes as they met hers. She couldn't tell what it was, but she was aware that her heart was beating loudly and that the air mysteriously seemed to have become thicker.

"Miss Baxter."

This was it, then. She must prepare to fight her first battle. She straightened herself and with a fair assumption of unconsciousness began down the stairs regally. As she reached his side, his words took her by surprise.

"May I say how extremely lovely you are this evening?" He swept her a handsome bow.

Drakefield himself in evening clothes was enough to make any girl's heart beat faster. She could not know that his own attire was in defiance of convention, that his breeches should have been in a pale color rather than black, or that he should have worn white silk stockings instead of black ones. She was unaware that he had fought his own private skirmish at Almack's long ago. She knew only that evening dress seemed to suit him better than any other, and that it was hard to tear her eyes away from the picture he presented.

To her surprise, he made no further comment about her garments, but instead offered her his arm and inquired whether she was ready. Outside, the duchess waited in her crested barouche. Although it was dark, it would be impossible for her to ignore the shade of Sarah's dress. To the latter's astonishment, the duchess appeared to notice nothing out of the ordinary, greeting her with pleasure, and also commenting favorably upon her appearance. As Drakefield took his seat beside Sarah, the duchess studied them. "You make a handsome pair," she observed.

There was little Sarah could say by way of reply, so she simply smiled her thanks. Her heart had not ceased its pounding, but she attributed it to nerves. Although Drakefield was lean, he was well-muscled and taller even than Sarah, and sitting beside him in the carriage she was uncomfortably aware of how close he was. My goodness, how warm the night was becoming—so odd for early spring. It was fortunate that she had decided against wearing her mantle, after all. She extracted her fan from her reticule and employed it. It would not do to be flushed when she entered Almack's. If she were really as vulgar as she wished to appear, she would give no sign of being embarrassed, for she would lack the sensibility.

It was going to be a dreadful squeeze, she could see. The line of carriages was shockingly long. Although the duchess kept a running patter of kindly small talk, and Sarah did her best to respond, she could feel her nervousness increasing. Was it possible that she was making a dreadful mistake? All of Eglantyne's warnings came flooding back to her. How many young ladies in London would give the world for a voucher to Almack's? And there was no doubt that the duchess had used all her influence to obtain them. It was well known that the haughty patronesses did not normally tolerate those whom they termed "mushrooms" within Almack's sacred portals.

This was the one *entrée* she would receive into a society which closed its doors to even wealthy cit's daughters. And she was throwing it away with both hands. She thought of the pride of her parents' faces as she had left this evening, and for a moment was close to tears. Perhaps it was not too late, even now. Perhaps they might turn the carriage around. She had many demure, if forgettable, evening gowns which would be suitable for this occasion. As the thoughts arose in her head, the carriage arrived at their destination.

She was near to trembling with anxiety as they waited their turn to be announced. She could actually feel her knees starting to knock together. The startled glances and whispers about them from others in line did nothing to improve her spirits. She had hoped to conceal her fright, but apparently Drakefield noticed, for now he leaned over to whisper in her ear.

"Courage. You look marvelous tonight. Stare down the old biddies." He gently patted the gloved hand which was resting in his arm.

She felt as if she had fallen into a dream when at last she stood by Mr. Willis, the keeper of the door, and their names were announced. There was an obvious lull in conversation, and she had the sensation that every face in the room was turned up to observe her. She read shock, surprise, and hostility upon them, as well as admiration from some of the male members of the company. She had never swooned in her life, but she felt as if she might do so now. The room was beginning to blur and . . .

A sudden pressure on her arm awakened her. She glanced to see gray eyes only inches from her own. There was a warning in them. She straightened herself to her full height. Unbidden, her chin lifted. She smiled at Drakefield. "A delightful evening, is it not, my lord?"

A dimple appeared in one cheek as he responded. How odd for a lean man to have a dimple, though it was rather endearing. She drew courage from his presence. There were virtues that he lacked, but given the circumstances, there was no other arm she would trade for that of the Black Dandy.

Below them, the conversation was rising in pitch. Her fate was being decided. She managed a splendid assumption of obliviousness as they traveled into the room.

Who was this latest flirt of the Black Dandy's? The same one he had driven in the Park? An heiress, is that what the gossip says? Her gown is lovely, of course, but most inappropriate. Well, if she is an unknown, perhaps she was unaware. Wait, she is on the arm of the Black Dandy, after all. He would not escort her in unless . . . She is rather beautiful, if far too tall, and she carries herself well. You would think she did not notice everyone whispering about her. But what if she *is* vulgar? Do you mean to refuse the introduction if—? No, of course, one would not wish to offend the duchess, standing beside her.

The scales tipped first one way, then the other as judgment was being formed against Sarah. A tall, handsome, and imperious lady crossed the room to bid their group welcome. It was Lady Castlereagh, that most haughty of all the patronesses, and seeing that she did not avoid Sarah's company, the scales tipped firmly in Sarah's favor. There were any number of persons who sought introductions, from fondness for the duchess, admiration for the Black Dandy, and many more from a lively sense of curiosity. Sarah saw the scarcely veiled enmity in some of the countenances, but she affected imperviousness.

Lady Jersey, another patroness, renowned equally for her scorn of cits and her love of gossip, drew Lady Castlereagh aside later in the evening. "You must tell me, my dear, what influence the duchess exercised upon you. Was it blackmail? I should so like to know. May we expect other persons of this type among us?"

The latter smiled thinly, "I should guard my tongue if I were you, my dear. The young lady has not wanted for introductions or partners this evening, as you may observe." She gestured to where Sarah was joined in a country dance line with Lord Drakefield. "A handsome couple, are they not?"

"Do you think that he does intend to marry her?"

"What else could it mean, particularly with the duchess here beside him? I confess that the entire affair is unprecedented, but one never knows, after all. I was quite taken aback when she requested the tickets. I had always thought she held Drakefield in dislike."

"Or so she had always said. Oh, how interesting."

"Yes, and despite all your brave words, my dear, I cannot imagine even you giving the cut direct to the Black Dandy."

At this Lady Jersey shook her head. "Not the cut direct, but . . . well, the girl does present a genteel appearance, after all. I shall suspend judgment. Mind, if anyone else even attempts to follow her example, I shall know what to do."

"So shall I. So shall everyone. Of course, I think it unlikely. Do you observe any gentleman here that are dressed in imitation of the Black Dandy?"

Sarah's dreamlike sensation persisted throughout the rest of the evening. Was is possible? The members of the *ton* had not avoided her; in fact, it almost might have been said that they sought her out. Several persons had openly admired her unconventional dress, although it must be admitted that most of them were male. Still, there were undoubtedly many high-born ladies that might have envied the success of the evening. It hardly seemed real.

Even though this success was contrary to her expectations, and indeed to her plans, she could not help glowing with happiness upon the ride home. Her pleasure in the evening was increased when they reached Tavistock Square and the duchess took her gloved hand and patted it in affectionate farewell, remarking that she, for one, was proud of Sarah's triumph.

Drakefield seemed different too. He hadn't sneered once, though of course, it must be observed that she hadn't given him cause. She could not have borne the thought of alienating her one firm ally. As he led her to the steps, he congratulated her on her conquest of society. He was smiling as he said it, and as the candlelight caught his eyes and that interesting white streak in his hair, she thought that she had never seen him appear more attractive. For the first time she felt like an awkward schoolgirl, stammering her thanks to him. He shook his head slightly.

"Ah, Miss Baxter. That will not do."

She looked at him, confused.

"You must remember your manner of this evening. *That* is the one you must employ. Tomorrow we will set a seal upon your success, shall we? I shall pick you up promptly at two. We shall return to Hyde Park."

She looked at him wonderingly, and the corner of his lip curled upwards once more. "I am certain that you must have other equally striking ensembles. It would provide a perfect opportunity to exhibit one of them." He bent over her hand. "Good night, Miss Baxter."

She had not thought to giggle or protest. What could he have meant? Was it just another chance for him to display to his creditors that his financial worries were soon to be over? She could have sworn that he looked amused as he said it. And his congratulations had seemed sincere.

It was puzzling and she might have devoted a great deal of thought to it, but the nervous strain had taken its toll. She was exhausted as she made herself ready for bed, and she fell immediately into a deep and dreamless sleep.

Her entire morning was spent recounting all the events of the evening to her mother, though naturally there was a great deal that Sarah dared not mention. Mrs. Baxter took a harmless pleasure in hearing the names and titles of all the persons Sarah had met, exclaiming with gratified pleasure at each one. She was also embarrassingly eager to know how her daughter had enjoyed herself at her first society function—and accompanied by a duchess too! Of course, nothing could be better than to have such a handsome gentleman as Lord Drakefield to escort one, could it? She cast a sly look at her daughter as she said it, and was gratified to see that Sarah pinkened becomingly. Still, Sarah was not about to tell her mother that she was embarrassed by the false picture she was creating, that of a happy young girl dazzled by her first grand ball. She could hardly confess that she had set out to scandalize society rather than to win its favor.

She managed to escape by protesting that the time was slipping away too quickly and that she must begin to dress for Drakefield's visit. The name held a magic charm. Her mother, smiling, released her. If Mrs. Baxter wondered why he had not yet made an offer, she at least knew that it was not for her to penetrate the mysteries of the *ton*.

It did not take much time for Sarah to reach a decision. It must be her new carriage dress in the blinding shade of blue and the new bonnet with the cornflowers upon it. Surely no one could think she looked anything but *outré*, but to make certain of things, she again added the yellow gloves and yellow kid boots. Today would be the real test. He had driven through the Park so quickly upon their last visit that she had hardly had time to embarrass him properly. The duchess would not be with them today to inhibit her. She stood before the mirror and attempted a simper, then drew up her mouth in distaste. If he meant to make her an offer today, she would know what to do. She was ready.

It was true that her heart began to race when Lord Drakefield was announced, but that was easily attributed to the spirit of battle within her. Her color was high as she swirled out to the top of the landing. Of course, he had seen the bonnet, but surely the entire effect of the ensemble would be enough to make him give a start of surprise. She was unprepared for his reaction.

Not only did he survey her with undisguised appreciation, he actually took a gloved hand and kissed it to her. "Superb, my dear Miss Baxter. Nothing could be better. You are truly magnificent."

She actually was frowning as she made her way down the stairs. What could he mean and why was there such a warm look, almost a laughing look, in his eyes? Disconcerted, she realized she was forgetting her part and she exclaimed, "La! How very flattering you are, my lord! It is enough to turn my poor head, I am sure."

He shook his head gravely, though the look never left his eyes. "A perfect indifference! I applaud you, but come, we must be going."

It would not do to let him see she was puzzled. She took up her act even more determinedly than before. She had made the mistake of remaining silent in his presence. Now she would talk until his ears fell off. She conversed during the entire drive there. She spoke of bonnets, of dresses, of a serial romance which she was reading in the *Lady's Magazine*, of the weather, of all the persons she had met the previous night, of his horses, of his carriage, of cricket, of any subject of which she might appear ignorant, though irritatingly sure of her own expertise.

Drakefield bore it all impassively; there was no sigh whatsoever to indicate his distaste, which must be certain.

By the time they reached Hyde Park, she was forced to surrender, too weary to continue. Was the man made of iron or was he merely deaf?

Truly, it was gratifying to see the heads turn in the other carriages as Drakefield drove expertly among them. Even though she could not admire the man, she had to concede that he had the power to command attention, and that no one could ignore the black curricle and black horses or the black-clad gentleman who drove them. It was also pleasing to receive so many civil acknowledgments from persons she had met at the ball the night before. They made an effort to indicate that their salutations were not for Drakefield alone, and she could not but be grateful. In fact, some of the young gentlemen looked as if they would like very much to approach the carriage and have conversation with her, but Drakefield did not allow them the opportunity. After the fourth or fifth time that it happened, she remonstrated with Drakefield.

"La, my lord. I do believe Lord Sandell wished to have speech with us, and now we have left him behind in the crowd."

A slight smile curved Drakefield's lips. "Miss Baxter, although I am more than willing to help you with your schemes, you are quite mistaken if you imagine that I would permit a want-wit like that to steal a march on me."

For a moment fear seized her heart. Surely he could not know of her plan to repulse him? It took only a moment for logic to assert itself. He would scarcely be driving her at the moment if he had divined her purposes. No, he must mean something else, though she could hardly guess what.

He flicked the tip of his whip near the ear of the off-side horse in order to catch the animal's attention, then eased past an elaborately gilt barouche, being driven at a sedate pace in order to accommodate the dowager within. A sound resembling a chuckle escaped him.

"You must take a certain amount of satisfaction in your success at any rate. I am afraid that young lady would be better off *not* following your lead, however. Not everyone can successfully attempt that style of bonnet."

She stared at him in puzzlement, and without flicking an eye in her direction, he added gravely, "To the right . . . in the brown vis-à-vis. Did you truly not notice?"

She glanced to her right and what she saw made her gasp. A young lady was wearing a bonnet which was very nearly a duplicate of the one she had worn on their previous outing to the Park. If anything, it was a trifle wider brimmed and higher crowned than her own, and it boasted *six* ostrich feathers upon it. Drakefield was right too. The young lady had far too small and narrow a countenance to permit the wearing of such an elaborate confection. It dwarfed her face, producing a comic effect. Sarah had to cough to hide a smile.

Drakefield had observed her reactions out of the corner of an eye, and now his own lips curled with amusement. "You did not notice! And I thought you had been taking it all into account, including every purple pelisse and pair of yellow gloves about us."

My word! Could he be serious? She tried to look about as discreetly as possible. What she saw startled her. There *were* lavender, lilac, and purple pelisses to be seen all about them, accompanied by yellow gloves and outrageous bonnets of many descriptions. Could it be? Certainly it did not seem mere coincidence.

He shook his head slightly, though his amusement lingered about his eyes. "Really, it was rather cruel of you. You might have selected a color scheme that was kinder to more of the fair sex."

Sarah could not help it. Her sense of the ridiculous was fully awake now. To think that in trying to appear vulgar, she had instead succeeded in creating a fashion! She broke into a spontaneous peal of laughter. "Oh, no," she gasped. "You cannot meant it . . . they are not . . . because of me . . . "

She caught a flash of white teeth. "Come now, you mustn't pretend innocence any longer with me. It is too clear that you are succeeding in your ambition. You meant to turn up society by its heels, but I daresay that even you did not know how very influential—"

He was not allowed to finish his words, for alongside his

curricle there had drawn a singularly beautiful barouche in dark green, picked out in gold. The lozenge on the side proclaimed its owner's position. Sarah followed his gaze and saw the dark-haired girl who had made herself unpleasant at the milliner's. She was smiling and nodding at Drakefield: he could do little but to pull up his horses. His face was set and pale.

If everyone in London had been quick to follow Sarah's lead, this particular beauty proved herself the exception. She was beautifully and most tastefully dressed in soft rose pink sarcenet, while a bonnet cap trimmed with rose pink satin framed those perfect features admirably. *Her* gloves, Sarah noticed sadly, were of a delicate buff.

"How do you do this afternoon, Lord Drakefield and, ah . . . I am sorry, but I have a terrible memory . . . " She gave Sarah a condescending smile. It was a slap in the face, but Sarah had no chance to protest, for Drakefield was already speaking.

"Perhaps you should say a convenient memory instead, your ladyship. Miss Baxter, you have met Lady Fernsbury. Lady Fernsbury, Miss Baxter."

"I saw that Lord Drakefield did not mean to share your company with the rest of us. I suppose he has his reasons." Sarah drew herself up stiffly, but again Drakefield prevented her from enacting a counterattack. He gave a thin smile.

"Just as I may suppose that you have your reasons for being *here*, Annabel."

Lady Fernsbury ignored his remarks as she studied Sarah, and again the latter had the sense that every part of her clothing was undergoing a critical inspection. Lady Fernsbury gave a little laugh. "My, you certainly are an original, Miss Baxter. Your bonnet! And the shade of your dress! Tell me, was it your own idea to accompany it with gloves in that particular hue?"

Sarah was finding it hard to contain herself. She was ready to explode angrily, but Drakefield cut in once more. He was still quite pale, but he spoke calmly.

"Miss Baxter is undoubtedly too modest to take credit for

her abilities. It is remarkable, is it not, how society has followed her lead?"

For the first time Lady Fernsbury allowed her anger to show. "Society is always ready to adopt some ridiculous whim," she said scornfully. "The one fortunate circumstance is that such things never endure." She rounded on Sarah. "I am certain that Miss Baxter is considered the arbiter of fashion in some circles." She gave a sneering smile. "You must share with me the name of your dressmaker, Miss Baxter, so that I will not seem out of the way if I ever fancy a journey East."

She had as much as accused Sarah of being a cit, which truly, no one could know. Moreover, she expected Sarah to be ashamed of it. Lady Fernsbury clearly meant for her to beat a mortified and frightened retreat. Sarah was blind with rage. This time she did not give Drakefield the opportunity to speak.

"I should be happy to, your ladyship, and if you like, I would also be glad to tell you exactly what it cost. A small fortune, of course, but one should never compromise on one's appearance, don't you agree? And I must exclaim against your ladyship's own modesty. I am afraid that you cannot help but seem as out of the way in the East as you do in the rest of town—you must always set yourself apart by your manners."

Sarah had spoken in carrying tones, but she hardly cared. Her scornful inflection could not be ignored. Lady Fernsbury, her pretty face flushed with rage, muttered something under her breath and directed her coachman to drive on.

Sarah suddenly remembered Drakefield. My word! She had mortified him for certain this time. The thought did not give her as much pleasure as it might have. She stole a glance at him. He was rigid.

"Do you wish to leave?" she asked in a soft voice.

"Lady Fernsbury is leaving the Park now," he said expressionlessly. "I mean to make one more turn about it before we go. Have the goodness to smile and acknowledge all of your acquaintances."

It was little enough to ask, so she did as he suggested.

The drive back to Tavistock Square was conducted in silence, much worse even than the first time. It wasn't until they had arrived and he had handed her down from the carriage that he spoke.

"I am sorry."

It was the moment for which she had been waiting. He was telling her that he could not overcome his repugnance. She had succeeded in her designs, even though it was by accident. Perhaps she was as vulgar as she had been pretending to be. She wished she did not feel so very miserable. She could not speak, but shook her head instead.

"Goodbye."

The carriage drove off. She turned and made her way slowly into the house. She was confronted by her maid, excited and secretive.

"Oh, miss," she whispered, "there's been another letter. I have it here for you."

She extracted it from a pocket and thrust it into Sarah's reticule. Another letter from Alan, at last! Her heart should be leaping with joy. She gave a heavy sigh and began to trudge wearily up the stairs.

5

ONCE SHE OPENED the missive, it proved to be every bit as disappointing as she had anticipated. Most of it was concerned with sport—he recounted proudly that he had shot four hares, which was a record for the camp. The game apparently provided a welcome supplement to army diet. He was excited also that the regiment had removed from Crato to Monforte, hoping that it meant they were to see some real action at last.

There was one sentence at the end which offered a crumb of comfort. He had received the first of her letters, and he wished to thank her for her kind thoughts. Kind thoughts, indeed! Letters from England would always be received with deep appreciation and gratitude. As a letter writer, he was no Abelard. She gave a sigh and laid the paper down. There might be a depth of emotion contained beneath these terse sentences, but her head was hurting far too much for her to think about it now. She must begin to dress for dinner.

The limping gentleman picked his way carefully through the puddles that had been left by an early evening shower. It was evident that his cane was no affectation. He was dressed with a fine, and possibly a premeditated carelessness, quite in contrast to the gentleman he intended to visit. His cane caught in a crevice, hidden by a puddle, and twisted, causing him to shift weight momentarily onto his bad leg.

"Oof!" He gave a curse, then continued on. There were few passersby to disturb his progress at this hour of the night—or, more accurately, the morning. He paused in front of a house and looked at the light emanating from a window with some satisfaction. Good! His guess was correct. He stepped up to the door, grasped the knocker, and let it fall.

It took some time, but at last a manservant appeared, still dressed, though he blinked with sleep. He stared at the visitor with pardonable surprise.

"I am here to see your master." He could not quite disguise his impatience.

The servant shook his head. "Lord Drakefield is not—"

"The devil with formality." He shoved his way in past the servant. "I'll announce myself."

The latter, only too happy to surrender, returned to his seat in the hall.

The gentleman crossed over to the dining room door and opened it. The Black Dandy was in an unusual state of disarray. His cravat had been torn off rudely and his shirt was open at the throat. His dark curls with the streak of white were disheveled far more than even fashion permitted. His coat was off and his waistcoat unbuttoned. He was sunk in a chair, a glass in his hand and a half-empty bottle on the table before him. He was staring blankly ahead of him and took a moment to react to the sound of his friend's entrance. He then glanced up at his visitor's face, though it was clear he had trouble identifying to whom belonged the shock of blond hair, the bright blue eyes, the leathered skin, and the beak of a nose.

"Clavering!"

"Am I disturbing your bacchanals?" He entered the room, closing the door behind him, and limped over to the table. He lifted the bottle to sniff it. "Whisky! Really, my dear Drake—"

"I had it from Johnson," remarked Drakefield indifferently.

"Serves you right for associating with Scots." He seated himself and eyed his friend with some concern.

A thought occurred to Drakefield's befogged brain. He

tried to focus on the Limoges clock on the mantelpiece. "Clavering—Good lord! It must be—"

The latter yawned delicately. "Just nearing three. I decided to make an early night of it. Always best to quit when you are ahead."

Drakefield was beginning to come to himself. "Made your fortune?" he said, at his most sardonic.

"No, though I should be able to live upon what I have for a few months. I understand that you are about to make yours, however," Clavering added carefully.

Drakefield shook his head, his expression bleak. "No. Won't work." He heaved a sigh. "Saw Annabella today."

"I daresay."

The casual words appeared to anger Drakefield. "Confound it, you know what I mean!"

"I suppose I do. You saw Annabella in the Park, only just avoided making a scene, and then probably were unforgivably rude to the only hope you have of repairing your fortunes. A fine day's work."

"You cannot understand." He picked his head up suddenly. "Who told you we met in the Park?"

"A little bird. One of your friends." He leaned forward before Drakefield could say anything else. "Devil take it! You never wanted for brains—or courage. Can't you see what you are doing? You are allowing an ungovernable passion for this chit to ruin your life."

Drakefield drew in his lips and said nothing.

"What is more, I and all the rest of your friends think that you were well out of it. Why must you be so blind? Marriage has not improved either her disposition or her temper."

"How can she be happy, any more than I can? Married to a septuagenarian—and the way he paws at her . . ." He gave a shudder.

Clavering shook his head. "She didn't marry the man—she married his title, and his wealth. She has precisely what she bargained for, and she has her cicisbeos to—"

Drakefield leaped up from his chair, his face black with rage. "Do not dare speak of her in that manner to me."

Clavering's face was expressionless for a moment, then he responded mildly. "You would inflict violence upon a crippled man? A hero of your country?"

Drakefield's anger faded as abruptly as it had risen. "You are the most absurd—"

"Let us discuss something more pleasant—the heiress, in fact."

Drakefield resumed his seat. "Whom do you mean?" he asked with an assumption of studied indifference quite remarkable for a man who had been drinking whisky all night.

Clavering could not help but be appreciative, but now he shook his head. "Unworthy, my dear fellow," he said gently.

"Who told you that she was an heiress?"

"It is what all the gossip says, but to be frank, I had it from Judith."

"I suppose she is telling the world."

"Not at all, though it could do nothing but benefit you if she were. Judith said that her fortune is vast. A handsome girl, isn't she?"

"I suppose so."

"And a lady of spirit. I heard that she managed Almack's in quite a remarkable fashion."

"Yes."

"It is said that society is beginning to copy her mode of dress—that she is beginning to set the fashion."

"Yes."

"And that she refuses to let herself be intimidated by the . . ." He paused, searching for a word for a moment. "By the dowagers and such." He watched his friend's expression carefully.

"Yes."

"There is nothing, then, that would prevent the girl from moving in the first circles were she so fortunate as to marry a peer."

"No."

He was studying Drakefield intently. "Judith would have it that even the duchess has approved the match."

"Yes."

"My word!" Leaning forward, he took his friend by the arm and gripped it hard. "What in heaven's name are you about, then? They began wagering on the possibility for a match as soon as you appeared together. The odds were in your favor, but they are beginning to lengthen every day."

"Gaming!" Drakefield snorted his disgust and disengaged his arm.

Clavering closed his eyes for a moment, then they snapped open again as he spoke. "Do not let your prejudices blind you to what I am saying. Your reputation was formidable enough to protect you at first, but now that the world has seen your hesitation, there are any number of fellows desperate enough to take the risk. Drake! I know that you are fastidious. I know that you have passed over any number of heiresses before. I have looked over the market myself, and believe me, I am not tempted. You must ask this girl to marry you as soon as possible."

Drakefield shook his head. "I cannot."

"Why not?"

"Annabella . . ."

"Forget Annabella for the moment. Do you like this girl?"

Drakefield met his eyes. "I do like her . . . I like her rather too well to—"

"Confound it, man! It is obvious that her one wish is to be a leader of society. There is no other gentleman of title that could elevate her to that position as easily as you. Why, undoubtedly everyone would simply have said her clothes were vulgar—except that she was driving with the Black Dandy. Now they all wish to imitate her. The girl does not have a love match in mind, that is obvious enough."

Drakefield frowned. "What you say is true, but—"

"I know that you inherited a bloody mess and that circumstances have been against you always, but each of us must play the cards we are dealt. Think of what you owe your family, your name, all those who depend upon you."

His expression softened. "I know it is late and that you are tired. Just consider what I have said. That is all I ask."

"I will."

His friend rose. Drakefield followed his example. "Clavering."

His friend turned to him. Drakefield took his hand and clasped it. "Thank you."

Clavering smiled. "I am not without self-interest. I am hoping the heiress will approve this bachelor friend also and that I may allowed to beg for scraps from your table."

"I-I am glad you had that run of luck."

"So am I. By the way"—he pointed at the whisky—"I should rid myself of the rest of that, if I were you. They invented it for the sole purpose of killing Englishmen, you know."

It was odd how the most favorable place for privacy was often public. With this in mind, Sarah had decided that she and Eglantyne might spend a part of the day strolling about the Green Park. Eglantyne had not yet had an account of Sarah's triumph at Almack's or the events that had happened since, so conversation between the two of them was imperative.

Sarah hardly liked to think of being accompanied by an attendant footman who might listen to their every word, and she knew that her parents would consider her maid an inadequate chaperone in such a public place. The only solution was to persuade Bertie to escort them. It had taken all her powers of persuasion.

"But dash it all, Sally," Bertie had protested, "there's to be a cockfight today in the pit on Tufton Street and I mean to go see it."

"Bertie." She had fixed him soulfully with her eyes. "Do not tell me that a cockfight means more to you than your sister's future happiness?"

"Of course not, but—stop looking at me like that, will you? Confound it! Isn't a man to have any pleasure in life?"

"Perhaps there will still be time to go after our walk?" she had suggested hopefully.

"I would be surprised. I am sure that you and that snip of a girl will probably talk for hours. I may fall asleep."

He was still protesting after their carriage had arrived and they had entered the Adstock house. "Dash it all, Sally. Why must you always drag me into your schemes? I daresay you and this shrimp—"

"Pray hush! Here she is." She poked her brother as Eglantyne approached, and shot him a warning look to ensure that he would have a polite smile upon his face. It was peculiar. His face had lost its peevish expression entirely, but he wasn't smiling either.

Eglantyne was wearing a muslin frock over a peach slip, with a cottage bonnet in peach crepe to match. She colored prettily as Sarah made the introductions and did not seem to notice that Bertie's response was merely a strangled sort of noise in his throat. Really, thought Sarah, if Bertie meant to enact his revenge by being rude, she would have something to say about it to him later.

"I could not try to imitate you, Sarah," said Eglantyne with a laugh. "I have heard how you have set the fashion for bright colors this year."

Sarah smiled but whispered, "I have so much to tell you—but it must wait until we are safely in the park."

Bertie was ominously silent during their entire ride to Green Park, though Sarah and even Eglantyne did their best to include him in small talk. Really, if he meant to be mutinous, he might as well have told Sarah so right at first. They didn't need a sullen escort. What a great fuss he was making over a simple cockfight. It was particularly unkind considering what an effort Eglantyne was making to show him attention. She kept casting glances his way and little smiles, but he might as well have been carved of stone. Well, if he wished to be that way, so could Sarah. She turned a shoulder to him and addressed Eglantyne exclusively. She would not even make the attempt to find topics that she thought might be of some interest to him.

She had asked the coachman to set them down near the

reservoir, so that they might enjoy a stroll around it before making their way past the Lodge, inhabited by the deputy ranger of St. James' and Hyde Parks. Sarah herself was a great walker, given opportunity, and the climb up Constitution Hill was one of her favorites. They had a fine day for it also, she noted. Last night's rain had freshened the air. The sky, now clear, was gloriously blue, the grass at its most verdant, and hollyhocks waved gently in the breeze.

As they left the carriage, she noted that Bertie at least had manners enough to execute the courtesies, even if he remained strangely silent. Perhaps it was for the best, after all. If she were free to ignore him, then she and Eglantyne could enjoy a more intimate conversation. Accordingly, she slipped her arm through her friend's and they began their walk. Bertie followed, unspeaking, behind them.

There was much to tell. Her unexpected triumph at Almack's had to be discussed as well as the duchess's evident graciousness. Eglantyne was just as astonished as she that no one had seemed to take umbrage at her conspicuous manner of dress. She asked Sarah if she had found it necessary to be very vulgar. Sarah shook her head. "I thought I was being vulgar just by wearing that dress. For a moment I did think that no one would speak to us . . . but then quite a crowd came up to be presented." She frowned a little when she thought of it. It was still so inexplicable.

"And then Cousin Everard took you for a drive in Hyde Park the next day?"

"Yes." Of course, the matter of dress had to be touched upon. Both Sarah and Eglantyne enjoyed several minutes of giggling over it.

Eglantyne was overcome. Imagine conservative Sarah of all people setting a fashion, particularly when she had instead meant to offend! She glanced at her friend and exclaimed between chuckles, "It is not that I mean to be critical at all, for you know that your taste is excellent, but as for creating the mode . . ." She could not finish the sentence.

Sarah was similarly affected. She had to extract a handkerchief from her reticule in order to wipe her eyes. She glanced behind them at Bertie. His face was just as grave as before. Well, really! What a stick he was proving to be!

". . . but of course," Eglantyne was saying, "I suppose we should have expected it, since you were with Cousin Everard. People always look to him to set the latest mode."

The thought was uncomfortable. "I suppose so," Sarah replied slowly. "But I have not told you all of it, Egg. It appears that I will not have to worry about his attentions any longer. I think I finally disgusted him so much that he will not bother me again." Wasn't it odd? A week ago she would have been laughing with joy as she said the words. Now she felt . . . she felt rather ashamed to say them. She thought of that grim, pale face as he had apologized to her. To her!

Eglantyne was all enthusiasm. "Well, why did you not say so at the first? How relieved you must be! Tell me what happened. What did you say? What did you do?"

The entire incident with Lady Fernsbury had to be recounted, and Sarah could not assume a lighthearted tone. The most mortifying thought was that she had not been *acting* vulgar; it was her own innate vulgarity rising to the surface that had so repulsed Drakefield. She was probably too low-bred a person to be able to keep company with an aristocrat. It was a depressing realization.

Eglantyne by now had caught Sarah's mood. She had dropped Sarah's arm and was frowning slightly as her friend concluded. "But surely this is for the best?" she asked. "Now that you are in no danger, you will be free to marry Alan."

"Yes."

"Have you had any more letters?"

"I had one yesterday."

Eglantyne seized her friend's sleeve and gave it a playful tug. "Then tell me, you goose! What did he say?"

Sarah tried to paint as rosy a picture of the contents as possible, but she could not continue to be entirely convincing. The faint crease still rested between Eglantyne's brows as Sarah concluded. Eglantyne leaned her head sympathetically toward Sarah, however, and addressed her in a cheerful tone.

"Well, I know that it is most difficult. I cannot imagine what it must be like, not knowing his whereabouts or his situation until months have passed. But I am certain that all will be well and that you will be able to be married, just as you wish. You already have overcome an impossible obstacle by ridding yourself of Cousin's Everard's attentions." She glanced back at Bertie as she spoke, putting a hand before her mouth.

"I hope I did not speak too loudly. Did your brother know of your plans?"

"Yes." Bertie had proven to be quite useless. Not only had he not helped her to eliminate Drakefield as a suitor, he had encouraged her to accept him. Well, she supposed it did not matter now, in any case.

They were nearing Constitution Hill, and Sarah was looking forward to its ascent. Perhaps a brisk climb up it would subdue the malaise she was experiencing. She gave a sigh and unconsciously lengthened her stride. In her eagerness, her pace also gradually increased.

"Sarah, wait!" Eglantyne, whose legs were not nearly as long, was some distance behind her. Sarah could hardly believe her own heedlessness. She stopped as her friend came panting up, followed closely by Bertie. It was the latter who addressed her first.

"For shame, Sarah! Leaving Miss Adstock in that way. Do you never think of anyone but yourself?"

She stared at him in open-mouthed surprise as he turned to address her friend. "I apologize for my sister, Miss Adstock. She sometimes has windmills in her head."

Eglantyne shook her head. "It is quite all right. It is only that—I think I must have a rest."

"Here, take my arm, Miss Adstock. Shall we repair to that bench over there so that you may recover? I scarcely like to leave two young ladies alone, or I would go to seek out our coachman immediately."

Eglantyne was shaking her head, though she did lean

heavily on his arm as they reached the bench. "It is unnec-
essary. I just need to catch my breath."

"Well, we shall stroll back at our leisure, then." He had
seated himself beside Eglantyne, never removing his eyes
from her, and Sarah wondered if she had suddenly become
invisible. She interrupted the conversation for the first time.

"Don't you mean to climb Constitution Hill?" she asked.

Two startled pairs of eyes met hers. They *had* forgotten
about her existence!

"Really, Sally, it's outside of enough, when you've already driven this poor fragile creature to the point of exhaustion."

What on earth was wrong with Bertie? And why didn't
Egg say something? It occurred to Sarah that it might prove
dreadfully dull to remain with these two, particularly if they
continued to exclude her from their conversation. Besides,
there was only room for two on the bench. Bertie might
have thought of that!

She shifted her weight from foot to foot impatiently. *She*
did not mean to miss out on her favorite walk. She loved
the view, even though it was not a great height. It seemed
to give her perspective, which was something she needed
badly at the moment. She straightened herself.

"*I* mean to go up Constitution Hill. I will not be long. I
suppose I may meet you here."

It was shocking for her to go off by herself in a public
place. Eglantyne did look at her for a moment with troubled
eyes. "Sarah, is this wise?" She did not add that they might
all go after she had recovered.

Bertie snorted. "Headstrong as usual. Well, if you have
any difficulties, you've a good strong set of lungs anyway."
His gaze returned to focus upon his far more interesting
companion. No further protests followed. They were again
in deep conversation.

"Well, I will be going, then." Neither took any notice.
Really, she had had enough of this. How ridiculous the two
of them were being—just like children. Sarah turned on her
heel and set off at a rapid walk.

As she progressed, she felt a great sense of release. This

was what she had needed to clear the cobwebs from her brain. Without her companions she no longer needed to dawdle, and the exercise felt good to her. She was certain that as soon as she reached the top of the hill, a great weight would lift from her shoulders. Surely her problems would seem insignificant then.

Her pace could not be described as ladylike, but then she did not care. There were not many people about, and she did not think that anyone would notice her. It was hardly likely that she should meet anyone she knew. She would not remain any great period of time. These thoughts comforted her as she hurried along. She was conscious of one or two curious stares as she went on her way. She did her best to avert her face, wishing that she had worn a close bonnet which would have somewhat concealed her features.

Still, despite a sniff of outrage from an elderly lady, accompanied by her footman, and an overly friendly remark from a young man not of the upper classes, Sarah had no real difficulties in achieving her objective. She soon stood on the top of the hill and drank in the fresh clean spring air.

It *was* doing wonders for her. Here there was no pressure being exerted upon her. She could forget the wishes of two doting parents, and those of her brother, and her friend. She might examine her own mind and try to determine the cause of her discontent.

She had hardly reached the top when she saw, a short distance behind her, a gentleman wearing a top hat, brown jacket, and fawn-colored inexpressibles. Drat it! When she so particularly wished to be alone. Discretion urged her to beat a hasty retreat down the other side of the hill, but stubbornly she ignored its promptings and remained where she was. If he came up the hill, as he apparently tended to do, she would pretend not to see him. If he were a gentleman, as it appeared by his dress, he would hardly force himself upon a stranger. If he were not—well, if he were not, she would leave! She caught sight of Bertie and Egg below her on the bench and felt reassured. She could still see them, after all. Of course, they couldn't see her since they were close in conversation, gazing earnestly into each other's eyes.

She sneaked a glance at the gentleman who was approaching. He was well dressed certainly, if a little too colorfully for her tastes. She could not quite like that red-and-yellow-striped waistcoat. There was something familiar about him—something about the way he walked, and that dark red hair and—was he smiling up at her? My word, it was Lord Sandell! She averted her face quickly and pretended to study the Queen's Gardens and, just beyond them, Buckingham Palace. Perhaps he would think she was trying to catch a glimpse of the royal family. She should be safe. He probably had not recognized her. Besides, no well-mannered gentleman would ever attempt to address a lady who had given no indication of wishing to recognize him.

"Miss Baxter?" The voice came from just behind her. The tone was polite, but Lord Sandell had just proved the insufficiency of his breeding. Or perhaps it simply was that he did not class her as someone deserving the courtesies due a lady. The thought made her flush with shame. Of course, it also might just be because he was desperate for funds, or so Eglantyne had informed her.

"Miss Baxter?" What was she to do? She had no choice. She must do her best to pull the thing off. A perfect indifference, was that what Drakefield had said? She would attempt it.

She turned and gave a slight smile.

"Miss Baxter? You may not remember me, but we were introduced the other night at Almack's." She had not forgotten that affected, drawling manner of speaking.

"Indeed, I remember you very well, Lord Sandell."

His handsome face smiled in gratification. "I had hardly dared to hope that you would remember me—" It was all empty flattery, of course. "—With such a crush of people there, though, of course, I could not forget you. By the greatest good fortune, I had decided to walk across the park to visit an acquaintance in Down Street, and I happened to see you ahead of me. I tried to catch your eye but failed, so I pursued you to this place."

A handsome, vain, and slightly silly dandy was what she had thought him. Shallow. Caring for no one but himself. Exactly the type of gentleman she most despised. It occurred to her that such had been her opinion of Drakefield also, and she blushed. Whatever his faults, Drakefield at least had more substance than this person—and better taste, she thought, studying his padded, wasp-waisted coat critically. And—could it be? Yes, he did have yellow gloves!

He had noted the direction of her gaze and misinterpreted her blush. His smile widened as he stretched a hand forward and took hers. "I wear them as a compliment to you. I could not help but notice what you wore in the Park the other day, though I was not allowed to speak to you. I have never met a lady of more refined taste than yourself. Others must always look to you to set the fashion."

It was so ludicrous that she could have laughed, except that it was also very annoying and his conversation was rather too warm for her. She attempted to withdraw her hand, but he only tightened his grip upon it.

"I have been in despair trying to hit upon a way that I might see you. I notice that you do not have your maid with you."

Blast! She had played right into his hands.

"So I thought that I would offer myself as an escort. A beautiful young lady such as yourself might suffer insult all on her own."

Just as she was now. She again tried to extract her hand. "You are too kind, your lordship, but I should not wish to put you to the trouble."

Her pulled her hand to tuck it in the crook of his arm. "It is no trouble, I can assure you."

"But my brother and my friend are waiting for me just down there," she said, trying to extract her hand gracefully and not succeeding.

It was clear that he did not believe her. "In that case I shall take you to them. I have long desired an opportunity for a tête-à-tête with you, Miss Baxter."

She was still trying to free herself, though she had given up any attempt at gracefulness. "But I do not wish your es-

cort. Please leave, Lord Sandell." The overpowering scent
he wore was beginning to choke her.

"I couldn't do that. No, I must see you safely . . . to your
brother."

His determination was beginning to frighten her a little.
Was it a misplaced confidence in the power of his own
charms, or was he just that desperate? She continued to
struggle with him. She was now breathing fast with the ex-
ertion. "Unhand me, my lord!" He smiled, not relaxing his
grip. He opened his mouth to speak, but had no opportunity
to utter a sound, for now a quietly menacing voice sounded
behind them.

"I should unhand the lady since that is her wish,
Sandell."

Preoccupied with their struggle, they had not noticed his
approach. Sarah turned to see Drakefield glowering at her
opportunistic companion. She was not usually a demonstra-
tive person, but she could feel her eyes moisten at the sight
of him. She had but rarely been so glad to see anyone!

Lord Sandell dropped her hand and leaped away as if she
had suddenly developed a fatal and highly contagious dis-
ease. "G-good afternoon, Drakefield."

For another moment Sarah was afraid, this time that
Drakefield might do something rash, but instead he stared
unblinkingly at Sandell for a long moment before speaking.
"I should not annoy the lady further with your attentions,
Sandell. It would be . . . injudicious."

"Yes, I . . . of course . . . I would never have dreamed . . .
just wished to be of help, that was all. If I had known—"

"Doubtless you have some urgent business that calls
you?" suggested Drakefield.

"I . . . Yes! That is . . . well, I . . . good day!" With his
last exclamation he swept the most hurried of bows and disappeared rapidly down the hill.

Sarah's heart was pounding. She turned to Drakefield.
"My lord, I . . . how can I thank you?" How odd his expression was. Did he always have to be so unfathomable? She
suddenly remembered that he now was only a former suitor

and blushed even more vividly than she had before. How irritated he must be at having to rescue her!

"Miss Baxter." He bowed slightly. "How is it that I find you unchaperoned?"

"Eglantyne tired before she could climb the hill, and my brother elected to keep her company." She raised her chin a little. After all, he already considered her to be vulgar. What could it matter if he caught her in another low-bred act? "I decided to make the climb by myself, since this is one of my favorite spots. They are still within eyesight." She gestured down toward the bench where Bertie and Eglantyne were deep in conversation.

"I wonder that they permitted you. Of course, they seem rather occupied."

"Yes," said Sarah stiffly.

An unexpected smile flashed across his face, revealing the dimple, and was gone. "I am sorry. I was merely surprised by their carelessness. This is one of my favorite spots also. I often come up here to . . . to think."

"Eglantyne did tell me not to go," admitted Sarah, "but I had no idea that—"

His face darkened slightly. "Well, you do not have to worry that Sandell will press his attentions upon you again. In fact . . ." He hesitated for a moment before continuing. "I had meant to come and speak with you about the subject today."

What subject? Did he mean to give Sarah her congee here and now? Her heart sank within at the thought.

"Although this is neither the time nor the place I would have chosen, if you have no objection to remaining here for a few moments, I would like to take advantage of this opportunity to converse with you alone."

A painful lump was rising in her throat. She could feel tears beginning to form in her eyes. She blinked them back defiantly.

"Perhaps you would rather not?" he asked, looking at her with some concern. "I know this recent experience must have been most trying."

No. If it had to happen, it was better to have it done. She

shook her curls. "No, I have no objection," she said huskily.

He took a deep breath. "Well, the truth of the matter is . . . it would be useless for me to pretend with you. You are far too clever a girl for that. You know as well as I do why we have been thrown together."

"Yes," she murmured almost inaudibly. She could not meet his eyes.

"Although our acquaintanceship has been brief, I think I have come to know you well enough to realize that . . . of course, we have our differences, and—"

She could not bear to wait any longer and so finished his sentence for him. ". . . that I should prove an embarrassment to you, given my background, that we should not suit."

"Good lord, no!" The note of surprise in his voice was evident. She looked up to see an expression of bewilderment on his face. "What I was about to say was that although we have our differences and we should not agree upon everything, I believe that underneath we have a great deal in common, that in many respects our likes and dislikes are similar, and that I think we are admirably well matched. Therefore, I wished to ask you if you would do me the honor of accepting my hand in marriage."

It was Sarah's turn to be surprised. What was this queer, spinning feeling, as if the grass she stood on had begun revolving quickly around her? Her heart was pounding and her mouth was dry. She could not tear her eyes away from his face and that countenance, so unusually earnest. She could crush him with a word. What a pity she had to say it.

"Yes."

6

As SARAH LAY in her bed thinking it over, she still could not quite understand it. She had known exactly what she intended to say. It had been as if she were standing nearby watching someone else say yes. The sound of the word had surprised her. Why had she said it? She had meant to refuse him. She was in love with someone else, even though his letters had been so unsatisfactory. It was not Alan's fault that he was inarticulate. She was as good as affianced to him; she had as much as said so in her letters to him. She had no right to even consider anyone else's proposal.

My word! And even if she were in love with Drakefield, which she certainly was not since she knew him far too well for that, she would never have simply accepted him like that. On a gentleman's first attempt, a proper young lady was supposed to protest and blush and refuse, while at the same time letting him know that there was hope. Her bald affirmation had undoubtedly added to his conceit, which was the last thing Drakefield needed.

She had to give him some grudging credit, however. At least, he had not looked smugly content with himself, as she had feared he might. Instead he had murmured the usual sorts of phrases about being honored, and the most fortunate gentleman, and such, so that she could not help but feel pleased. Neither had he attempted to embrace her, but had simply kissed her hand and led her back to Eglantyne and Bertie, who seemed reluctant to see her. There had been no knowing looks, no pressing of her hand as he bade her farewell, nor had he divulged their secret to the others.

He had simply informed her in a low voice that he would call upon her father the next day. She had to be thankful for his restraint.

Of course, she might also wonder why she herself had not shared the news. She was too embarrassed to admit that she had been so stupid, she supposed. Moreover, they had made little attempt to include her in their conversation—really, Sarah knew she was a sister and a best friend, but it was rather ill-bred of them all the same.

Why had she done it? Her head was beginning to ache as she tried to puzzle it out. She might tell herself that she had accepted with the notion of breaking the engagement later, but she knew that was not truly the thought that had been in her head. Nor was obedience to her parents—the proposal had occurred in such an unexpected place and time that they would never have suspected its existence. It was certain that if she had refused, Drakefield would not have mentioned it to them. She knew him well enough now to know that he would not use coercion to win her hand. Of course, he had not been forced to either!

She groaned aloud as she puzzled over it. It was true that the proposal had been unexpected, most unexpected, and perhaps that was a part of why she had accepted it. She had been caught off guard. It had been all the more surprising since she had been expecting him to say that he did not wish to see her any longer. She had thought he would state that she was too vulgar to be associated with (although of course he would have phrased it more politely). He had startled her instead by remarking that they were well matched. The thought of the words could not help but bring a little glow to her cheeks. To be honest, she found it gratifying that he considered her to have a great deal in common with him, a peer, a leader of fashion, and one of the most notable gentlemen in London. It was quite an achievement for plain Sarah Baxter to have succeeded where so many better-born damsels had already failed. She could just imagine the expression of aristocratic disbelief on the face of her old schoolmate, Miss Draymore, when she heard of the engagement. How many airs Miss Draymore had given herself over the fact that the Black Dandy had deigned to *dance* with her at an assembly, and how angry she had been when he omitted to do so at the next. She had always treated Sarah with annoying condescension. How pleasing it would be to meet her as Lady Drakefield . . .

What on earth was she thinking of? She would never marry Lord Drakefield! She loved Alan, and she would be his wife or no one's. How disappointed in her he would be if he knew. She could almost picture his dear face—at least she almost could if she concentrated. It was the smile she remembered particularly. A broad smile, not at all like Drakefield's.

Alan had winked audaciously at her when he entered that ballroom last fall, and had lost no time in securing an introduction. He had proceeded to dance two dances with her in a row! When she had protested, feebly, against such a violation of decorum, he had said that it elevated his credit to be seen with the prettiest girl in the room. His intentions could not have been more plain, particularly when he had repeated the performance at two subsequent parties. In fact, if only he had not had the bad fortune to be sent abroad, she might well be married to him by now. She gave a sigh. He was not the graceful dancer that Drakefield was, but . . . but he put more feeling into it perhaps. Naturally, when she danced with Drakefield, she was aware that every eye in the room was upon her, an agreeably flattering sensation.

She bolted to a sitting position. Was it possible? Was this why she had accepted Lord Drakefield? She *had* liked the sensation of so much envious attention. It *was* gratifying for the daughter of a cit to be thrust so prominently into the *ton*. It was even more satisfying to be looked to as a leader after having made only two appearances among them.

She sunk her face in her hands and groaned again. It was all vanity, wasn't it? She had accepted Drakefield because she wished to be Lady Drakefield, to move among the first circles, and to play further audacious tricks upon society. She *liked* the position he had conferred upon her and all it entailed. She was as shallow and self-centered as she had ever believed Drakefield to be! Still cradling her face in her hands, she began to weep silently.

When Drakefield presented himself the next day, Mr. Baxter could not fail to be astonished. It was true that the earl had taken Sally driving twice and to a ball once, but Baxter had already written him off. If only Sally hadn't become tangled with that young military fellow, she might have seen what a prize she was throwing away. A pleasant enough young gentleman, handsome, titled, well thought of and without those vices into which the decadent aristocracy were all too apt to fall. Mr. Baxter had made inquiries most closely into that. Not that he would have objected if the fellow had enjoyed an occasional game of cards, but it was as well that he had a strong aversion to gaming. Sally need not fear that she would be beggared after her marriage as so many heiresses were.

Still, he could not blame the gentleman for wishing to avoid an unwilling bride. Sally was a great deal too set in her ways. Though she had promised to cooperate, Mr. Baxter had lent no weight to this statement. "Mark my words," he had informed his too hopeful wife, "Sally will say and do just as she ought but leave the poor lord with the feeling that he'd be better off marrying an icicle. I know the gel too well. She'll never budge an inch, once she's made up her mind." He had shaken his head at the thought. They would probably have no choice but to let her marry this Grenfell fellow, if he wasn't already married before his return. An accomplished flirt, if not an out-and-out bounder, that was Mr. Baxter's opinion. The type who'd break Sally's heart before breakfast and have it served up to him for dinner. And as a younger son, it was all too clear that her fortune would prove welcome. Clever girl, Sally, but not a particle of sense where men were concerned.

His astonishment was therefore pardonable when a card arrived from Lord Drakefield, asking for permission to call upon him the next morning. He had meant to ask Sally what all this portended, but she had refused dinner and closeted herself in her room, pleading a sick headache.

There was always work waiting for him at his office, but Mr. Baxter was not about to let this chance escape. He waited at home and kept himself busy by demanding why Sally was still abed, poking his nose into every room, frightening the little upstairs maid so much that she burst into tears, and generally finding items he might criticize in his wife's domestic management. Mercifully for Mrs. Baxter, Drakefield called at the unusually early hour of half past ten, obviously a pretty concession to Mr. Baxter and his work. By now the entire household was aware of the lord's visit and was all curiosity to learn the outcome.

Anyone might have guessed it from the broad smile upon Mr. Baxter's face as he personally escorted the lord outside after their meeting. He improved upon it by calling for his lady as soon as Drakefield had left and proclaiming the news loudly as she came running down the stairs. It was a gratifying moment for Fraley, the butler, who had wagered a large amount of cash upon this outcome. A young footman, two pounds the loser, was heard to remark bitterly that it had been an idiotic bet. What they should have done was to wager upon the marriage's actually coming off. Fraley, a light gleaming in his eyes, quickly offered the opportunity for a second wager, but the takers were fewer in number than before.

For Sarah, the most unendurable part was receiving her parents' enthusiastic congratulations that evening. She had remained upstairs for the better part of the day, before deciding that she could not hide forever. Their anxious questions about her health smote her conscience.

Bertie, who had returned from parts unknown only just in time for dinner, had given no indication of surprise, nor of sympathy, nor of dismay. In fact, Sarah would have said that his mind was elsewhere as he spoke. "Best wished and all that, Sal. I say, what's for dinner?"

She supposed she was fortunate. She had been dreading what he might say, the questions he might ask about such inconsistent behavior. It would be equally hard, if not worse, to face Eglantyne.

* * *

Her friend, when Sarah called upon her the next morning, did appear more surprised than Bertie had, but, oddly enough, seemed as little disposed to ask questions, for which Sarah must be grateful. She had borne enough today with the delighted good wishes of Eglantyne's mother, Lady Adstock, who took personal pride in the match, regarding herself as chiefly responsible for it. She had exclaimed that she knew just how excited and happy Sarah must be, and reminisced over the way she herself had felt at such a time in her life. She had inquired about the announcement, and the engagement party, and the date for the wedding, and had been horrified by Sarah's ignorance. She had made Eglantyne promise not to keep Sarah long, for there were hundreds of things she must do, "Conferring with her fiancé being the primary one, of course!" It had all been quite depressing.

"The worst part of it," she confided to Eglantyne, "is that I think I cannot be any more vulgar than I already have been. If he has not found me to be underbred so far, I hardly can imagine what would give him a disgust of me."

Eglantyne looked at her, startled. "Do you mean that you do not wish to marry Cousin Everard?"

"Of course not!" Sarah gazed at her friend in some shock. "Why should you think I would?"

"Well, it did seem to me that you were rubbing along tolerably well, and you did accept his proposal—"

Sarah cut her off hastily. "I was startled and could not think what else to do. I told you already that I thought I had succeeded in repulsing him." She sighed. "Now my problem is to try to imagine what might make him break our engagement."

Eglantyne shook her head as she sewed placidly on the piece of fine muslin. "I cannot imagine. There would be a terrible scandal, and your reputation would be compromised. I do not think Cousin Everard would break the engagement. No gentleman would."

She was being far from helpful. "Well, he must, or I shall be forced to run away—or something of the kind."

Eglantyne paused in her sewing. "So he asked you while your brother and I were waiting for you at the bottom of the hill, and after rescuing you too?"

"Yes, I was grateful to him for that," admitted Sarah grudgingly.

"Do you know, he is so utterly delightful? I felt I could have stayed there for hours. I know we were there for a long while, but it seemed only a few seconds to me."

Eglantyne was one of Drakefield's supporters, but even this seemed excessive. "Your cousin?"

Eglantyne laughed. "No, of course not! I was speaking of your brother. It is a pleasure to meet a young gentleman of a serious turn of mind for a change, not given over to frivolity like every other one I know."

"You are speaking of Bertie?" asked Sarah uncertainly.

Eglantyne had to laugh again. "What a goose you are! And you his twin! Don't you know him at all?"

Sarah was beginning to believe that she did not. To her dismay, her problem was shelved as a conversational topic in favor of a discussion of all the many virtues of her brother.

When she arrived home, her mood was somber. It was not that she objected to her brother and her best friend falling in love; it was just their timing that she found difficult. She needed every resource she could muster in order to find a way out of this dilemma, and their minds had ceased functioning for now.

To cap her misery, her maidservant informed her of the arrival of another letter. Delightful. Alan would probably tell her what he had been eating and how deep the mud was once more.

It was a shock therefore when she made her way to the bedroom, sank down wearily on a fauteil, and opened the letter. It was written in a state of high excitement. His regiment was on the march. She examined the date. It was three weeks newer than the one she had received just a few days ago, owing no doubt to neglect upon someone's part. He thought at last to see some real fighting and could not help but hope for it. "For, my dear Sarah, that would be my only means to a promotion, since my resources are so limited and a promotion I must have, if I am ever to be deserving of you."

This was quite a change in tone. She gave her head a little shake and read on. "Your letters have been my constant companion. I have read them over and over until they have worn thin. Thoughts of home are most precious at such a time as this, when one does not know whether or not he is facing death. I should never have dreamed of the possibility of your being mine except for your constant and repeated assurances. I feel I may dare anything for your sake. Please send me a lock of your hair so that I may carry it beside my heart as I go into battle."

There were several troubling aspects to this missive. She squinted at the paper. No, it was his hand. Was it possible that someone else had helped to dictate the flowing phrases to him? There obviously must have been some serious misunderstanding between them. She had thought of herself as practically affianced to him ever since his departure. He clearly had seen things in a different light. Only her letters had made him view their relationship as a serious one. He also asked for a lock of her hair, which was an insult since they had exchanged locks before he left. His was still in the locket she wore about her neck. She fingered it thoughtfully. Had he forgotten or was he merely careless? Most disturbing of all, though, was her own reaction. She had been hoping for a letter such as this ever since he left. Now that she had received it, she found herself slightly repulsed by the warm phrases. She could not imagine why. She thought of her letters and cringed. She could not have realized—she need not have considered herself as betrothed to him all this time. She might have been free to do whatever she wished. The thought was as upsetting as it was novel. What should it matter if he simply realized things rather later than she did? He was facing death now, as he had said. He deserved her loyalty more than ever, and she in turn had betrayed him by becoming engaged to another gentleman. She was filled with guilt. She thought of Drakefield with some resentment. He was the author of all her troubles! If it were not for him . . . but that was not quite fair either. She might have said no. She turned to finish the letter. "I count every hour and every day apart from you as torment, but I hope that I may return as one more worthy to receive your hand. In the meantime, your devoted regard sustains me. I ask that you keep me always in your thoughts, as you are in mine. Yr. Most Affectionate—A. Grenfell."

Sarah crushed the paper in her hand. She did not merit such a gentleman. If her feelings had cooled, it was just the fault of distance. She would do her best to stir them up again. She had made a mistake, it was true, but she would strive to be worthy from this moment on. Vanity would have no hold upon her. "I promise you that I will, Alan," she said softly as her eyes filled with tears.

Drakefield had spent two long (and to his mind rather arduous) days. Asking Sarah for her hand had been the easy part—it had taken a great deal more than that to be closeted with his future father-in-law and to have to listen to his effusions. He felt as if he were a trophy of some sort to be displayed upon the mantelpiece for all the world to see. The next step involved sending for his man of business, in order to confer about the financial settlements to be made upon his marriage. Drakefield spent much of the evening closeted with this efficient person. He did not understand most of what they discussed, and despite his best efforts to attend, he could not shake his boredom. It made him feel like a horse being auctioned off at Tattersall's, so he did his best to avoid allowing his mind to dwell upon it.

When he rose the next morning, there was an obligatory trip to Sackville Street to select an engagement ring for Miss Baxter. The jeweler, whose concern had handled all the Drakefield family business for at least two preceding generations, bowed deeply when his noble customer arrived, even though much of that same business in more recent years had involved the purchase rather than the sale of jewelry.

He bowed even more deeply when Drakefield explained his business. Might he be permitted to congratulate his lordship? Certainly, he would be honored and delighted to help his lordship select a ring for the most charming Miss Baxter. Such a beautiful lady . . . no, he had not yet been privileged to meet her, but surely all of London knew of her? A lady of such matchless style and elegance must deserve a ring both beautiful and unique. He would be happy to show his lordship all his most striking creations. As he went into the back of the shop and began barking orders, Drakefield shook his head wearily. How fast news traveled around London. There were no queries about his credit. Everyone already knew that he was to marry an heiress.

It occurred to him that he had thought at another time to be selecting a wedding ring for a very different hand—a tiny, translucent one, so fragile that it bruised at a slight pressure. He thrust the thought from his mind. He must concentrate upon the business at hand.

Selecting a ring was much more difficult that he had imagined. There were diamonds, rubies, which he refused out of hand, and emeralds, which he considered, then declined. No, certainly not topazes, he would hardly wish to insult her. A sapphire? For the first time he felt a hope that his visit might meet with success. After he had seen every ring in the shop and rejected them, he was about to give up, but the jeweler had another suggestion.

"Perhaps you would care to see my loose stones, my lord? I have several very fine ones. If you find one you approve, I would be happy to place it in a setting." Drakefield agreed readily.

It did not take long for him to make a selection. He found a large sapphire of unusual clarity and brilliance. It would make the perfect engagement ring. The jeweler, smiling, could not help but agree, and to applaud his lordship's choice. Now as to the setting, perhaps just a simple circle of diamonds . . . not of diamonds? My lord, I . . . He was left speechless as the earl informed him that diamonds were too insipid for a lady such as Miss Baxter. He made an attempt to recover, but his lordship scoffed at the idea of pearls. He cast about in his mind wildly for an idea, and mentioned the first that popped into his head. Rubies? Of course, not rubies, really, he was not sure why he had said that, it was just . . . He was beginning to feel a measure of desperation. He could not like the scowl upon Drakefield's face. He did not wish to lose a third-generation client, and even more pertinently, he wished to assure himself of the future custom of the wealthy bride to be.

Drakefield rose, throwing the poor man into a panic. He was offering fluttering protests when he realized that his client was simply asking a question about a ring which reposed in the case before him.

"Why, that is a yellow sapphire, my lord. Quite an unusual stone, is it not?"

Drakefield studied it. "I have an idea."

At first it seemed far too outrageous to a jeweler accustomed to bowing to even the oddest whims of the aristocracy. As his lordship continued to explain, however, touching upon the necessity for the exact hue, the tastefulness of the gold setting which would include only four small stones at either end, the jeweler had to recognize that this was genius. After all, it was not any ordinary peer that he was dealing with, it was the Black Dandy, an acknowledged leader of fashion. How dense he had been! He apologized profusely to his lordship for being so slow to follow him and promised that he would execute it personally. And when would he wish for the ring to be ready? This question caused Drakefield to pause.

"I do not know as yet. As soon as possible, I should think. I shall let you know when our plans are made final."

The jeweler bowed very low and conducted Drakefield out of the shop personally, after thanking him again for his patronage. As soon as the door had closed behind his client, however, he began rubbing his hands with glee. "It will start a mode!" he informed his minions. "Mark my words, all the fashionables will be flocking in here for rings and brooches like my Lady Drakefield's. And I've no doubt that she will be able to think of even more novel designs, if only half of what I've heard of her is true."

Drakefield felt drained after his visit, and wished most to return home and perhaps partake of a cold collation, but

duty called him elsewhere. There could be no better way of
ensuring the duchess's hostility to the match than by letting
her learn of it from another quarter first. Accordingly, he
stoically whipped up his horses and in a short time had
crossed town to arrive at the duchess's home.

She evinced no surprise when he was escorted into the
room and she listened to his announcement in silence,
though her lips were curved in an expression which might
be taken for a smile. After he had shared his news, she remarked kindly that he might have done far worse, and as
further evidence of her being pleased, she offered to host
the engagement party, since Sarah's own home could not
be considered anything other than ineligible and since
Drakefield's quarters were obviously inadequate.

Though his face remained impassive, he breathed an inward sigh of relief, for he had feared that she meant to bur-
den him with hours of unasked-for advice. She questioned
him as to the date, but did not seem surprised that it had not
yet been set—it appeared that it was a matter that should
wait until after the lawyers had finished their work. She did
command him to let her know as quickly as possible so that
she could begin plans for the party.

He promised to do so and would have bowed his leave,
but she halted him, a piercing expression in those gray
eyes.

"I have something I wish to tell you. Daresay you don't
care to hear it, but you will anyway. You have found a gel
of spirit, which fortunately suits your disposition." She
cocked her head to one side and studied him for a moment.
"Daresay you think you know everything about females,
but you have not been married to one yet. I have a word of
warning for you—a high-strung gel like this is going to jib
at any little obstacle that blows across her path."

Drakefield's brows drew together in a frown. She gave a
dry chuckle.

"So you don't believe me—any gel would think it an
honor. Well, must simply take my word for it, then. I have
seen it happen over and over again. When she sees that
you mean to slip that bit between her teeth, she pins her

ears back and refuses it. Besides"—her eyes narrowed slightly—"the gel may not be as fond of marriage—or you—as you think."

"What do you mean?"

"First of all, I mean that you should set the date as soon as the documents have been signed. Make certain that you do not neglect the gel in any way. An engaged gel is apt to be oversensitive." She saw that her words had not convinced him, so she gave a bark of a laugh, though her expression remained mirthless. "Well, I suppose you will learn soon enough, one way or the other."

He could not fathom what she meant, and she refused to explain herself further. All he could do was to take his leave. Back at home, he found his man of business ready with notes on the tentative agreement they had reached. Quite hungry by now, he called for some cold meat and devoured it as the settlements were discussed, point by point. He was exhausted by the time the fellow departed, giving assurances that everything could be drawn up and copied the next day.

He felt that it was insufferably rude to have passed two days without calling upon his bride to be, but unfortunately, it was out of the question to do so now. The hour already was well past nine. He asked the servant to draw him a bath. He would read the paper while it was being prepared. Peace and solitude were all he asked.

Neither were to be granted, for he had hardly stretched out upon the sofa, slippers on his feet and the paper in his hands, when a knock on the door presaged a visitor. He was a little surprised when he read the engraved card that his servant handed him, but it was not a visitor that he could refuse. Repose would have to wait. Accordingly he rose, and smiled as a young gentleman in rigidly correct evening dress entered the room nervously.

"Mr. Baxter, a pleasure to see you." He held out a hand, but his visitor was already bowing.

"My lord—Oh, I say!" In bowing, his quizzing glass had slipped from his pocket to dangle upon its ribbon. Bertie straightened himself awkwardly and began to stuff it back into his pocket, saw the outstretched hand, blushed, and abandoned the attempt, causing it to fall free once again.

"Dash it! Oh, I beg pardon, your lordship." Having succeeded in fitting it back in, he began to bow again, recollected himself, and straightened rather self-consciously. "Too kind of you, I say, your lordship," he said, giving the still outstretched hand a tentative press before releasing it.

"Won't you have a seat, Mr. Baxter?" asked Drakefield, indicating a somewhat worn but decidedly comfortable-looking leather wing chair.

"What? Oh . . . thank you." Still rather flustered, and keeping a close eye upon his host, he lowered himself gingerly into the chair, making certain that his posterior was the last to touch down. He gave Drakefield an imploring look. "Beg you not to call me Mr. Baxter—makes me think my father's about and gives me quite a start every time. Might as well call me Bertie—everyone always has, even in school, you know."

Drakefield smiled again, but there was no mockery in it. "Very well, Bertie. How d'you do? Can I be of service to you in some way?"

Perhaps it was just that his cravat had been tied too tightly. He was slowly turning purple and his words were seeming to choke him. "Came to beg a favor," he at last gasped. "Hate to intrude at this hour, but missed you earlier today. Errand couldn't wait. Daresay you're wishing me at the blazes."

"Not at all. I had no plans for the evening," returned Drakefield courteously. "Would you care for some refreshment? A glass of wine perhaps?"

Bertie was clearly too overcome to reply, so Drakefield took the situation in his own hands and called for the servant to bring them a bottle and two glasses. Perhaps the wine might put his visitor at his ease. If not, he was likely to be here the rest of the night trying to learn what his future brother-in-law wanted.

7

WHILE HE WAITED for the wine to take effect, he asked no more intrusive questions of Bertie, but kept his conversation limited to the commonplace. Bertie was singularly uncommunicative. Drakefield's inquiries about how Sarah did, which might have been responded to at length, drew no more than: "She is well, thank you." Queries about his parents met with a similar fate, as did a more detailed investigation into how Bertie himself did. After a half hour or so, Drakefield was beginning to fear that he would have to fall back upon the weather as a topic, when a transformation began gradually to make itself evident in Bertie.

At first the change was quite subtle. He no longer sat rigidly upright in his chair as he had before. He crossed his legs and began to swing one casually. He smiled at Drakefield and tapped a finger upon his glass.

"Good stuff, that."

Drakefield heaved an inward sigh. At last he would learn what Bertie wanted. "I am glad you think so. But tell me—"

"Cozy place you have here, what?"

"Yes, I find it to be, but as I was going to say—"

"No one to answer to—you may come and go as you wish, eh?"

"Bertie—"

"That's the life! Do what you please, rise when you like—"

"Bertie—"

The sharp note in his voice caused his visitor to blink at him in surprise, but at least it had the effect of halting

Bertie's soliloquy for the moment. Drakefield continued more gently, "Bertie, I think you said that you had a favor to ask of me. What is it?"

Perhaps he had overestimated Bertie's capacity. Was he having trouble focusing? His visitor leaned forward dramatically in his chair. "Lord Drakefield . . . I need your help!"

"Please, just Drakefield will do."

"You see . . ." He glanced around the room as if making certain that no one was listening. He paused for effect before speaking. "You see, I am in love!"

Drakefield had his suspicions as to what sort of female Bertie might had fallen in love with, and he could see that it would present a problem. What he could not perceive was how Bertie imagined he would be of help, and he told him so.

Bertie shook his head vigorously, thereby shaking his glass of wine also and causing it to spatter generous drops about the room. Drakefield removed it from his hand gently and set it out of reach as Bertie spoke.

"You don't understand. It's not that sort of thing at all. I am in love with your cousin—Eglantyne."

Drakefield's brow cleared. He should have remembered how occupied the two were in Green Park—but then he himself had more weighty matters to consider that day. "Well, then I cannot see your difficulty. I know you are both rather young, but I cannot imagine that either of your families would have any objection if you were willing to—"

"No, no, no!" Definitely too much wine. "That's not it. My problem is horses."

"Horses?" Try as he might, he could not see where this was leading.

Bertie clenched a fist in his effort to make Drakefield understand. "Yes! Horses . . . and a carriage. Can't take her about without one, can I? Not in Mother's stuffy old barouche. Besides, she uses it most of the time for her meetings and such. In any case, wish to cut a dash—drive her myself—"

"Can you not drive a carriage?"

"Dash my wig!" Bertie was assuming a purplish color, of outrage this time. "D'you take me for an infant? Of course I can drive—just need the proper equipage, that's all."

Drakefield was frowning in bewilderment. "Then I still do not see how I may be of help."

Bertie drove his fist into the arm of the chair. "*Dash* my wig! Just what I'm trying to tell you. Sarah already asked you—want your help choosing horses at Tatt's."

Finally the mystery was made clear. "I should be delighted to accompany you there, although as I have said, I am not an acknowledged expert on horseflesh."

"*Pater* was in the best of moods what with the engagement—congratulations and all that, by the way—so I seized my chance and asked him the day before yesterday. Only too happy to let me have a carriage of my own. Daresay I might have asked him for the moon."

There was not a polite way to halt this fresh burst of confidences, so Drakefield, who was feeling extremely weary, simply cut him off. "That's all very well, and you may tell me all about it, but as for now, if we may simply set a date to visit—"

"Confound it, that's what I've been trying to tell you. Must go tomorrow—Sheepnose say that Exham's grays are up for sale."

"Sheepnose?"

"Pal of mine at university. We're forever going upon some lark together, like the pig—did I tell you about it?"

"I think you are wandering from the point," suggested Drakefield mildly.

"Oh, yes. Anyway, he arrived in London just a few days after me. Rusticated, same as I was. He's the deuce of a fellow. Quite up to snuff, and if he thinks Exham's horses are good—"

"But I must call upon your sister tomorrow."

"Confound it! She can wait. She is there every day. Only day Exham's horses for sale."

"My lord, you have another visitor."

"This is not the time," Drakefield said, waving his manservant away.

"But he says it is most urgent, my lord."

It must be an unusually persistent visitor. Drakefield heaved a sigh. "Very well, show him in."

In another moment an extremely disheveled man entered. His casual trousers were stained and his muslin was far from spotless. His jacket showed an inattention to current modes, and it stood in need of a good pressing. His hair, though apparently some attempt had been made to brush it, stood up wildly upon his head. There were dark smudges upon his face and hands, and his eyes burned with excitement. Bertie goggled at him.

"Drakefield, I've done it, I think. My theories seem to work. With only a small investment I think I can build a working model and then—" He halted as he noticed Bertie draped across the wing chair.

Drakefield gave a weary sigh. "Johnson, this is my future brother-in-law, Bertram Baxter. Bertie, this is Donald Johnson, who is, er, one of my old pals from university."

They acknowledged the introduction with mutual surprise. Johnson turned back to Drakefield. "Then it has happened!" he said eagerly. He took Drakefield's hand and shook it. "Congratulations! This means that we should have no obstacle in—"

Drakefield's eyes narrowed and he shot a warning glance in Bertie's direction. "No one but the family knows yet, as it has not been officially announced."

"Oh, I see." He hesitated for a moment. "I am sorry to burst in like this, but I was so excited that I had to share my discovery with you immediately. You know the problem, of course, is to keep the gas from exploding and—"

Drakefield gave his head an almost imperceptible shake, but he said, "Yes, that is capital. I am quite as happy as you are and would like to discuss it with you further, but this is not the place or the time."

Johnson and Bertie were still eyeing each other with curiosity. "Yes, you are right, it can wait." Without further ado, he flung himself down in a chair. "I will be only too glad to tell you about it later." He stared at Bertie, who stared back. Clearly each was determined to outwait the other visitor. So much for peace and solitude.

Drakefield resigned himself to the inevitable. "Gibbons, another glass."

Johnson looked at the bottle in some disgust. "Wine? Where is the whisky?"

"My lord—" Gibbons didn't get another word out of his mouth before the next visitor, a slender gentleman of the medium height, painfully made his way into the room. In marked contrast to the previous one, this was dressed with exquisite care. His cravat was perfection, his coat extremely well cut, and his inexpressibles fitted him like a glove. Bertie gaped at him in admiration.

With one gloved hand the exquisite carefully flicked an invisible bit of dust off the right sleeve of his dark blue coat before crossing the threshold. He took one limping step forward, then paused as he surveyed the group.

"My dear Drakefield. A thousand pardons. I had no idea that you were entertaining a party." He did not add that it was an ill-assembled one. "D'you know, when I saw the candle burning in the window at this hour, I had rather a different picture in my mind." He acknowledged Johnson with an inclination of the head. "How are you, my dear fellow? Unchanged as regards your attention to appearances, I see." He turned to Bertie with a look of curiosity. "But perhaps I am intruding and should take my leave?"

"Clavering, this is Mr. Bertram Baxter. Baxter, my friend Gervase Francis Molyneux Clavering."

"Baxter, did you say?" he asked, raising his eyebrows at Drakefield. "But I am delighted, my dear fellow, absolutely delighted."

Bertram, having staggered to his feet, could only accept that hand with the same kind of awe that had earlier marked his intercourse with Drakefield.

"But my dear Drakefield, you have not said whether or not I am intruding. Shall I go?"

Drakefield would have liked to tell him to go, and to take the others with him so that he might at last enjoy some qui-

etude. It was deucedly late. He saw from Clavering's expression, however, that he had read the situation at a glance
and was deriving considerable amusement from it. Despite
all of his protests, there never was a way to make him leave
once he had clearly determined to stay.

"Please yourself," he said ungraciously. "Gibbons, one
more glass."

To say that the conversation which followed was halting
was an understatement. Clavering, who might have main-
tained it with ease, was enjoying himself too much to con-
tribute. It was tedious in the extreme.

He could practically see the thoughts forming in Bertie's
head. If this was the sort of evening that the Black Dandy
usually spent, then clearly he had been regarding him with
too much awe. Drakefield stifled a yawn, and to make his
feelings even more obvious, refused to call for another bottle when the present one had been drained.

The first to surrender was Johnson, who evidently was
still disgruntled at the fact that there was no whisky. He informed Drakefield that he would expect him to call the next
day. Bertie put up a good fight, but was yawning himself
by the time the clock chimed two. He looked over at the
other visitor, but Clavering, still fresh as an oyster, had extracted a pack of cards from his pocket and was busy playing against himself at vingt-en-un.

"By gad! That hand has taken three out of four games already. I'd wager on its taking the next three also."

Bertie yawned again. "I suppose I had better go. You will
come tomorrow, won't you?"

"I will come to call upon your sister, yes."

"But the other—" His eyes were pleading.

"We shall have to see about that tomorrow. Good night,
Bertie," said Drakefield firmly, showing his guest to the
door.

Bertie had to be content with that.

As Drakefield reentered the room, Clavering turned to
him, his eyes alight with amusement. "My dear fellow!
What rare entertainment."

"You are the only one who found it diverting," Drake-field informed him as he regained his seat upon the sofa.

"I hardly liked to say anything in front of your other guests, but Judith informed me today that congratulations are in order. So that was your future brother-in-law?"

"Yes, unless as my grandmother predicts, the girl takes it into her head to cry off and leave me at the altar."

"I shouldn't think that likely." His eyes narrowed. "What is it, Drake?"

He gave a hollow laugh. "Why, nothing! I am as happy as any man can be. I am told that I fetched quite a pretty price."

"This is the wine talking." Clavering began gathering up his cards. "I will come and see you when you are in a more rational mood. Who is hosting the announcement party?"

"The duchess."

His eyebrows flew up in surprise, but he merely said, "Indeed?" He put the deck back into his pocket. "I hope you will beg a card for me. I should like to have the privilege of meeting *La Colonne D'or* myself."

"What?"

"It is the nickname that has caught society's fancy, including, as it does, her stature, her elegance, and her fair beauty and her wealth. Do you not find it apt?"

"No, I do not." He gave a snort. "And neither will you once you've met her."

"Oh." He gave his friend a thoughtful look. "Do you know, Drakefield, the duchess is a singularly perceptive lady. It just may be that the girl *will* cry off and end all your troubles. Farewell."

Drakefield would have asked him just what in the devil he meant by that, but Clavering had already made his limping way from the room. He lifted a hand to his forehead—it was pounding. It was too late for his bath. All he wished was for sleep and oblivion. He called for the servant. "Gibbons, I'm going to bed."

"Very good, my lord." The servant blinked his weary relief.

* * *

She had avoided seeing him ever since he had asked her for her hand. She might have congratulated herself upon her success in evading him except for the fact that he had not called upon her either. Could it be that he had as little wish to see her as she had to see him? The thought was a troubling one, but she shrugged it off. It did not matter even if it were true. She would be no one's bride but Alan's, and therefore Drakefield's feelings were unimportant. She had evolved a daring plan during the night. If she could think of no way to break the engagement, and if Alan had not returned before the wedding (which was unlikely), then she would merely run away. In accordance with this resolve, she had risen and told her mother that she had some shopping to do and would take her maid. Even Eglantyne would be unwilling to lend support to this plan. Mrs. Baxter, still euphoric about the betrothal, had no objections to the announced activity.

Sarah had chosen a plain dress of gray watered silk and an unobtrusive bonnet with a veil to go with it. She meant to go to an inn to inquire about fees. As the time for the wedding came nearer, she would flee in a postchaise to Dover, and then if her nerves held steady, find a boat to take her to Spain. She had heard that some officers' wives followed their husbands to the Peninsula. She would be there to nurse Alan if he were wounded. Of course, the life he had described was not exactly appealing, but she felt herself bound in honor to be his spouse. The thought of trying to procure passage was daunting also. She wondered how much it would cost, and how she would manage for accommodations. It did not occur to her to consider the difficulties she would encounter trying to find one British soldier in the midst of a war-torn country.

She might be intimidated by the prospect, but she could comfort herself with the notion that few people had more determination than she did. She would show all of London how little she cared for prestige or social position. From a leader of fashion to a social outcast. Her lip trembled a little at the notion. She hoped that Drakefield would not be too humiliated. Despite all his sneering arrogance, he could be kind also. She gave her head a shake as if to dispel these ideas. After all, no sacrifice was too great for love, or so the books always said. Even if her parents cut her off without a cent, she and Alan could be happy living in a cottage, she thought. Of course, it would be better if they did not cut her off. She would write them a most earnest farewell letter, explaining matters as best she could. Perhaps that would help.

She drew on her gloves as she stood before the mirror in the hall. She was just tying her bonnet when the door opened, and Drakefield stepped inside, followed by Fraley. Drakefield looked as startled as she felt.

"Miss Baxter. Were you going out? Have I called at an inopportune time?"

"I did not think you'd wish for his lordship to have to wait outside to be announced," said Fraley excusingly.

"Lord Drakefield! No . . . that is, I was going out, but it will not matter if I delay for a few moments." Drat it! Why did she have to be so agreeable to him? She could have sent him upon his way. And why did she feel so breathless when he was about? Well, they hardly could stand in the hallway and talk in front of the butler, even though he was beaming upon them most benevolently.

"My lord, would you care to come into the drawing room?"

"Thank you."

"And shall I ring for some tea?"

"No, thank you." He eyed her ensemble. "Your dress, it is most elegant, but not in your usual style, is it?"

Well, she had not planned upon his catching her. "I find that people become easily bored unless you introduce the unexpected."

There was that same sparkle deep in his eyes. "Very true. I would never presume to dictate style to you, my dear, since you are perfection itself."

As she took a chair and he followed suit, she reminded herself that she was supposed to be repulsing him. "Really, your lordship, I did not expect to see you at this hour of the morning." It was not so terribly early, being some time after eleven o'clock, but the usual hour for morning calls for some inexplicable reason was in the afternoon.

His brows drew together. "I hope that you will call me by my given name, which is Everard," he said gently.

Never, she determined, but she smiled slightly. "As you please, your lordship. Was there something particular you wished to discuss with me today?"

Good. The frown was slightly more pronounced. "I consider that we have a great deal to discuss. I am sorry that I have not been able to see you since the day I spoke to you."

She could feel herself coloring, which gave the lie to her indifference. Blast! She tried to cover it as best she could by smiling and giving an airy wave of her hand. "Oh, you need not concern yourself with that. I am certain that you must have been very busy with all sorts of important matters."

"Yes, I have, but none is so important as this."

It would have been nicer if he had said "as you," but she promptly chided herself for the thought. Why should she care what he did or did not feel for her? It was all beside the point, anyway.

"In fact, I think that perhaps we should discuss the date for our wedding. My grandmother wishes to host our engagement party. I think it a generous and appropriate gesture, and hope that you have no objections."

What a party it would be! In the Duchess of Wiltham's monstrous town house, they could select from the cream of society for their guests. She was lost in visions of glory and forgot for a moment that she might well be gone by then.

"Miss Baxter?"

"Oh—"

"Have you any objections?"

"No, of course not. It is most kind in her to offer to do such a thing."

"Very well." He could not quite suppress a sigh. "Had you given any thought as to a date? Have your parents expressed any wishes in the matter?"

She had to shake her head.

"Well, since May has just ended, I suppose we may set a date in June, before the Season ends."

A month or less for an engagement was quite usual. She must think of some way to delay it. "Oh, no, my lord!"

He frowned a little as she began improvising. "The preparations, the trousseau, you know that everything I wear must be out of the ordinary, and so it will take some additional time."

"The end of June?"

"Oh, no, I-I, um . . ." An idea struck her. "I wish to be married in August. It is a family tradition." Her mother and father *had* married in that month. Although she had never heard of anyone else in her family marrying then, it was always possible that they had.

"August?" He did not like it, she could tell, but he managed to be polite. "But town will be dreadfully thin of company—and it can be quite warm."

She forced a little laugh. "What better way to arouse society's curiosity? And to rid ourselves of some of the dead bores who might otherwise attend?"

He frowned again. "But does this mean that you also wish to delay the announcement of our engagement?"

She did wish it, but she could not immediately think of a reason why they should. "No, I suppose not. After all, if our engagement is so unusually long as to occasion remark, we may simply set a new fashion."

He smiled and his dimple showed again. It was a singularly attractive smile, she had to admit. She felt she would be happy to remain by him forever as long as he smiled like that. Why was her heart pounding so?

"Drakefield!" The door swung open and Bertie popped into the room, still busily engaged with tying his cravat. "I knew you wouldn't disappoint me. Thought I heard your voice out in the hall. Morning, Sal." He obviously had overcome his diffidence.

"Bertie, I am attempting to have a private conversation with your sister," said Drakefield in a voice which was not quite even enough for someone who was not beginning to lose his temper.

"But I told you," replied Bertie, aggrieved. "It is today or never! I have to buy those grays."

"Then it is never if you must have my company. London is full of horses and—"

It was a golden opportunity and Sarah did not know why it had taken her so long to seize it. "Oh, pray, gentlemen, if you already have made an appointment for today, do not let me delay you. I understand how such matters are."

"Good girl, Sal," said Bertie enthusiastically. "You see, Drake—"

"I have no intention of going," Drakefield was saying simultaneously. "I consider our plans to be of primary importance—"

"Oh, pshaw! As if we could not wait to settle things later today, or tomorrow, for that matter. What difference could a few hours make? No, you gentlemen must have your little pleasures and I—"

"But my wish is to be with you—"

"You see, Drakefield, Sally can talk to you at any time. The horses will only be there today—"

"Go on. I have my own errands to run, after all—"

"But—"

"Come on! I'll wager Sheepnose is waiting there for us already."

"Goodbye! Enjoy yourselves."

"I'll speak to you at the first opportunity. I promise you that."

He shouted the words as Bertie hustled him through the doorway and out into the hall. Sarah could hear him complaining about the appearance of Bertie's cravat as they departed. Good! He was gone and their wedding day was not yet set. She had been successful. She wished, though, that her eyes were not smarting so. She had to extract a handkerchief from her reticule to dry them. She supposed she was crying from happiness.

8

IT WAS ODD, Drakefield thought, how one could set such simple goals and yet not achieve them. All he had wished to accomplish today was to have a conversation with Sarah and set the date for their wedding. Instead he had found himself hustled off to Tattersall's by her brother. Instead of the pleasing scent she wore, his nostrils were filled with the overpowering odor of a multitude of horses.

True to Bertie's prediction, a young gentleman was waiting there for them. The spotted kerchief about his neck proclaimed his sporting blood. Drakefield had wondered at the nickname, but when he saw the individual, he had to admit to himself that it was singularly apt. Sheepnose had a slightly somnolent expression, protuberant ears, and a well-fed sleekness which made him resemble the animal; but it was his nose, long and broad, that sealed his fate.

"Drakefield, I would like you to meet my friend, Arthur Sheephouse. Sheep—Sheephouse, this is Lord Drakefield, who has kindly consented to accompany me here."

Consent had little to do with it, thought Drakefield. To his relief, he saw that at least this individual was not going to fawn over him. After muttering the minimum dictated by politeness, Sheepnose turned to the matter at hand. "Exham's grays in the box over there. Care for a look?"

Drakefield had been rather worried about the sorts of horses Bertie's friends might choose for him, but when he saw the pair, he realized his fears were groundless. Intelligence might not radiate from Sheepnose's face, but clearly he knew a thing or two about horses. Drakefield examined the animals appreciatively.

"Well proportioned, nice light necks, broad, deep chests, straight, short backs, clean hocks—and well matched besides. A handsome pair of animals."

"Groom looked them over already. Found them sound. Cursed rare good fortune," offered Sheepnose anxiously, overcome by this praise.

Drakefield shook his head. "I would say you have done well. You have no need of my help, so I will bid you good day and—"

"Wait!" Bertie's face was anxious. "There is the matter of the carriage too." This proved to be somewhat more difficult, since the relative merits of a curricle versus a phaeton must be argued, as well as variations upon them. The importance of make, color, and the necessity for *C* springs as opposed to the older style of *S* springs then had to be discussed.

After giving his opinions, Drakefield gladly would have departed, but found he was not to be permitted to do so. Despite all their bravado, the young gentlemen were clearly nervous about making such an important purchase, and desired the presence of an older and more experienced companion. He submitted to his fate with only a sigh, foreseeing that he had a long, dull afternoon ahead of him.

So it proved to be, and matters were not improved by the fact that his head was still aching from the late hours he had kept the previous night. When at last the purchases had been made successfully, he thought that he would escape, but found that he was expected to accompany them to Limmers' Hotel for a congratulatory glass of daffy.

It was not a beverage he enjoyed, but he found there was no escaping their importunities. When he crossed the threshold, he could not help but be aware of raised eyebrows and whisperings. It was unusual for a pink of the *ton* to find himself in the gathering place of those of the sporting fancy, and judging from their expressions, they found it every bit as singular. His two young escorts, however, were oblivious to these undercurrents and settled down to their celebration in great good cheer. Drakefield was actually forced to drain a glass before mentioning his need to leave once again. Magnanimously they insisted that he join them for dinner. This was taking goodwill a bit too far.

The hour was approaching nine when he made his escape at last. He had to breathe a sigh of relief as he did so, for the gin was having an unwholesome effect upon both Bertie and Sheepnose, and they had begun to reminisce sentimentally about the various larks they had kicked up at school. Drakefield, catching the wistful notes in their voices, feared to remain. London would not be the same once these two were unleashed upon it.

Once more it was far too late to call upon Sarah. He cursed his luck. Upon returning home he found a stack of missives waiting for him. One was from the duchess and one from Judith, demanding to know the date of the wedding so that they might set their plans into motion. Surely he would wish for the party to be next week or the week after at the latest? There was little he could tell them, so he simply laid their notes aside for the moment. There were the usual sorts of invitations and one quite irritated scribble from Johnson, demanding to know why Drakefield had not called upon him this morning. Drakefield shook his head. He could not possibly see him tomorrow, for he should try to have an audience with Sarah again instead. A note would have to suffice for now. Johnson was a brilliant fellow, but not always understanding about the demands society made upon one.

In order to discourage any visitors, he took to his bedchamber immediately, but once there, found it hard to sleep. The central problem occupying his mind was how he would be able to have conversation with Sarah alone. Why should such a simple thing be so difficult? He was tired of having matters unsettled between them. He must speak to her tomorrow. He would kidnap her, if necessary, so that they might talk. As the thought occurred to him, he smiled. Kidnapping. It might prove the perfect solution to his problems. With that in mind, he closed his eyes and peacefully drifted off to sleep.

Had he but known it, his intended had experienced a day that was every bit as frustrating as his own. She had ridden in her mother's barouche to the vicinity of an inn, but had left her carriage some distance behind. She was aware that her destination might occasion some curiosity in the mind of her family's coachman, and so she and her maid were forced to make their way to the inn upon foot. Even worse, a coach had just arrived, full of passengers, and Sarah had to endure a great many rude remarks and questioning looks as she shoved her way through the crowd.

Once inside, matters did not improve. She found that it was difficult for a heavily veiled young lady to be taken seriously as regarded the hiring of a postchaise. It wasn't until she had extracted a gold coin (which might very well be needed for her journey) from her reticule and laid it upon the counter that she found anyone would even pay attention to her.

The landlord, a good-natured man, enlightened her ignorance. Posting charges were exorbitant. She had not had any idea that it would cost so much. Persistent, she inquired about coaching fares. This was somewhat closer to the realm of possibility. The worst blow came when she asked if he knew what the fare from Dover to Calais was likely to be. He could not help chuckling out loud.

"Eh, miss, that's a good 'un. From Dover to Calais, you say? I'm not sure why you're wishful to be going to France, but you won't find a packet to take you there. Service is suspended because of the war."

She flushed, but luckily her veil covered it. "Well, of course, I do not wish to actually go to France. I am going to join my—my husband, who is fighting in Spain. I just need to know how much it costs for the packet from Dover to— to wherever they go in Spain."

He shook his head. "I've never heard of a packet to Spain."

"Well, there must be one . . . to Portugal, then?"

He sighed. "There's a packet to Lisbon, but if I were you, miss—that is, ma'am—I should wait here in London for your *husband* to return. 'Twould be easiest."

She drew herself up to her full height. "What you think

does not concern me. Do you have information on how much the packet to Lisbon costs?"

He shook his head. "I can't say, other than that it's bound to cost a pretty penny. The trip to Falmouth is dear, also, but then it's about two hundred seventy miles."

"Falmouth? But why—"

"Because that's where the Lisbon packet sails from—not Dover, miss." He gave her a pitying look and turned to help a large, red-faced man who was demanding a room.

She left the inn in a state of shock. This seemed to be the end of all her plans. Falmouth was two hundred miles farther away than Dover. There would have to be money to pay for beds at inns along the road, as well as the coach fare. And the length of the trip! Why, Alan might return while she was still on her way there.

If she had enough funds, of course, she could just hire a postchaise and a boat of her own in Dover. Her parents gave her pin money to purchase trifles she saw here and there, but since all her clothes went onto their accounts, there was no need for her ever to have any great sum about her. The little she had managed to save would hardly carry her out of London, and certainly not abroad. It seemed an insurmountable obstacle.

Her maid, more knowledgeable in worldly affairs than she, informed her that rides upon carriers' carts could be had very cheaply. Sarah, who had seen the vehicles in passing, shook her head at the idea. Not only were they the slowest form of transportation available, they were apt to carry persons who made the coach passengers appear positively genteel by contrast. It would take some time to recover from this blow. She rode back to her house in stunned silence.

A restless night did not bring any fresh ideas into her mind. She awoke early, still trying to hit upon some way to salvage her plan. She did not linger in bed, but dressed and breakfasted. Perhaps she would call her maid and go for a walk. Perhaps the exercise would stimulate her brain.

She had just reached her decision when a visitor was an-

nounced. She glanced at the clock and saw that it was nearing ten. Was this some new eccentricity of Drakefield's, to
call upon her when all the fashionable world was still abed?

Dressed in driving clothes, he was as handsome as ever,
though she thought she saw evidence of a new strain about
his eyes. He bowed deeply and apologized for calling so
early. He had wanted to make certain to catch her. Would
she care to take a drive with him today? He would be happy
to wait while she made herself ready.

There was no polite way to refuse, and besides, it did
look as if it would be a beautiful day for a drive. Perhaps
the fresh air would clear her mind. She could not imagine
where they would go at this hour of the day, but it did not
concern her overly much. She hurried upstairs, and so did
not see him hand a sealed envelope to the butler.

She dressed quickly but carefully, wearing her signature
yellow gloves and an outrageous bonnet. It was odd how
one became accustomed to things. Perhaps it was because
she had seen all the fashionables similarly garbed but her
ensemble now simply appeared daring rather than *outré* to
her.

It was also peculiar how eager she was for this drive. She
had been glad to see Drakefield, she was forced to admit.
She supposed that with her spirits as low as they had been
and not a shred of sympathy anywhere, the arrival of even a
total stranger would have been welcome to her.

In any event, as they set off, she could feel a distinct
lightening of her heart. Surely, everything would work out
for the best. She glanced at the handsome profile beside
her. That was another strange thing. She had thought
Drakefield not at all handsome when they met, but now he
seemed quite prepossessing. Perhaps that was because she
had discovered that he had a kind side, even if it were well
hidden.

She gave her head a shake. So much analysis would
hardly be of help to her. She would ignore such thoughts
and abandon herself to the pleasure of the ride. Drakefield
made no effort at conversation, and she was happy to
dream mindlessly as they drove along.

They passed through Holborn and Cheapside, and had almost reached the Tower before she realized that anything was out of the ordinary. They were headed east! Surely, they should have been traveling west, toward the fashionable part of town. She glanced at her driver with some unease. "Where are we going?"

"I thought we'd make a little excursion to Kent."

"Kent!"

"Yes. After yesterday it became clear to me that if we ever meant to be married, I should have to kidnap you."

"Kidnap—!" Her head was spinning. She had read of these sorts of abductions in novels, but then the bride was always an unwilling one. She had already consented to marry Drakefield. Why would he wish to make a runaway match? That is, why would he unless his creditors were hounding him and he had become desperate . . . ?

It was rather inconsiderate too. He had not even given her the chance to pack a bandbox. She realized just a moment later that the proper course of action would have been to scream and try to throw herself down from the carriage, dangerous though it might be, but instead she issued a practical objection. "But don't you have to go to Scotland instead?" She had made rather a study of runaway matches in the past several months.

"Scotland?" He was frowning.

"Yes, to Gretna Green?"

"Gretna—oh!" His dimple appeared and he gave a shout of laughter—a sound which she had never heard escape him before. What did he mean by laughing she wondered angrily, though she had to admit there was a certain boyish attractiveness about him in the throes of amusement.

He still had not recovered. She hoped that the groom was not paying undue attention to all this, but then Drakefield undoubtedly had paid him well before setting off on this expedition. Drakefield shook his head, not yet master of himself.

"Forgive me," he at last gasped. "I did not mean to frighten you. It was a joke—a poor one, admittedly. I am driving us to Greenwich to spend the day. I hope that there we may escape interruption long enough to plan the details of our wedding."

"Oh." Color flooded into her face. What must he think of her? She looked away as if to admire some interesting object in the distance.

"I am sorry," he said quietly. "We will talk later."

There was a great deal she might have said and did feel like saying to him, but she must contain herself for the moment, at least. She could not discuss it further in front of the groom. A perfect indifference. Well, she could assume it.

"Greenwich. Do you know I have never been there? How long is the drive?"

"It is only five miles from London, so it will not take us a great deal of time."

"I hope my parents will not worry."

"I left them a note, telling them of our destination and when we should return."

His own assumption of composure, though she hated to confess it, was a help to her. It was much easier to pretend that the misunderstanding had never occurred, and far preferable not to dwell on the fact that she must appear a perfect idiot.

Fortunately, there was a great deal to see, though not all of it was terribly picturesque as they passed through Southwark and on to the village of Deptford. At the dockyards here, Drakefield informed her, the royal yachts were generally kept. It was a large town, and possessed a good many fine houses, though in general it seemed very dirty.

"We are now in Kent," he added, "so Greenwich will not be too terribly far—just perhaps another mile."

Sarah was ashamed to admit that she had but rarely been out of London in her life. It was all very interesting and different from what she was accustomed to seeing. As they approached Greenwich, she could not help exclaiming at its beauty. Drakefield slowed the horses.

"There are many fine sights to see—the Greenwich Hospital, the Royal Observatory, the Naval Asylum. The park has many fine walks. I had my man pack a picnic for us and so if you prefer—"

"Oh, I don't care about the rest," she exclaimed. "Let us go to the park."

It was a delightful area, far more scenic than any she had seen in London. The hills were much steeper than any she remembered being near before. Drakefield had told her that the view from the Royal Observatory was particularly fine, but in the interests of privacy, One-Tree Hill seemed a more suitable destination.

Accordingly, they made their way thence, the groom trailing along behind them with the picnic basket. In response to Drakefield's inquiry, Sarah had to admit she was ready for a nuncheon. Worry had driven away her appetite at breakfast this morning; sunshine and fresh air had returned it to her with a vengeance.

A suitably shaded area was chosen. The groom spread out a cloth and laid out the comestibles before vanishing discreetly. There were figures strolling about in the distance, but otherwise they were quite alone. Sarah for no reason abruptly felt shy.

Drakefield solicitously helped her to the viands, cutting her a piece of a cold gammon pie, inquiring if she cared for a slice of the pickled tongue or any of the potted pigeon. He was dismayed when he realized that he had nothing but wine to offer her to drink. He knew that she was unused to spirits, and if she preferred, he would send his groom to procure—

All her troubles had put her in a rather reckless mood. She shook her head and said that she had drunk wine before and was sure it would do her no harm. She had been given a glass of wine before, it was true, on the occasion of a relative's wedding. It had been a small one and she had been only twelve at the time, but there was no need to go into such detail.

The taste was, as she remembered, not particularly pleasing, but it was bearable when one used it just to wash down food. Really, the picnic was delicious. She had never dined al fresco before. It was delightful and quite relaxing. She only wished she might untie her boots and unlace her stays.

Once one became accustomed to it, the wine was not really so disagreeable. She commented upon it to Drakefield.

There was something different about him too. That harsh look had gone from his face. "It is from the last of my father's cellar. Whatever else, he did have good taste in wine. I suppose I should be grateful, since there will be no more until after this war is over."

The war. She didn't wish to think about it. There was a warm glow spreading over her. She delicately wiped the last crumb of a gooseberry tart from the corner of her mouth. It had all been simply delicious. She told Drakefield so. He responded with a smile.

It was a perfectly marvelous day. The air was perfect. The clouds were perfect. The sunshine was perfect. It was wonderful to be alive. She looked at her companion and it appeared that he, too, was enjoying himself. Propped against a tree, he reclined upon the grass. The breeze ruffled his dark curls. She had never had a chance to study him so closely before now. In fact, they had never really had a chance to talk.

"How long has your hair been like that?" The sound of her own voice surprised her. She had been wondering the question to herself, but had not intended to voice it. He looked at her, surprised.

"The white part, I mean. Was it like that when you were born or . . . it is rather unusual," she concluded lamely.

To her relief, he smiled, evidently not offended. "It began to turn white when I was about fourteen, I suppose. It is a Drakefield characteristic. When you see the portraits of my ancestors, you will see that many of them shared it."

"Oh."

"This is a great part of what I wished to do today," he said, suddenly serious. "The lawyers have settled everything between them, but it seems to me that you must have a great many questions that you wish to ask of me. We have never really had an opportunity to be alone. I would like you to ask me anything you wish to know."

The question that popped into Sarah's mind first was, Who is Lady Fernsbury and what is she to you? Fortunately, her tongue did not betray her this time, and she simply remained silent, gazing at the ground.

He misinterpreted her reticence. "I am in earnest. I should like there to be open communication between us, Sarah, if you do not dislike my using your first name."

She shook her head to show that she did not mind. It seemed natural somehow.

"There must be something you wish to ask me. Please do."

She raised her eyes shyly to him. "They . . . society has a name for you. I have often wondered about it. How did you come to be the 'Black Dandy'?"

He turned his head away, and for a moment she was afraid that she had asked too personal a question. He plucked a blade of grass and began to twirl it in his hand mindlessly.

"I . . . when I was a child in London—that is, some of my earliest memories are of tradesmen calling, asking for money. I don't know that I can explain it. The humiliation of going somewhere and not being able to buy anything, because the shopkeeper will no longer extend credit, despite all the grand titles you may possess. And when I went to school . . . well, it was worse. I was never sure if I would be there the next term . . . if there would be sufficient funds."

He looked up, gazing off at a scene visible to no one else. "I fell in with a group of boys—I suppose you would call them odd fish, like myself. None of us had money, but what little we could save we squandered on dress."

The champion cricketer, the brilliant scholar, whom everyone admired an odd fish? What a peculiar picture he had of himself.

"I suppose I felt the need to set myself apart, so I adopted the mode I wear now. It was inevitable. I learned early on that no matter how poor one's finances were, the tradesmen were always a little more inclined to deference if one were well dressed. Then too, doors open that would otherwise be closed." He gave a sigh. "When I was younger I occasionally wished that I had been born into a different situation, where I might earn an honest living instead." He shook his head. "But I cannot help being what I am." He gave a bittersweet smile. "We all must play the cards we are dealt, as a friend of mine is so fond of saying."

He looked up at her. "You ask most probing questions, my dear. I do not think I have ever told anyone else that. What else do you wish to know?"

It was an emotional bravery to which she was unused and which she did not know he possessed. Without any ado to lay his soul bare for her to see. She could only shake her head in wonder at it. "Do you have any questions of me?"

He smiled and there was such unexpected tenderness in it that her heart turned over. "No. I have to admit that when we first met I would have had many questions to ask of you. But I know you now, you see."

She blushed as she thought of her former scheme to drive him away.

He rose and held out a hand. "We are wasting a beautiful day and a fine hill. Do you care to climb it with me?"

She nodded and he pulled her to her feet, where she felt surprisingly unsteady for a moment before recovering. He tucked her hand in his arm and they began their walk. They climbed in silence for several minutes. She was glad of his assistance. It would have been difficult to ascend so steep a hill by herself.

When at last they reached the summit, she was slightly breathless but exhilarated. The prospect was magnificent. They looked down upon the tops of the trees, and the cattle grazing upon the fields beneath. Before them lay the Greenwich Hospital and the Thames, with the Isle of Dogs beyond. All about them was picturesque countryside and villages, with London rising past them in the distance.

"I would like for us to settle upon a date for our wedding. My grandmother and my aunt are all impatience to host a party for us, with your mother's approval and help, of course."

How considerate he was. Her heart was racing so. Was it still from the effects of the climb?

He spoke again. "I was afraid that you might be angry with me because of our misunderstanding earlier."

Now she truly could not help blushing. In unconscious embarrassment her hand clenched, tightening upon his arm.

"Oh, Sarah. I did not mean to laugh, truly. It was just—"

She could not look at him and she loosed her hold of his arm. "I know," she said in a small, tight voice. "It was simply ridiculous. You could not help laughing when I had made such an absurd—"

"My dear, it was not that—"

". . . Figure of myself. I am certain that you—"

"Sarah!" He had taken her by both hands and turned her to face him. He said nothing further until she finally lifted her eyes to gaze at him.

"My dear, it was unexpected, that was all," he said gently. "I only wish I had had the ingenuity to think of the scheme myself."

Tears were welling in her eyes and one escaped to slip slowly down her cheek. He released one hand and lifted a finger to wipe it away gently. "Please, my dear, don't—"

The touch of his hand on her face sent a novel and thrilling sensation through her. Her vision was somewhat blurred from the tears, but it seemed to her that there was an unfamiliar look in his eyes. He was very near to her. She could hear him breathe, could smell the masculine scent of him.

"Sarah." It was little more than a whisper, but it seemed to signify something that a part of her understood with no further explanation. She was inclining slightly toward him as his face drew nearer. She saw it very close for a moment, and then she was in his arms and his lips were upon hers. It was bliss. It was heaven. She concentrated all her energies upon the project at hand. It was as if she had awakened an ever increasing thirst deep in herself.

"My dear . . . my dear . . . we must stop." In another moment he had pushed her back from him slightly.

It took just a moment for everything to register. She gazed at him in horror. My word! Her arms had actually snaked about his neck! She had behaved like the veriest wanton. "Oh!"

She would have attempted to flee, but he caught her by the shoulders and drew her to him once again. "Sarah, stop!"

She was still trying to tug away. "You must release me!"

"No!" Surprised by the sternness of the word, she looked up into that face again. It was grave. "You . . . you and I have done nothing wrong. We are affianced. I admit that we were indiscreet, but there is no one else in the immediate vicinity, after all."

She could not face him. With nowhere else to turn, she sank her face into his shoulder and began to dig blindly in her reticule for a handkerchief. He extracted his and handed it to her.

"My dear. . . . my dear, I am glad this happened. It is easier to embark upon a marriage with the certainty that each partner finds the other . . . pleasing."

She was wiping her eyes with the handkerchief when she saw what havoc her impulsive action had wreaked. "Oh, your coat!"

"It is nothing." He had her firmly by the hand now. "I had to stop it before we—before we overstepped the bounds of propriety more than we already did."

"Oh!"

He tilted her tear-stained face up firmly to meet his. "I enjoyed kissing you, Sarah, and I hope that we shall do a great deal more of it and as soon as possible. Shall we move the date of the wedding up?"

How handsome and how dear that face was. She wanted to marry him tomorrow, today, if possible. But there was something she had forgotten. It was important to marry in August. She could not remember why.

"No," she breathed.

He shook his head. "Very well, then, but I mean to marry you the first week in August then, perhaps the first day." Still holding her face in his hand, he stroked her cheek with his thumb. "And I shall tell my grandmother to hold the engagement party as soon as possible." He leaned down and briefly saluted her lips once more. There was warmth in that gaze and concern. Sarah basked in it. She loved him. Why hadn't she realized it before? He was her ideal of what a gentleman should be. He offered her his arm once again, and they began slowly down the hill.

9

SEATED AT HER escritoire, Sarah dipped her pen in her ink glass and hesitated. She had known that this job would be difficult, but surely it should not be impossible. With her other hand she fingered the locket she had removed from about her neck, the locket which she would never wear again, the locket which contained one of Alan's curls.

"Dear Alan," she wrote.

There, it was a beginning. She waited patiently for the next words. None arrived. "I hope you are well?" No, that would be terrible if he were wounded. Perhaps she should just come right to the point. "I am engaged to another." That might be rather too brutal.

She wished she could rid herself of this sense of guilt. Really, it was ridiculous. Alan certainly hadn't written *her* any fond letters, at least he hadn't until after she had written several effusive ones to him. She blushed at the thought. If his affection for her was based upon a few silly letters, then he would hardly be crushed by one more.

The worrisome thought, of course, was that he could receive her letter on the eve of a battle. He had seemed to think that there would be one soon in his last letter. It would be horrible to send him off with a callous farewell letter, perhaps in his breast pocket. And although it was too terrible even to consider, there was the possibility that he could be killed. Could she send him to his end with such a letter?

No, she was not inhuman enough to do it, she decided, crumpling the piece of paper before her. If she did not write (well, she had not for several days, after all), he would be able to draw his own conclusions. He would know that her ardor had cooled. Time would help to ease the sting of her rejection. She had until August. Why, that was still two months away! She laid her pen down.

The unanswerable question was why her ardor had cooled. When had she ceased to think of Alan as her ideal and begun to center her thoughts upon Drakefield instead? She had only grudgingly admired his looks in the beginning. He had won her gratitude with his support at Almack's; she could not have endured the ordeal without it, particularly given her headstrong choice of dress. It was then that she had first seen his kinder side. That night she had caught a glimpse, and the next day she had a confirmation of his sense of humor. She had seen that his delight in the absurdity of bending society to conform to his rules was equal to her own.

She shook her head. No, she could not think of a single instance when she had "fallen in love," and it certainly had not happened at first sight. It had been a slowly growing affection, tenacious and powerful enough to have revealed that what she felt for Alan was no more than a schoolgirl's infatuation. How absurd she had been! To have been ready to declare her undying love for Alan when she did not even know him at all.

She closed her eyes abruptly. She was surely the most fortunate girl in the world! To have become engaged to the handsomest, the most estimable of gentlemen. She thought of their kisses at Greenwich and blushed, but not with embarrassment this time. A warm glow spread over her at the thought. Who could have dreamed that a mere kiss could affect one so deeply? Alan had stolen a kiss from her before, it was true, and it had been exciting simply because it was forbidden. But she could remember nothing of it, whereas she could remember every detail of the life-altering embrace she had shared with Drakefield. She thought of his words afterward and glowed. He had enjoyed kissing her. He had wished to move up the date of their wedding.

She basked in the memories for several minutes before

her brows drew together in a slight frown. He had *not* said that he loved her. Probably he took her knowledge of such a thing for granted. He could not have kissed her like that if he had not, she thought. He had been every bit as moved as she was, she was sure.

Her brow cleared. The unspeakable fear was removed, the one she had not even been able to admit to herself. This would not be a marriage of convenience. At least, she did not think so. It was true that the ways of the aristocracy were different, but . . . Well, it must be a needless worry. She resolutely banished it from her mind.

"Well, I am glad that at last you found the time to call upon me—and just when I was in the middle of an experiment too. How convenient."

"I am sorry, but I have been rather busy, you know." The words were penitent, but a smile curled one side of Drakefield's mouth and a sparkle of amusement shone in his eyes.

Johnson, who was not blind to these subtle signs, gave a sniff. "Hmph. Well, I suppose that you don't mind keeping the world waiting for this discovery either."

Drakefield sighed. "I am afraid that I am out of funds at present, what with expenses such as engagement rings. Why don't you show me what you have accomplished?"

Johnson was tempted for a moment to spurn this offer scornfully, but he was overcome by his own enthusiasm. He led Drakefield over to a table in a corner.

"Here, d'you see? I think that if I make a cylinder of wire gauze, so, it will conduct the heat away from the flame." He gave a discouraged shake of his head. "But of course, I will not know for certain until I have experimented with it, and that will cost more money."

Drakefield's face was alive with interest as he examined Johnson's work. "It looks to me as if you have solved the problem. I cannot see anything that should prevent it from functioning." He put it down with a sigh. "I am sorry about the money, but financial matters will improve after my wedding in August."

Johnson's face was concerned. "You do not think that your wife will object?"

Drakefield smiled. "I have found her to be a remarkably intelligent and also a rather visionary young lady. I think that she will gladly lend her support to our project once she learns about it."

His friend looked at him curiously. "You have certainly changed your tune. It sounds as if the prospect of marriage no longer depresses you."

Drakefield raised an eyebrow. "Let us say, at least it is less depressing than formerly," he returned softly.

The Season was at its apogee, curiosity was at its peak, and nearly every invitation was accepted for the Duchess of Wiltham's ball. Society guessed that there might be an interesting announcement made before the end of the evening. If so, there might perhaps be the added pleasure of meeting and judging Miss Baxter's parents.

There was some petulance in certain circles over the notion of the Black Dandy's being removed from the list of eligibles. More than one beauty remarked sourly that of course no one could be expected to compete with someone of Miss Baxter's fortune. Those who were rich as well as pretty had no such excuse.

There was one individual readying herself who was motivated by more than simple curiosity or envy. Lady Fernsbury looked in the mirror one last time to make certain that her ensemble was perfection. Let the gaudy thing wear her obnoxious colors. Annabella intended to dazzle society by contrast in pure white. She wore an expensive and spectacular gown of white lace worn over a white satin slip, cut very low across the bodice, the short puffed sleeves exposing the flesh of her upper arms. It was a dress that could not fail to attract the eye.

The sad crush of carriages lining Bruton Street and spilling out of it to fill Berkeley Square boded ill for those who could not endure crowds. Indeed, one guest stepping into the huge ballroom was heard to remark that he was unsure that it could hold another person. The heat made the gathering even more intolerable, but no one gave any sign of leaving.

Miss Baxter, as one might have predicted, had forsaken the idea that a white dress was the most suitable for the occasion. Instead she was attired in a striking gown of bright blue satin, cut very simply and unadorned except for the blue ribbon about her waist. The most shocking part of the ensemble, though, was that she was not wearing the required white gloves. Instead her long kid gloves were of the very palest shade of lemon, with lemon-colored kid slippers to match. It was daring, it was different, and the liberal minds in the crowd had to admit that it was also rather pretty.

"She'll set another fashion—lay you a wager upon it," one young gentleman remarked to another. The latter, more perspicacious, replied, "Daresay she won't. There will be those who try it, of course. It's the sort of style only La Colonne D'or can manage. Anyone else will look ridiculous."

To society's delight, both of Miss Baxter's parents indeed were present, and it was immediately apparent that they might be classed as belonging to the mushroom sort. There were mutterings of discontent at the necessity of sharing a ballroom with such persons, though apparently no one was offended enough to leave. It was generally agreed that only the duchess could have succeeded with such a bold stroke.

To society's disappointment, Miss Baxter's parents were both soberly dressed and well mannered. There were no obvious faux pas, and no hints that they were overwhelmed by the situation: nothing, in short, that might have provided delightful fuel for gossip. It placed several social leaders in a quandary. Without knowing her background, they had raised Miss Baxter to the heights. Could they now abruptly change their minds and cut her?

At least one dowager announced her intention of doing so. A friend's voice at her elbow stayed her. "You may intend to cut her, my dear, but I do not dare. To cut Lady

Drakefield, the granddaughter-in-law of the Duchess of Wiltham and the wife of the Black Dandy? I lack the nerve."

The dowager considered these words thoughtfully. "You may have an excellent point," she admitted judiciously. She gave a sniff. "Well, I shall make up my mind when we see if this marriage actually takes place. I cannot understand this delay. Everyone knows that he's wedding the gel for her money. I am sure that I wish him the best, but we all know it is an arranged marriage, after all. There is no need for all this pretense, as if it were something else."

It was unfortunate that the dowager's deafness, combined with the buzz of the crowd, forced her to raise her voice to such a volume. It was even more unlucky that she happened to be standing in such proximity to Sarah. Her friend shushed her quickly, but those carrying tones could not be ignored. Miss Baxter must have been afflicted with a similar deafness, for she gave no sign of having heard, but instead laughed brightly at an admirer's compliment.

No one could know what an effort such apparent indifference cost, or how tautly her nerves were drawn. This was her real test, she knew. The announcement that she was to be Drakefield's wife would inspire enmity among all those who aspired to the position, or whose daughters or sisters or nieces had. Judith had suggested that she might prefer a small family party to announce her engagement, as was more usual, but the duchess had shrewdly remarked that it was best to have the ordeal over with now. Sarah might have hoped to have counted upon the support of her brother and her best friend, but Bertie and Eglantyne were so besotted that they had hardly a thought for anyone else. Even now they were seated in a corner, conversing earnestly and generally monopolizing each other. Really, they had become quite boring. At least both sets of parents smiled upon that possible match.

It was reassuring to have the duchess beside her, and Drakefield, of course. Her eyes softened at the thought as she looked over her shoulder to see him. He was gazing far beyond her, with the most peculiar look upon his face.

Some new arrivals were being announced. Lord and Lady
Fernsbury.

Sarah had not wished for the inclusion of this couple,
though she could hardly have said so. The duchess seemed
to divine something of her feelings, for she had remarked
sympathetically that there was nothing to be done, since
Annabella's family's lands marched with Drakefield's. She
had added in an undertone that perhaps she'd have the
sense or good taste to stay away, but Sarah had been too
shy to ask her what she meant.

The look on Drakefield's face was piercing. Sarah was
forced to look away. The sudden silence followed by a rising hum of conversation told her more than she wanted to
know. She lifted her chin proudly. No one should guess
what she felt. She greeted both Lady Fernsbury and her elderly husband warmly, and tried not to notice when Lady
Fernsbury stood on tiptoe to murmur in Drakefield's ear.
She tried not to hear her extract a teasing promise for a
dance, and did her best to ignore Drakefield's affirmative
reply.

She did not know what was the worst part—to bear the
glances of naked hatred in that sea of faces when her engagement was announced, or then to lead out the first dance
with Drakefield as if she had been blind to them. His face
was wooden, his expression preoccupied. There was no
comfort there, though he replied with mechanical civility to
her attempts at conversation.

The most crushing moment of all came after their dance
was through and he led Lady Fernsbury out onto the floor.
The latter seemed to be enjoying herself immensely, smiling and laughing, and apparently making jesting remarks.
Sarah could comfort herself with the observation that
Drakefield seemed scarcely more happy than during their
own dance. The problem was that despite his grimness, his
eyes never left his beautiful partner's face; they practically
burned holes in it. Unable to watch any more, Sarah turned
to Lord Sandell, standing in her vicinity, and began a determined flirtation with him, to that gentleman's surprise and
obvious dismay.

Her heart was breaking, but still she had to smile and pretend that nothing was wrong. She affected not to notice when Drakefield and Lady Fernsbury both disappeared from the ballroom at the same time. She would not have been reassured had she known what was occurring.

"Drake!" Annabella looked beautiful in the moonlight, and she looked far more like the nineteen-year-old he had loved than a married woman of twenty-one. She held out a hand imperiously to him. "Come here!"

He had never been able to refuse even the least of her commands. He walked over and seated himself beside her upon the marble bench, overlooking the duchess's garden.

"Why did you wish to speak to me, Lady Fernsbury?" he asked, carefully keeping his voice even.

"My, we are formal. You might as well call me by name. There is no one about to hear us," she said scornfully.

He expelled a deep breath. "Very well then, Annabella. Why did you wish to speak to me?"

"Oh, Drake. Couldn't you guess?" Her large brown eyes were emotion-filled. She laid a hand upon his knee. He rose.

"No, I cannot even imagine what we have to say to each other now." Only by a tight hold upon himself was he able to keep the anger from his voice.

She looked at him. "Do you really mean to marry that— that vulgar giraffe?"

He turned to face her. "I do mean to marry Miss Baxter, and I cannot imagine what you suppose you have to say in the matter."

"Can you not? Oh, my darling—"

He bowed slightly. "If you have nothing further to say, I will take my leave." His face was a bitter mask.

She leaped up and seized his arm with surprising strength for one so deceptively small and fragile-looking. "Don't be stupid, Drake. I know that she cannot make you happy— any more than I am happy myself." She gazed into his eyes. "I understand, you know. We both have had to do what we must."

He looked at her coldly without speaking.

"It's all very well to blame me for everything, but you know very well that you should not have been a contented pauper any more than I could be."

"We might have been comfortable with a great deal less than that to which we were accustomed. I was willing to sacrifice anything, but you, Annabella . . . Well, there is no point in discussing it. You have your fortune now and both our futures are settled. I hope you are content." He could not help his voice's shaking somewhat. He would have left, but she tightened her hold upon his arm.

"For heaven's sake," she hissed angrily. "For once in your life, can you be less pigheaded? I am willing to let bygones be bygones, you great idiot!" As she spoke, her voice softened and she abruptly leaned up to kiss him. He could not help but respond to those lips, those curves so familiar, the nostalgic odor of the scent she wore. It took just a moment for him to realize what he was doing, and he thrust her forcefully away.

"You see?" She was speaking breathlessly now. "It is just as it was before. It will never change between us. Don't let your bitterness stand in the way of our present happiness, my love."

He stared at her. "You wish to leave your husband?"

"Don't be a fool!" She tried to smile, to lessen the effect of the harsh words. "I mean that I have what I need. You shall have what you need too. Why shouldn't we steal what joy we can from life?" She held out a trembling hand to him.

She was not prepared for the look of revulsion that crossed his features. "By God, madam, I pity your husband!"

Too late she saw the damage that had been done. "Drake! It is your anger speaking. You must not leave matters like this between us."

"That is your mistake, Annabella." He spoke quietly, his features shadowed. "There is nothing between us, and there has not been since your marriage. I am sorry if it took you so long to realize it."

There was an awful finality in his voice. She snatched his hand and pressed it to her. "You cannot pretend, even to yourself, that you are not in love with me. The kiss just now—"

He laughed sardonically and gently withdrew his hand. "Is that what you imagine love is, Annabella? That is what the beasts of the field have, nothing more."

Her eyes flashed with anger. She stepped forward to slap him, but he caught her hand. "It is odd. We have known each other all our lives, but I do not think I ever really knew you until this moment, Annabella, and it is equally clear that you never knew me."

He released her hand gently.

"Annabella, my love?" The quavering voice drifted over to him. A silhouette appeared at one of the ballroom windows.

"You'd better go," Drakefield advised her.

She pressed her hands to her cheeks as if to drive down her color, then straightened herself. "Go to the blazes, Drake. I hope you'll be very happy with that overgrown mushroom. Perhaps her father will take you into the family concern. Shall I look for your barrow to come down my street?"

Her wrist was abruptly caught in a grip of iron. "I should be more temperate in your remarks about the lady I am to marry and her family," he suggested. "It should be unfortunate if this night's doings were to become common knowledge, wouldn't it? Even doting and elderly husbands have been known to repudiate faithless wives."

"Drakefield!" Her fear showed in her face.

"Annabella, my dear. Are you out there?"

He released her and without any further ado she fled toward the safety of the ballroom. He walked over to the marble balustrade and, leaning upon it for several minutes, stared out across the garden. At length he heaved a sigh and, turning, walked back into the ballroom.

Sarah did not know what had occurred, though something obviously had. Lady Fernsbury, pleading a sick headache, had left the party with her concerned husband. Sarah could not help but be glad, but the worrisome part of it was that Drakefield was still missing. When at last he reentered the ballroom, she was struck by the look of preoccupation upon his face. When he caught her eyes, he smiled and crossed over to her.

"Is anything amiss?" she whispered to him.

"No, why do you ask?"

"You were gone from the ballroom so long."

"I will tell you about it later."

He pressed her hand reassuringly and turned to the elderly gentleman at his elbow who was demanding his attention. Sarah herself was forced to respond to a question the duchess was asking her.

It seemed as if the night would never end. Her curiosity was about to consume her. She was heartily wishing all her guests would depart some hours before they did. When the last guest left, she slumped in exhaustion.

"Congratulations, my dear. It went off very well, I think. If you do not mind, I will bid you good night. I am no longer accustomed to keeping such late hours." The duchess saluted her on the cheek and departed for her bedroom, after taking leave of the rest of Sarah's family.

"Mr. and Mrs. Baxter, if you do not mind, I will bring Sarah home. There is something which we need to discuss."

It was true that her parents failed to exercise any discretion at all where Drakefield was concerned. They smiled and simpered and departed with no objections. Bertie and Eglantyne had left some time since, it being of necessity that he drive her in his new phaeton whenever he could.

Drakefield took Sarah's hand in his, then glanced around at the servants who were busy clearing away the food. "Let us go out to the back balcony. It will be more private."

As they sat together upon the marble bench in the moonlight, Sarah could not help trembling. He had been so moody, not at all like a man in love. And what could those burning glances at Lady Fernsbury have meant? Could it be that he had changed his mind about their marriage?

She was waiting for him to begin when she finally real-ized that he was waiting for her to start. She cleared her throat.

"I noticed that you were gone from the party a long time," she began.

"Yes." He had drawn away from her slightly and was frowning. It was not a good sign.

She waited for him to elaborate. After a few moments he did so. "Lady Fernsbury drew me aside and asked me to speak with her, so we came out here for a short while."

His features were unreadable, shadowed as they were. He had crossed his legs and pulled his hands about his knee. He was staring at the ground.

"You may as well know that we were, ah, sweethearts at one time. I have known Annabella since childhood. Our parents planned for us to marry, but when the time came, our situations would not permit it."

Sarah was having difficulty mastering her emotions. What was he going to tell her? That Lady Fernsbury had convinced him not to marry her?

"I suppose you are wondering what she wished to speak to me about," he said rather absently. He drew a deep breath. "She . . . she, as an old friend of my family's, had questions about our marriage. I think I was able to put them to rest." The sensation of relief was overwhelming. He did care about her, at least enough to go through with the wed-ding.

He turned his face to her, but the shadows still hid his eyes. "Is there anything else you wish to know?"

Are you still in love with her? The question was scream-ing within her, but she didn't have the courage to say it. "No."

The smile lightened his features. "Very well." He rose and held out his hand. "Come with me."

Putting her hand in his, she stood up also and followed him inside to a secluded alcove. He reached into his breast pocket. "I hadn't had an opportunity to give you this ear-lier. I hope it meets with your approval."

She opened the box and gasped. Inside reposed a stunning and sizable sapphire mounted upon a ring. A small spray of diamonds at each end made the setting most unique. She extracted it from the box. "It is beautiful."

He smiled and, taking her left hand, slipped it upon the third finger. "Hold it up to the light."

Obediently she held it up to the candelabra burning on the wall. Why hadn't she noticed it before? Those weren't diamonds on the end. "Why, they're yellow," she exclaimed unthinkingly.

"Yes, they are yellow sapphires. I asked the jeweler to set them as a compliment to you and your unusual taste. I hope you like it. If not, we may exchange it for something else."

This must have cost him a great deal of thought and trouble. Her eyes misted over at the thought. The idea sounded outrageous, but really the pale yellow harmonized with the deep blue magnificently, particularly in the setting of gold. "No, it is lovely. It is the perfect ring," she said sincerely.

She looked at him and was conscious again of that same magnetic pull that she had felt at Greenwich.

"Sarah." Again, it was hardly more than a whisper, but it seemed to draw her closer to him. Their faces, their lips were just inches away. The creak of a door startled them. They leaped apart as a servant entered, then apologized for intruding upon them.

Drakefield shook his head and assured him that they were about to leave. He turned to Sarah. "It is past time for you to go home, my dear." He took her by the arm and led her from the room.

It was clear to Sarah that the worst thing she could do was to allow her mind to dwell on the incident. Drakefield had given her a full account of his past relationship with Lady Fernsbury. There was no reason for doubt, except of course, for the fact that he still had not told Sarah that he loved *her*. Still, what did words matter, after all? If he did not care for her, he would not have sent Lady Fernsbury packing as he had—or at least as he said he had. She tried to think the most optimistic sorts of thoughts, but the nagging worry would not leave her.

To make matters even worse, another letter had arrived from Alan, a missive equally as fond as the previous one. He had been given his first real taste of war at last. His regiment had been engaged in driving the French from the city of Salamanca, where the famous battle had been fought the previous year. They had accomplished their purpose with surprising ease, though of course there was the sadness of losing some of one's comrades in arms. It was expected that they would continue to pursue the French, and he reported optimistically that he thought they should be able to drive them from Spain altogether. Also, although he did not wish to be thought immodest, his colonel had had some particular praise for him, and he felt that with luck and a major engagement, promotion would be inevitable. Need he say it again? His hope was to prove himself worthy of her. As always, his thoughts were with his dearest Sarah. He kissed her hands. He hoped she might write him of the latest news from home. Also, although he did not like to mention it, there had been some misunderstanding with his family. At such a distance, he naturally was unable to defend himself against malicious lies that had been brought before them. He hoped that Sarah would disregard anything she heard of him in that quarter. His fondest love and it was agony to be parted from her.

What could she write him? She could hardly send him a farewell letter when it sounded as if they were on the eve of a major battle. It was particularly unfortunate that his family had also deserted him. Perhaps if he did distinguish himself and win a promotion, it might prove a more opportune time to write. She hoped so.

10

THE NAGGING FEELING of unease which had disturbed Sarah's sleep the night before remained with her still. It would have been a perfect opportunity for Drakefield to demonstrate his devotion by appearing that morning or even that afternoon, but she knew that he had a cricket match. She supposed she might go shopping, but that activity did not hold any of its usual allure. She gazed down at the sapphire which sparkled upon her finger. Really, it was a lovely ring as well as a most unusual one. Her mother had been in ecstasies over it.

She sighed. She always could go to call upon Eglantyne today. Bertie had surprised them both by accepting Drakefield's invitation to watch the game. It was a mark of the slavish adoration he felt for the Black Dandy, since Sarah did not think he had spent a day apart from Eglantyne since meeting her.

Having reached a decision, she was preparing to go out when a visitor was announced. She stared at the card in some surprise. None of the fashionable world would ever come to call upon her here, and she was certain that the news of the engagement had driven off even the most desperate fortune hunters. The name was not familiar. Well, she was not in any great hurry to go anywhere.

"Show him into the drawing room," she told the footman as she began to remove her bonnet.

When she stepped into the room, she saw a well-dressed, slender gentleman of medium height, with blond hair and a beaked nose. When he smiled at her and took a limping step forward, she recognized him as someone whom she had met at the ball last night. Drakefield had introduced him as a particular friend, she remembered.

"Mr. Clavering, how good to see you."

He took her hand and pressed it. "Charming of you to say so, my dear. The pleasure is all mine."

"Please, won't you be seated?"

He hesitated for a moment, then followed her example.

"I hope you will forgive my forcing myself upon you in this way. I know it is unprecedented."

"Any friend of my fiancé's must also be a friend of mine," she told him smilingly. "I am delighted that you decided to visit."

He gave a chuckle. "Very liberal-minded of you, Miss Baxter." His brows drew together slightly and, leaning forward, he added, "There are many who would say that I am intruding in matters that do not concern me, but I am afraid that it is one of my vices. Everyone knows me for a meddler."

Sarah tried to keep from appearing startled.

"If you would care to take a drive with me—it is a borrowed carriage, I am afraid—I would like to have a chance to speak with you."

What could she do but assent? Her maid fetched her bonnet, but after she had tied it on, she saw a warning look in Clavering's eyes. "I am afraid that the carriage does not accommodate more than two," he said gently. "I hope that the coachman will prove a sufficient escort."

Again she had to agree. As he limpingly escorted her to the carriage, he whispered in her ear, "This way we shall not be overheard. I was careful to borrow one with an elderly coachman—he is nearly deaf." The individual mentioned turned to smile ingratiatingly at them, revealing some gaps between his teeth, as Clavering loudly gave him his orders. They were to go north, to the countryside and privacy.

As they set off, he glanced at Sarah and remarked ruefully. "I suppose you are wondering who the deuce I am and why I made it my business to call upon you. I should begin perhaps by telling you that Drakefield is one of my oldest friends. We were boys at school together. Since I was a year ahead of him, I am afraid I have always taken a paternal interest in his affairs."

He had told her more than he thought. This must be one of Drakefield's "odd fish." Yet he looked the very picture of fashion. He smiled at her. It was an electric smile, and it made her realize that here was a person who could rival Drakefield for charm.

"So, I was quite interested to learn of his impending marriage. I hope you will forgive my being so personal, but after all I have learned of you, your character, and your conduct, I am convinced that Drakefield could not make a better match."

It was not what she had expected to hear. She had expected rather the opposite, in fact. The kindness of it made the tears spring to her eyes.

He hesitated for a moment. "I suppose that perhaps I am in the habit of reading worlds of meaning into slight nuances of expression and actions, for you see, I am a gamester by profession." He smiled in a self-deprecating way, and Sarah found that she was not at all shocked, as she should have been, but rather smiling back at him.

"You see, I had—well, I do not know how to say it, but I had formed certain . . . ideas about you that were dispelled when I met you last night." He regarded her earnestly. "It may seem foolish to you, since we exchanged nothing more than a few words, but my livelihood depends in a great part upon my powers of observation and interpretation. I received the impression last night that you perhaps were not entirely happy—you hid it very well, of course, and I would doubt that anyone else would have a suspicion—but it occurred to me that it might not have been your wish all along to marry Drakefield, but rather that of your parents."

She would have responded, but he stayed her. "You need not confide in me, if you do not wish. I merely wished to assure you that if such were the case, you need not fear to admit it to Drakefield. He has his faults, and he can sometimes be rather . . . intimidating, but he also can be extremely kind and he would not want to make you unhappy. You may share the truth with him without fear."

His gentle concern was too much for her. The tears that had been welling in her eyes now overflowed. He extracted an exquisite linen handkerchief from his breast pocket and handed it to her. "I am so sorry. Would you like to return home?"

She shook her head as she wiped her eyes. Here at last was the sympathetic confidant for whom she had been waiting. "No, it is just—you are so very kind . . ." He waited patiently for her to finish. She lifted clouded blue eyes to his. "You see, I did not wish to marry Lord Drakefield at first. You were right. I-I tried to give him a disgust of me, so I acted as vulgar as I might." Despite herself, she could not mention Alan. No one need ever know about that error on her part, after all.

He smiled. "Obviously, you are not very good at being vulgar."

She sniffed. "But as I grew to know him better—I had a mistaken impression of the sort of person he was, you see—I-I want to marry him now." She inadvertently gave a little sob. "I love him."

"Oh, my dear!" He patted her shoulder as she once again dissolved into tears. "Then I am so sorry I said anything at all. I certainly did not mean to upset you."

She shook her head again. "No, it is not that." Her lower lip trembled, but she willed it to hold firm. "You see, I know what my feelings are for him, but I am not certain what his are for me." She forced herself to meet her companion's eyes bravely. "Sometimes I am certain that his sentiments are the same as mine, and other times I think that he simply is too well bred to allow me discover the truth."

His brows drew together. He gave his head a single shake. "I wish I could be of help. But I am not sure that Drakefield himself actually knows his own sentiments." He paused, then continued. "I am sorry that I do not have some assurance to give you." He paused again before meeting her eyes squarely.

"There is one matter . . . which perhaps had best be discussed between you and Drakefield alone. However, you are far too clever a young lady not to have made observations and drawn some conclusions of your own."

"You mean Lady Fernsbury," said Sarah. "Drakefield and I had a conversation about her last night."

His astonishment was plain. She elaborated: "He told me that their families had intended for them to marry, but that when the time came, their situations did not permit it." She looked at him questioningly.

A corner of his mouth drew upward, but it was not with amusement. "Magnanimous as always," he said softly. "You must forgive me, my dear, but I had not expected Drakefield to have spoken to you about this. He is generally so reticent about his affairs."

"What did happen?"

"I don't suppose I will be telling you anything you might not learn from another quarter. Very well, then. As he said, their families had intended for him and Annabella to wed practically since their infancy. The estates march together and she is an only child, so it was thought to be a fortunate alliance."

He drew a deep breath. "I do not know what he has told you about his past, but as you no doubt know, his family had always wanted for money. Apparently, his father did a masterful job of concealing his situation, for hardly anyone had an inkling. It was known that he wanted ready cash and that he was careless in the extreme about money, but no one suspected that he was so heavily in debt or dreamed that the estates were mortgaged. The family remained in London throughout the year, so disrepair was blamed upon the incompetence of the estate manager."

He met her eyes again, as if trying to make certain that she understood. "So, naturally, no one cast any rubs in the way. He was raised to consider himself as nearly affianced to Annabella from his earliest years, and certainly she must have considered herself in the same light. It was a pity that the late earl chose to reside in London. Drake might otherwise have come to know Annabella better." He paused again, and Sarah had the feeling that there was something he was not telling her.

"In any case, her parents wished for her to have a Season. He was her frequent, well, almost her constant escort. He had already made a reputation for himself, and they were considered a handsome couple. I daresay Annabella planned for them to rule society together. Everyone knew that the date for the wedding would be set at the Season's conclusion. Drakefield's father, the fourth earl, died in the midst of it. Almost immediately all his embarrassments came to light." He leaned forward, emphasizing his words carefully. "Annabella's engagement to Fernsbury was announced within a week of the fourth earl's death."

She stared back at him speechlessly.

"There are those of her friends who would insist that it was her parents' doing. The truth is, their situation was a comfortable one. She might have married where she chose. Her parents have never been known to oppose a single one of her wishes."

There were a few moments of silence before Sarah stammered, "B-but Lord Drakefield, perhaps he was too proud to live upon her funds?" Her face flushed as she finished the question. Whatever he had felt for Annabella, he was not too proud to propose to live upon Sarah's money.

Fortunately, her companion did not appear to notice. "She didn't even give him the opportunity to see how matters stood. He had enough of an income left from the estate to enable him to live in a modest manner. He has increased it gradually by his own hard work, though without his marriage to you it is unlikely that he could ever clear the estate of debt. He feels an obligation to those dependent upon him. He cannot bear to see his tenants with their cottages falling in or with their fields in shambles."

He shook his head again as if to clear it. "But I wander from the point. When it became clear to her that marriage to him would entail sacrifices and economies, reduction in the grand life that she was planning, she rid herself of him without a backward glance. He learned of the engagement by reading the paper." He sighed. "I know, because I was with him at the time."

"How horrible!"

"Yes, particularly since she gave out that he had deceived her all along as to his expectations. She published that he had been callous, calculating, and indifferent to her welfare, anything she could think of that might make her actions appear in a more favorable light."

Sarah's eyes flashed. She would have exclaimed aloud, but then she remembered how once she had been only too eager to believe this sort of talk, and she had to bite her lip.

Clavering made a noise suspiciously like a snort. "Of course, she claimed that she was the one whose heart had been broken. Drake kept his thoughts to himself. I myself thought it was an act of Providence. Marriage to the creature would have been difficult in the best of circumstances . . . and unbearable in the worst."

The awful truth had to be faced. "But he still loves her?"

To his credit, Clavering did not turn away from that questioning gaze. "He persisted in an attachment to her. I suppose it is difficult to break old habits. And despite his anger with her, he truly wanted to believe that her parents had forced her into the marriage against her will. I suppose he is too credulous. He has even told me that she had a right to be angry with him since his father had deliberately concealed their circumstances."

Sarah gave a small, sad smile. "You still have not answered my question . . . or perhaps you have."

He considered the matter for a moment before speaking. "I cannot tell you what is in Drakefield's mind . . . or heart. I do know that he respects you and has an affection for you." He sighed. "I know that if he has not already, he will someday come to see her for what she is. It is hard to give up the dreams of youth, after all."

That was a subject Sarah knew something about. Of course, the dream she had clung to so stubbornly had been replaced by a far more wonderful one. It was too bad that it was proving to be nothing more than an illusion also. Her throat constricted at the thought. Her fairy-tale picture of a romance was over.

Her companion was studying her closely. "I do not wish to upset you further," he said gently. "As I have said, I think you and Drakefield are admirably suited. I think perhaps there is some part of him that understands that already. He will come to realize it, given time."

Could she marry him knowing he did not love her? It was a terrible question, but as she confronted it she had to admit to herself that the answer was still yes. She *would* be good for him. Their love could grow with time. Clavering did not know about the interlude at Greenwich, after all. Many married couples must have started out with less than that. Something in her expression must have troubled her companion.

"Miss Baxter, are you—?"

"I am quite all right."

"In that case . . ." He reached forward with his walking stick to tap the box next to the coachman. "Back to town," he shouted. He turned to Sarah. "I am parched by the heat. Do you care to go to Gunther's for an ice?"

It was odd to realize how quick she had been to share the deepest secrets of her heart with a veritable stranger, but she had to confess that she had been longing to do so with someone for weeks now. Bertie and Eglantyne both had been too preoccupied with their own romance to be good confidants. And Mr. Clavering, besides being so agreeable, was in a position to tell her much she had been longing to know about her fiancé. Clavering was simply one of those people who combined sympathy and an unwillingness to elicit confidences in a manner which released a flood of them. It was easy to talk to him. It might have taken a lifetime, but to her surprise, when she glanced at the clock upon her return, she found that only three hours had passed. There was still time to call upon Eglantyne.

She found her friend a trifle low in spirits, and quite ready for conversation. It was her first taste of being deserted for sport, and she was taking it to heart. Sarah, having been raised with a brother, was able to explain to her that it was just the way that gentlemen were.

She recounted her own adventures of the afternoon, though without discussing the content of the conversation. To her surprise, Eglantyne's eyes widened when she mentioned Clavering's name. Inquires elicited the information that she had been spending the afternoon with a personage. He was a notable exquisite, a pink among pinks. What was more, having been interestingly wounded as a result of the war, he had achieved even greater *éclat*. He was one whom the pretenders to fashion watched in order to ape his manners and dress, but always unsuccessfully. Sarah had to admit to a certain feeling of surprise. Certainly, he had seemed well dressed, but not as strikingly as Drakefield. Of course, the latter's height and physique would always make him noticeable, almost as much as his habit of appearing only in black.

"Oh Sarah," gasped Eglantyne, "no one might aim higher than that. To spend the afternoon with Mr. Clavering, particularly when one knows how fastidious he is about female company. Those who didn't envy you already certainly will now."

Just what she needed, thought Sarah, more envy.

Eglantyne shook her head as she poured milk in her cup before carefully adding tea. "I daresay Cousin Everard himself would be jealous if they were not such good friends." She stirred in a spoonful of sugar and looked at Sarah with a troubled expression.

"I have not been able to talk with you for such a long time. Have you heard from Mr. Grenfell?"

Sarah smiled at her. "Yes, but that need no longer concern you. Lord Drakefield is the one I wish to marry. The other was a schoolgirl's infatuation."

Eglantyne's eyes brightened. "Oh, Sarah, I am so delighted to hear you say that, for it is what I have often thought myself. In fact, Bertram and I were in perfect agreement on that point, that Cousin Everard was the perfect gentleman for you—that you were admirably suited." Her eyes fell upon Sarah's hand, and she exclaimed in remorse. "Your engagement ring! Oh, let me see it. I am so sorry—I had not thought of it until just now. I am afraid I have been too preoccupied today."

The ring had to be duly held up and admired. Eglantyne was quite as startled by it as Sarah had been, but upon studying it, she declared that she quite liked it and predicted that it would set a fashion. "And such trouble as he must have been to in order to design it, it is evident that he must care for you." She smiled into Sarah's eyes. "I am so happy for both of you. Who could have imagined that things would work out so well?"

Of course, she did not know what Sarah knew. Should Sarah dispel the illusion? The liveried footman entered the door. "Mr. Bertram Baxter here to see you, miss."

Their conversation came to an abrupt end. A moment later, Bertram burst in, in exuberant spirits. He rushed forward to take Eglantyne's hands, but stopped short upon catching sight of Sarah.

"Please be seated. Would you care for a cup of tea, Mr. Baxter? I did not expect to see you today." Eglantyne's words were formal, but the glowing smile upon her face conveyed the true message.

"Er, yes," said Bertie, taking a place upon the sofa next to her. "The game just finished, so I thought I'd pop round to see you."

"How kind of you. Did you enjoy yourself?" Eglantyne, Sarah noted with amused suspicion, did not need to ask Bertie how he liked his tea, but was already pouring milk into the cup.

"By Jove! I'll say I did. What an inning!" He magnanimously included Sarah in the conversation. "You should have seen Drakefield, Sal. He was magnificent! What a slashing hitter. It looked a little grim at the beginning, for the first batter was bowled out without a run and the second made only three, but then Burke scored some fifteen, which put heart into me, and the next scored fourteen more. But Drakefield was coolness itself. You have never seen anyone so steady. He scored seventy-three runs, and knocked the ball out of the ground twice."

Sarah's eyes were beginning to glaze over with boredom, so she took the opportunity to cut him off. "And the other six?"

"When we were done we had one hundred and eighty-five runs. What an inning. Of course, the other club will have their turn tomorrow, but they were pretty dispirited, I can tell you."

"They must have been wanting in the bowling department," remarked Sarah knowledgeably.

"You are going to watch it again tomorrow?" Eglantyne's face expressed her dismay.

Bertie was equally taken aback. "Of course! I'll have to see them finish the inning."

Sarah had to smile at her friend's revealing expression. "And they play two innings, you know, Egg."

"You are going to watch a cricket match for four days?"

It was clear than an altercation was brewing, so Sarah mercifully stepped in to rescue Bertie. "This inning was an unusually long one. With luck, the match could be over tomorrow, isn't that right, Bertie?"

Eglantyne's stormy expression faded as Bertie's brow also cleared. "Yes, you are right." He leaned forward to address Eglantyne very earnestly. "It is such an exceptional match, you see. One that people will be speaking of forever, I daresay." Reassured by the renewed warmth in her eyes, he continued. "D'you know, it reminded me of our grand match against Eton. Have I ever mentioned it to you? Not that I scored seventy-three runs, of course, but I did hit forty-eight off my own bat."

Eglantyne, recognizing a cue, sighed enthusiastically. Sarah, who had heard the story at least a hundred times, rose. "I think I had better go," she said brightly. "There was a parcel I meant to collect upon my way home." She made her farewells, and the two allowed her to depart without the least sign of reluctance.

Upon awakening the next morning, Sarah experienced a pang of disappointment when she realized that she again would not be seeing Drakefield today. She knew better than to let her mind dwell upon it, however, and so she rose and dressed without further delay, while she considered how she might best occupy herself. To sit about the house and brood would only serve to nourish those doubts that had already been troubling her and so encourage them to grow out of all proportion.

She might visit Eglantyne, who would probably be sitting at home again, but to tell the truth, Sarah had no great desire for her friend's company at the moment. Sarah loved her brother, but one day of enduring him as the topic of conversation seemed quite enough to her. Neither Bertie nor Egg were very good company for anyone else at the moment.

Accordingly, she decided to spend the morning shopping. Her mother was a willing and indeed an eager companion, and Sarah realized with shame that she had been neglecting her lately. She had no right to criticize Bertie and Egg. In her own way, she had been just as preoccupied with her own romance. She said as much to her mother, but the latter only patted her arm forgivingly as they rode in the carriage together.

"Now, you mustn't feel that way. It's natural for your mind to be on Lord Drakefield, just as Bertie's is on Miss Adstock, though we'll have to wait to see what comes of that." She could not quite conceal her joy at the thought of another prestigious match in her family, but she turned back to the topic at hand. "Why, I recall when I married your father—well, I was just beside myself, that's all, just giddy with happiness."

Sarah wished that her own emotions about her upcoming marriage were as uncomplicated.

"I was in a whirl, what with choosing bride clothes and having them made, and of course, some of the fancy sewing I liked to do myself. But then, I had only three weeks to prepare . . ." She paused for a moment before beginning again. "It seems odd that Lord Drakefield preferred such a long engagement, but I suppose he knows his own business best."

Sarah flushed guiltily. She had not told her parents that

the August wedding had been her idea. In fact, now she did not quite remember precisely why she had insisted upon it. She supposed that Alan had been in her mind. It was too late to change the date, however.

Still, they spent a happy morning looking over fabrics and designs at Madame Vauban's salon as they discussed their ideas for a trousseau. Sarah was fortunate in having a mother who was so understanding. All the designs she approved were accepted uncritically by Mrs. Baxter, who had the greatest faith in her daughter's taste. She had never said a word about the sudden change in Sarah's clothing or about all the new frocks that had been purchased, and Sarah had to wonder why. She broached the question as they rode back to Tavistock Square. Her mother smiled wisely, but hesitated for a moment before beginning.

"Well, my dear, I've never seen you choose a dress that didn't become you. I knew that you were still thinking about the young gentleman that went into the army, and that being with Lord Drakefield made you unhappy at first. I thought that if some new frocks, and perhaps a change of style, helped to lift your spirits, there was no reason you shouldn't have them. Your papa can afford it."

She gave a sigh of satisfaction. "I thought that as long as you were willing to just be with Lord Drakefield that we should make things as pleasant for you as we could. And then I hoped that you should come to see him for the worthy gentleman that he is—and of course you, you clever girl, did." She squeezed her daughter's gloved hand. "It makes your father and me both very glad and proud. I knew that Lord Drakefield was the sort of gentleman who could make you happy—and he has."

Tears started to Sarah's eyes, but she did her best to blink them away. She was not successful in evading her mother's sharp eyes, however. The latter scolded her gently. "Now, what's this—tears! That will never do." She extracted a handkerchief from her reticule and handed it to her daughter. The carriage came to a halt. They had reached their house.

"All the servants will think I've been giving you a scold.

Now smile at me, my dear. I wish I could go in for a comfortable coze right now, but I dare not miss this meeting. Mrs. Aldwich told me it was most important for me to attend. We will speak later."

As Sarah stepped into the hallway, she saw that the drawing room door stood open. A questioning look at Fraley elicited the information that a friend of her brother's was waiting to see him.

"If that is the case, I had better see him myself. He'll have several hours to wait if he wishes to see Bertie."

"He's been here two already, miss."

She stepped into the room and saw an individual perched dejectedly upon the edge of a green and gilt satin sofa. When he saw her, he lifted his face hopefully and rose. Meeting that countenance, she could not doubt who it was.

"Why, you must be Bertie's good friend, Sheep—" Mercifully, she caught herself just in time.

He bowed. "Arthur Sheephouse, at your service." He straightened himself and shook his head. "Don't worry, everyone calls me Sheepnose. Used to it."

It was a pity that his hair had to be both extremely fair and curly, she thought, studying him critically. The resemblance might be less pronounced if . . . She recalled herself suddenly and smiled at him. "I am Bertie's sister, Mr. Sheephouse. Please do have a seat."

"Pleased to make your acquaintance. His twin sister? Bertie's told me about you."

They were words which always struck fear into her heart, but she tried to appear serenely indifferent. She seated herself as she asked him if he cared for tea.

Following her example, he sat once again and shook his head. "Just came to see Bertie. Haven't seen him about lately. Missed him at Limmer's and the cockfight. Thought he'd be at the mill the other day, but he wasn't. Called a few times but always missed him. Cursed luck, I s'pose. Thought I'd wait this time."

"I do not think he will return for some hours yet. He is attending a cricket match today." He also would undoubtedly cadge a dinner invitation from the Adstocks, if he hadn't one already. "Is there a message you would like me to give him for you?"

He rose, shaking his head disconsolately. "Just wanted to see him. That's all. I s'pose he's been spending his time with that girl, er, I mean that lady—driving her in his phaeton and such. Just that town's cursed dull without his company. Thought he might like to cut a lark now and again. Tell him I stopped by, won't you?"

"Yes, I will."

She rose also, showing him to the door. Despite the fact that she deplored his influence upon Bertie, she had to feel rather sorry for Sheepnose. She thought it likely that the message would go in one ear and out the other.

She did not expect to hear from Drakefield that day, for despite her reassuring words to Eglantyne, she thought it most likely that the match would run for at least three days. Therefore she was surprised to receive a note from him late that afternoon. His cricket match had come to a successful conclusion. He apologized for neglecting her for so long. Would she care to take a drive with him tomorrow? Bertie and Eglantyne had thought they might drive out with them also, and so they could make an outing of it.

Her heart leapt with happiness. Despite appearances, he had not forgotten about her as soon as they had become officially engaged. The cloud that had been hanging over her the past two days began to lighten. Perhaps he did care, after all.

11

DRAKEFIELD PRESENTED HIMSELF the next morning promptly at ten-thirty, and Sarah's heart swelled with joy at the sight. Surely he was the handsomest man in London. She tried not to let her gladness show, but apparently she was unsuccessful, for upon seeing her face, the frown upon his gave way to a smile.

"My dear! How charmingly you look, as ever." She had decided to attempt a new mode today, and her dress and pelisse, her bonnet, and her gloves were all in the same bright shade of buttercup yellow.

"What a sad scoundrel you have affianced yourself to. It was inexcusable for me to abandon you for two entire days after our engagement party and I apologize. Unfortunately, it was a vital match and . . ."

She shook her head playfully. "You forget that I have a brother. I know full well that a female should never interfere with anything as important as a cricket match."

He kissed her hand. "Ah, perfection itself as usual. Still, I must humbly beg your pardon."

His words were light, but there was preoccupation in his tone. She looked closely at his face as he straightened himself and was dismayed to see that the frown had returned.

"Is—is there something wrong?"

He stared at her blankly for a moment. "Why do you ask?"

"Your face, your voice . . ." There was no way to explain it. She must sound absurd.

He dropped his gaze and forced a laugh. "I am sorry, my

dear, if I let other matters intrude upon my thoughts. I assure you it is nothing of import."

"But it must be if it is worrying you." She crossed the drawing room to close the door. "Please, can you not tell me?" She gave an uncertain smile. "I am afraid that I will imagine horrors worse than any truth if you do not." Annabella was in her mind, but she did not dare breathe the name aloud.

He raised his eyes to hers. "As I have told you already, it is nothing of import." Meeting the earnest eyes before him, his countenance softened. "It is probably just some idiotic alarum. An eccentric friend sent me a note asking me to call upon him this morning." He lifted one shoulder slightly and dropped it. "He seemed to think it an urgent matter, but everything seems so to him."

"But you are concerned."

"My dear, after abandoning you so shamelessly and so soon, I would not wish to do so again. Johnson and his emergency can wait."

She had picked up her bonnet, but now she set it down upon the table again. "Our expedition may be postponed until later. Do go see your friend."

"Absolutely not." His voice was jesting, but there was seriousness underneath it.

"I shall not mind in the least."

"I would not consider doing so."

"I am quite earnest."

"So am I."

They had reached an impasse, and Sarah could see that he was every bit as determined as she was. Clearly a compromise was in order. "Come, it is early in the day. Can we not do both? You may see your friend and we might still have our outing."

She could see him considering the idea. "I will wait for you here," she added.

"But what of your brother and Eglantyne?"

"He is already at her residence. I will send him a note telling him that we will be slightly delayed." She smiled. "I can promise you that it will impose no hardship upon them."

He did not speak and finally he shook his head. "Johnson is far too apt to detain me."

"Then take me with you." The words were impulsive and she regretted them instantly. She had merely been trying to find a solution to the problem and instead had succeeded in sounding like the most odious, managing female alive. She knew that his silence meant that he was trying to think of a polite way to refuse.

It came as a shock when he abruptly smiled. "Why not? An excellent idea, my dear. I have wished for you and Johnson to become acquainted." He hesitated again. "Of course, it is a bachelor establishment."

She smiled back at him. "I should think that my fiancé's escort would be sufficient. My parents will not object."

"That is true, and it is unlikely that anyone will see us, after all. Very well, since you are willing, let us go."

She tied her bonnet upon her head eagerly. She had a feeling that a hitherto unrevealed side of Drakefield was about to be exposed. It would be one more piece to the puzzle of the man.

A half hour later, as she stood in a dark, dingy hallway, she wondered why she had been so eager. Although it was sunny outside, just a few rays of light penetrated the gloom from the cracks between the curtains. Of course, though there was not much light, it was still enough to reveal that the wooden banister was in need of dusting, the rugs begged for a beating, and the floors fairly demanded to be swept. Unfamiliar acrid odors wafted to her nostrils. Drakefield had not been exaggerating when he had said that his friend was an eccentric. Unconsciously she took a step closer to him. He smiled at her reassuringly.

In another moment an individual rushed up the stairs, pushing his way hurriedly past the elderly manservant who had been sent to announce their presence. He was tall, thin, and pale. His clothes were stained and wrinkled, and his hair stood up wildly upon his head. He did not even appear to notice her. Sarah found it easier to class this old school-mate as an "odd fish."

"It's at an end—all our work—we're too late—if only we'd had the funds—"

"My dear fellow, please calm yourself. I would like for you to meet my fiancée, Miss Sarah Baxter. Sarah, this is my friend Donald Johnson."

"How d'you do—oh, she's the one then—well, never mind, it's too late—"

"You should really ask us in, you know. Shall we go into what passes for a parlor so that we may speak?"

"What? Oh, very well." He allowed himself to be led by Drakefield, still ignoring Sarah, who trailed after the two. Drakefield seated her before thrusting his friend into a chair and taking one himself. She perched gingerly upon the edge of her chair, wishing she had worn a pelisse in a dark shade rather than yellow. Johnson was still babbling incoherently. Drakefield shook his head.

"You're not making any sense, you know. Try to gather your thoughts and speak more slowly."

Johnson made the effort. He drew in a deep breath. "They've already invented it. A fellow from Sunderland—his name's Clanny, I believe, but what does it matter? He's produced a working model. It's all at an end." His voice was full of despair.

His explanation made no more sense to Sarah than his babblings had. Whatever it meant, though, it apparently was bad news for the man she loved, and her heart contracted with fear.

Drakefield gave a sigh. "My dear fellow, I don't mean to criticize, but honestly I think it would be to your advantage to find your way out of your laboratory occasionally. Then you might discover what has been occurring in the world."

"You knew about it." Johnson was clearly shocked.

"Yes, of course and—"

"You knew about it and you didn't tell me. You let me work all those hours on a useless project when my time is so limited."

"It is not—"

Sarah was beginning to resent Johnson's tone.

"If I hadn't happened to receive a letter, who knows how many more months I might have wasted?"

"But you haven't wasted them." The authority in his voice finally managed to silence Johnson temporarily. "You have been making a great piece of work over nothing. Of course I have known about the lamp for some time, as has probably everyone else in the world except you. It works, yes, but it is not really a practical solution. A fellow has to stand with a hand bellows in order to feed the air to the lamp through a container of water. It is a cumbersome thing to take down into a mine. From what you have told me, your model would prove far superior."

Relief was written across Johnson's face, but this time it was Sarah who spoke. "A mine—this lamp has something to do with coal mining, then? A lamp that will not explode if they encounter gas, is that it?"

Johnson turned to look at her in surprise, but Drakefield smiled at her appreciatively. "Just so, my dear. My friend Johnson here is trying to invent a safety lamp."

She blushed and in answer to the inquiry upon his friend's face, murmured, "My father had some mining interests, and though I do not know much about it, of course I have heard about fire damp and how it explodes." She gazed at their faces earnestly. "Why, there was that terrible accident at Gatehead—last year, was it not?—where over ninety men and boys were killed. I think that was why my father decided to sell his interests."

"Remarkable." Sarah did not care for Johnson's scrutiny.

"I did tell you so," said Drakefield softly, before adding in more normal tones, "Yes, there is a desperate need, for it could save many lives, which is why a Society of Coal Owners is being formed to study the problem. Of course, it also might make its inventor and his supporters wealthy."

She was catching on, but slowly. "Do you mean . . . do you need me to . . .?"

Drakefield shook his head quickly, crossing the room to take her by the hand. "No, my dear, not at all. I simply wished for you to be informed about this project so that after our marriage, hopefully you would approve my continuing to support Johnson's experiments, and perhaps we might be able to lend him more assistance than before."

She could not contain her shock. "You are asking for my approval?"

He misinterpreted her words. "I know that it is a gamble, but once you see Johnson's work—"

She shook her head. "No, I mean—I meant that you do not have to ask my permission."

"I would not wish to invest the money contrary to your wishes."

"But it is a wonderful idea—an admirable idea. Why should I have any objections?"

She had forgotten entirely about Johnson's presence, but now he intruded himself by springing up and exclaiming, "You are right, Drakefield, she is a marvel. Come along, Miss Baxter, and I will show you my laboratory. I think you will be particularly interested in—"

She was ready to go along with him, but Drakefield shook his head. "Another time, I am afraid. We are already late as it is."

His words recalled her and she bade Johnson a regretful farewell, while promising to make a visit to his laboratory soon. After they had settled themselves in the carriage once more, she turned to Drakefield.

"But surely time is of the essence. Don't you wish me to speak to my father about—"

"No." His mouth was set. He added more kindly, "August is little more than a month away, after all, my dear."

She closed her mouth abruptly. She was the one who had ruined his plans with her wedding date. If they had already been married, his friend could have been funded, and he might well have produced his invention by now. She glanced at Drakefield's profile from under her lashes. Was that why he had wished to marry her soon? It was just one more thought to trouble her.

As Sarah had predicted, Bertie and Eglantyne did not appear at all upset by the delay. If anything, they seemed startled to see Drakefield and Sarah. One might have thought that the expedition had slipped their mind. They bore the interruption of their pleasures with good grace, however.

Sarah, who had not seen Bertie this morning, informed him about his visitor of last night. He shushed her hurriedly, casting a worried glance at Eglantyne. Sarah's surprise must have appeared upon her face, for he whispered to her, "That is, Sheepnose is the best of good fellows, but a trifle unrefined. Prefer not to introduce him to Miss Adstock anytime soon if I can avoid it."

She was startled and a little disappointed. She could not help but let her eyes rest warmly upon Drakefield again. He, at least, was not ashamed of his old friends. She had met one today who was far less presentable than Sheepnose. Of course, the meeting had concerned business also.

"Miss Adstock, please allow me!" Bertie, adoration in his eyes, rushed over to fetch her bonnet which had been lying upon a side table.

Sarah frowned. Drakefield never looked at her with that sort of devotion. It was obvious that Bertie fairly worshiped Eglantyne. Perhaps if Drakefield felt that way about Sarah, he would not have wished to introduce her to Johnson either. She had to wonder if Annabella knew him.

Drakefield's voice recalled her straying thoughts. "All right, then, if we are ready, we may begin." He conferred briefly with Bertie, then offered Sarah his arm, leading her outside to the carriage before helping her inside it.

"Where is our destination for today?" she asked him playfully.

"Have you ever visited Hampton Court Palace?"

She could only shake her head by way of reply as they set off.

"It is just under fourteen miles away, so if it is agreeable to you, I think we may as well wait until we get there to eat. I instructed my man to pack us a picnic luncheon."

"You enjoy dining al fresco."

"Yes, don't you?"

"Yes."

He gave her a smile as he returned his eyes to the road,

and Sarah returned it, feeling a warm glow spread over her. It was a beautiful day, perfect for an outing, and she was determined not to let anything spoil it. She would thrust those doubts to the back of her mind for now.

There was much to see, after all. After they had passed from the familiar grounds of Hyde Park, they traveled into Knightsbridge, the first village outside London, which soon gave way to Brompton, then Chelsea, then Parson's Green and Fulham. She had never seen a single one of these villages before and they delighted her. Fortunately, Drakefield seemed not at all averse to answering her questions at length.

"Fulham is famous for the Episcopal Palace of the Bishop of London, which is here. The manor dates back before the Conquest. You can see the park as we cross the river."

They were approaching a timbered bridge. "What bridge is this?"

"It is called Putney Bridge, for it connects the village of Putney with Fulham. For years it was the only point close to London where one could cross the Thames west of London Bridge. Of course, that changed when they built Westminster Bridge. We cross into Surrey, by the way."

They had traveled on through Putney and Roehampton when they suddenly reached a vast expanse of rolling green countryside, surmounted by magnificent houses. Sarah gasped in admiration. "Where are we now?"

"We have reached the edge of Putney Health. Many notables have constructed homes upon it. Just behind us is Wimbledon Park, the property of Earl Spencer, whose late father formed it into one of the finest parks in England. Just to the south of Putney Heath lies Wimbledon Common, but we will not have time to visit it today."

As they left the grounds of Putney Heath, he anticipated her next question. "And this on the right is Richmond Park—the New Park, that is. As doubtless you know, it at one time contained a royal palace, though much of it was pulled down during the Commonwealth. Still, there are several houses on lease occupying part of the palace itself. The

Old Garden, which adjoins Kew, is well worth visiting on a Sunday afternoon."

It occurred to Sarah that she had been asking questions in the manner of a three-year-old child. "I am sorry. You must think me terribly ignorant."

He smiled. "No, I think you eager to learn. It is a very good quality, and unfortunately, an unusual one."

How skilled he was at setting her at her ease. "You have just given me license to ask all the questions I desire."

"I am at your service."

It was a pleasure to take a drive with such an informative and entertaining companion, not to mention such an attractive one. She had forgotten all about Bertram and Eglantyne. She looked about behind them to see the other carriage a short distance back.

"I asked my groom to keep an eye on them so that we should not lose them," Drakefield informed her.

"Well, we are supposed to be their chaperones," remarked Sarah in a practical manner, "even though Bertie does have his groom. It is fortunate for them that we are engaged, since Eglantyne's parents are so much stricter than mine."

"Not only fortunate for *them*," said Drakefield with some amusement, his dimple appearing as he spoke.

His words made Sarah catch her breath. He considered himself fortunate to be engaged to her! Of course, he might only be speaking monetarily. Words of love had never crossed his lips. Those annoying doubts kept rising to the surface despite all her best efforts. She pushed them angrily away.

They were nearing a village, and now Drakefield commented, "At last we are in Kingston-upon-Thames. We will cross the Thames again at Kingston Bridge and reach the village of Hampton Wick and Bushy Park."

"Bushy Park?"

"Yes, it is a royal park which we must traverse to reach Hampton Court. The Duke of Clarence's residence is here. Some years ago, a shoemaker from the village won the right of free passage through the park for the public."

Sarah was all eyes as they entered the park. "Oh, look, a deer!" she breathed.

"Yes, it is said to be tolerably well stocked."

"It is the first deer I have ever seen."

He did not reply and she could have bitten her impulsive tongue again. Why must she always be reminding him that she was a commoner?

"I have been told . . . that in my great-grandfather's day, Drakefield Park was stocked with deer also. Perhaps some day we may wish to do that also—so that our children may see deer."

He was concentrating upon the road ahead of him, but Sarah's heart turned over inside of her. Our children. Suddenly she did not think that she could wait until August for the wedding.

Her thoughts were abruptly recalled as she caught her first glimpse of the palace. "Oh!"

He glanced at her and smiled, though she did not see it. "The grounds occupy some three miles. We shall have to drive all the way around it to reach the main gate."

She did not speak for several minutes, being fully intent upon catching glimpses of crenelated towers and turrets of red brick, dressed with white stone in the Tudor manner. She also could steal brief sights of sculpted formal gardens in the style of a later period.

"Oh, this looks wonderful. Thank you for bringing me," she exclaimed.

"I thought that perhaps you might not have seen it before . . . and the grounds are among my favorites in England." They had reached the main gate, but to her surprise, instead of driving through it, he pulled up the horses.

"I thought that since it was so late, you might care to eat before we explore the palace and its grounds."

Sarah suddenly realized that it had been hours since breakfast and that she indeed was famished. As the grooms spread out the picnic lunch, she spent her time peeping at the grand sight that lay before them. Drakefield neared her side. "I do not think I have ever seen anything as beautiful," she told him.

"Perhaps you will care for Drakefield, then. It is also in the Tudor style, though of course not as grand as this." He gave a sigh. "The gardens unfortunately are in a shambles now."

She faced him, her eyes shining. "I shall love it, I know, for it is your home and together we will make it whatever we wish it to be."

He did not say a word, but held out a hand gravely to her. She clasped it and he drew her near to him. They were interrupted by the groom, who gave a discreet cough before announcing that their luncheon was ready.

Sarah did not expect that Bertie and Eglantyne would provide much conversation, and her expectations were fulfilled, though Eglantyne did make a few halfhearted attempts. After one such, when she forgot what she was saying in the middle of the sentence, Sarah could not help giving her head a little shake. As she did, she felt Drakefield's eyes upon her and caught his shared amusement. It set her heart to racing.

As soon as the meal was over, they attempted to reach a decision about which area to visit first. Sarah did not find it odd that having declared an interest in the gardens herself, Bertie should immediately express a wish to visit the house. She looked at Drakefield for a decision. They were supposed to be accompanying the other two, even though this was a public place. On the other hand, she would prefer to be alone with Drakefield.

Apparently, he felt the same, for he offered her his arm and said that he wished to show her the gardens. They arranged a time to meet at the gate, and the two couples parted amicably. They turned to their left and began to make their way toward the kitchen gardens. The long, orderly avenues of trees, the bright sun above, the flowers in bloom about them, all combined to make Sarah feel as if she were walking through a fairy tale. The nearness of him was overwhelming. Her throat felt tight. She attempted to clear it, and in order to maintain a semblance of normalcy, she asked him another question. "Can anyone come here?"

"I suppose, with an introduction, anyone may—and of

course, with a suitable tip for the servant who acts as your guide. We will have more privacy in the gardens, though several residents of Hampton Wick have keys to it."

"It is so beautiful. Why do they not use it as a royal palace any longer?"

He gave a chuckle. "It is said that the king has disliked it ever since he had his ears boxed here as a child. Of course, that is one of the prince regent's stories, so one never knows the truth of it." He paused for a moment, then added, "Of course, I myself would never question anything he has to say, since my greatest wish is to emulate him. Else I would never 'study everything he wears' so earnestly, would I?"

Sarah's confusion turned to embarrassment. "I had hoped you had forgotten that," she said quietly.

He laughed and the sound cut her like a knife. "Never, my dear. Never as long as I live will I forget those words of yours."

He suddenly saw that she was looking troubled and stopped, taking her by the hands. "My dear! I was not laughing at you. I was laughing at myself. It took your prodding for me to see the error of my ways."

Her head was still drooping. He lifted her chin with one hand. "I was an arrogant fellow in those days. If you had not given me such a rude awakening, I would not have come to realize that I was marrying someone with a brain and spirit and heart and . . . and a sense of humor of her own. It did not occur to me that there were two of us entering into this bargain—can you imagine that I was ever such a heartless, selfish fellow?"

A tear slipped down one cheek. "I was worse than you. It was all a plan to drive you off. I didn't wish to marry you, you see." Now was the time to tell him about Alan. She drew in a deep breath, but he interrupted her, drawing out a handkerchief to wipe the tear away.

"And why should you have? No, I cannot blame you, my dear. To be sure, you were sometimes outrageous, but I grew to appreciate that about you. It is a quality which we have in common."

She could not let him accept all the blame in that generous way. "But I didn't even know you, and yet I had formed an opinion against you, in direct opposition to the advice and wishes of my family and friends. I refused to give you a chance. It was stubborn prejudice and nothing more." She took his handkerchief and wiped her eyes. Now was surely the time to tell him.

"Perhaps we simply should agree that all of it is forgotten. I assure you that I do not like to think of the sort of self-pitying fellow that I was then. We shall put it behind us and pretend that it did not happen. Agreed?"

It was her last opening. She should mention Alan now. "Agreed," she said, a little shakily.

"Come, then." His dimple flashed at her. "We are not far from my favorite part of the garden—the maze."

As they approached the structure of hedges, clipped to some six feet high, he took her hand and they fairly ran toward it. They came to a stop as they reached it. Sarah eyed it uncertainly. "I haven't been in one since I was a child, and then I became hopelessly lost."

He laughed. "You cannot get lost in a maze. Don't you know the secret?"

She shook her head.

"You first turn to the left, take the next two turns to the right, and keep left thereafter. To get out, you do the same. That will get you in and out of any maze. Hadn't you ever heard of it?"

He gave her a little push. "Very well, go on, then. I will be behind you. See if it does not work."

She took a few unwilling steps into the darkness of it. Well, he would be behind her, after all. She turned to the left, then, finding two places to turn right, she did so. She prayed that he was correct.

After several minutes of keeping to the left, she did at last come to the benches which stood in the center of the labyrinth. She sat down upon one and waited for Drakefield. He appeared just a moment or two later, his eyes shining. "You had no trouble?"

"No, none at all."

To her surprise, he reached out an arm and pulled her to her feet. Without another word he clasped her in his arms and his lips met hers. She was all unprepared, but it was delightful. He abruptly drew back a step to look at her.

"Do you know, I have been wanting to do that for the longest time?"

Her heart was racing. She should protest this treatment, of course, but how could she, when she was longing for it herself?

"Sarah," he barely breathed her name. A thrill ran up her spine as he drew her to him once again. She could feel the goose flesh rise upon her arms. His face was so close. His mouth was so close. She closed her eyes and the world vanished as their lips met.

"Nanna—Nanna—" There was a sudden rustling and they opened their eyes. A small boy in a linen shirt and nankeen trousers stood regarding them interestedly. "Nanna!"

A middle-aged woman, flushed and with her hair escaping from her bonnet, came panting into the center of the maze. "Now, Master Robert, I am certain that your Uncle Gervase will never bring you anywhere else again if you persist in being so naughty—" She noticed Drakefield and Sarah, and dropped a curtsy while taking the boy by the arm.

"I beg your pardon, I am sure. Now, Master Robert, come with me."

"But Nanna, you should have seen them. He was—"

Her face assumed a darker hue. "Now, Master Robert."

"But he was—"

"That's enough." The voice was mild, but it had the effect of silencing the boy immediately. A blond gentleman came limping into the center of the maze, murmuring, "I do beg your pardon, but—"

"Clavering!"

"Drakefield . . . and Miss Baxter." He bowed to them. "How pleasant to see you, though the circumstances are so unfortunate. This imp of Acheron happens to be my nephew, whom my sister somehow persuaded me to take charge of for a few days. Make the gentleman and lady a bow, Robert."

As the latter complied, he continued lazily, "He has already completed the destruction of my rooms, so I thought to offer him a project of greater scope. I took him to the Park, but an unfortunate incident involving a pebble and a horse persuaded me that we should range farther afield. He had not managed to break anything yet or set anything afire, so I had high hopes, but I see that they must be dashed."

"Oh, Uncle Jerry," laughed the boy, obviously interpreting his uncle's mood as a jocular one.

"Do you know, I think I should have left you at home so that you might have caught the measles from the twins. It would have been no more than you deserved."

"Uncle Jerry!"

He nodded graciously. "I am sorry. I did not mean to involve you in our little domestic disputes. Can you say goodbye to the lady and the gentleman nicely, Robert?"

He bobbed his head. "G'by." In another second he was running back through the maze with his little legs moving as fast as they could carry him, and the nanny shrieking in pursuit. Clavering heaved a sigh. "I am in for it. The next time those babies become ill, I will put my foot down and refuse." He tipped his hat to them politely, remarking, "Good day," before strolling off.

Drakefield and Sarah looked at each other ruefully. Should they begin where they had been interrupted? Another voice was approaching, and another. " . . . Now see, this is where you must turn—oh dear me, it's a blind alley. Well, there's nothing for it, Mother, we must go back the way we came."

Drakefield offered her his arm. Giving a last adjustment to her bonnet, Sarah took it. "Do you know," he said loudly just as they encountered the elderly couple, "with your interest in horticulture, I think you would enjoy seeing the Great Fountain Garden, too, as well as the Privy-garden, which is terraced, and boasts an extensive grapehouse . . ."

"Thank you, I am certain that I would," she returned demurely.

12

IT HAD BEEN a marvelous day, a perfect day, and nothing could mar it. They had not seen the inside of the palace, it was true, but what did she care for that? They might easily do so some other time. And although she had regretted being interrupted in the maze, upon reflection she realized that it was just as well. She might easily have allowed herself to be overcome by her emotions. Sarah did not trust herself. Not for the first time she wished that she had not insisted upon being married in August. As if fate wished to improve matters even further, the duchess had sent an invitation to the theater tomorrow night, to include both Sarah and Drakefield. Sarah was assured of seeing him tomorrow. She could hardly contain her bliss.

She was in a sunny mood when she arrived home, and greeted her parents with unexpected and enthusiastic hugs. She went tripping up the stairs singing and rang for her maid so that she might change for dinner.

Her maid came in and began laying out her dress. As she did so, she commented, "There's been another letter come for you, miss. I left it on your pillow."

Sarah experienced an abrupt sinking sensation. She said nothing, but after the maid had helped her off with her old clothes and on with her new, she dismissed her and crossed over to the bed. There lay an envelope with the familiar handwriting on it. Drat it! Why couldn't Alan disappear from her life as completely as he had from her mind?

She might easily have thrown it away unopened, but the thought did not occur to her. The missive read:

Dearest Sarah,

I am writing you upon what we all sense is the eve of a great battle. We camp upon the plains of Vittoria tonight. Our actions tomorrow could turn the tide of the war. I hope that, whatever happens, I may act in a manner so as to make you proud of me. I regret more than ever my estrangement from my family, and I hope that you will choose not to believe any of the malicious lies that are being told of me. I cling to your letters as they are all I have of home. You have seemed strangely silent of late—but I know how unreliable the mails are. I pray that I may distinguish myself so that I may someday return to England as one entitled to claim your hand. I cannot tell you how happy it makes me to have your assurances that I already have your heart. Whatever the outcome tomorrow, dear Sarah, please hold me in your thoughts as you are in mine and if I should die, know that I died loving you.

She could not help the tears that rose to her eyes. This was all her own fault. How could she ever explain to Alan that she did not love him? She had certainly done everything she could to convince him of her affection in her letters. He would never have had a thought of it in his head except for her. To think, however unwittingly, that she had deceived him in such a terrible fashion. How heartbroken he would be if he learned the truth. When he learned the truth.

She looked at the date on the letter. 20 June. Why, there might already have been word of the battle by now. She would ask her father at dinner. No, perhaps it was better not to ask her father. It was better not to rouse his suspicions unnecessarily. She would visit the lending library tomorrow and see what she could learn.

Inevitably, she was delayed. She had been ready to start out that morning when she realized she had forgotten her reticule and was forced to go back upstairs for it. When she came back downstairs, she encountered Fraley, who looked at her hopefully. "The young gentleman who is a friend of Mr. Betram's is here, miss. Do you wish to see him or shall I send him away?"

She gave a sigh of exasperation and began untying her bonnet. "Show him in, Fraley."

She had remonstrated with Bertie when he had returned last night but had made no progress with him. She had argued that only a vulgarian would simply forsake such an old friend. Bertie had protested that he didn't mean to cut the acquaintance entirely. "It's just that I wish to make the best sort of impression upon Miss Adstock. She thinks I'm a fellow of high ideals—and Sheepnose is a rackety sort, you must admit."

Sarah shook her head. "You cannot hope to deceive Eglantyne forever. She is far too clever for that."

"Only for a little while. Daresay she'll know about Sheepnose—and the pig, and all the rest—but I wish her to be exposed to it gradually rather than all at once. Might come as a bit of a shock, what?"

As much as Sarah deplored his actions, she was forced to concede the uselessness of further argument, and so she had abandoned the discussion. Yet even though she strongly disapproved, she was reluctant to expose him to his friend. When Sheepnose was escorted into the drawing room, she therefore greeted him as if nothing were wrong.

"I am afraid you have missed Bertie again today, Mr. Sheephouse. I did give him your message, but we all went out of town yesterday. Today he left rather early, so I do not know where he went."

The latter, who was still holding onto his hat, gave a sigh. "I s'pose I won't be seeing much of him. London's so cursed dull when you're on your own. The cursed part of it is that I can't even return home at the moment. *Pater*'s still too cursed angry about the cursed pig."

It was difficult, but necessary. Sarah managed to repress a smile in the face of such dejection. "I am sorry."

"Well," he gave a sigh, "thank you for seeing me anyway. You might tell Bertie that I stopped by again. Perhaps

I'll see him at Fives-Court next week. Perhaps you might mention it to him?" he added hopefully.

Sarah didn't know what Fives-Court signified, though she was certain it was something unpleasant. "I will," she promised.

"Thank you. Most kind." He seemed struck by an idea. "If I may be of service to you some time, just call."

She could not imagine how he would ever be of service, but she smiled warmly at him and thanked him.

Owing to the delay, the lending library was already crowded when she reached it. There were several gentlemen gathered around the papers, and Sarah clearly had no hope of reaching one. She was about to give up in despair when she picked out a few significant words of conversation.

"It's the end of the war. They've had them on the run since May, and when they tried to make a stand, Wellington ran over 'em."

"Much you know about it. If Bonaparte himself had been at Vittoria instead of his fat brother, the French would never have defeated. He's the craftiest general alive," argued the devil's advocate.

"He's driven them out of Spain. What's more, he's broken the back of the French army. They'll never recover from it, never. Why, the war will be over in a year, perhaps less."

"It's the same sort of talk we've heard all along. Then Wellington retreats and it begins once more—" the other was retorting when Sarah broke into their conversation.

"Gentlemen, I am sorry, but please, could you tell me which battle you are discussing?"

The group stared in amazement at this female who dared to interrupt them, but one elderly gentleman replied kindly, "Why, the battle of Vittoria, my dear—the great victory. Surely you heard the news yesterday?"

"I was gone from town yesterday. Please, can anyone tell me if the 13th was engaged?"

One gentleman stared down at his paper and read for a moment. "Yes, according to this account they were."

Sarah's face grew pale. "Is—are there lists of who has been . . . of the wounded . . . and—"

The old gentleman drew her away from the group. "Now, my dear, you do not want to worry yourself unnecessarily. They say our casualties were only half those of the French. There will be no lists for some time, you know. Do not fret yourself. The best thing for you to do is to go home like a good girl and wait for word to come."

It was clear that there was nothing further to be learned. He was beaming at her with kindly concern. "Thank you." She called for her maid and they departed from the shop.

Now, in addition to everything else, Sarah had an unspeakable worry as she strolled homeward. Yesterday had been the best of days. Today seemed as if it might be the worst. She tried to make her thoughts more cheerful. She had not heard that Alan had been wounded—or worse. All was probably well. Of course, that still left her with the problem of how to explain her engagement to him. Perhaps it would be easier now that they'd had this great victory. She must not allow her spirits to become lowered so easily. After all, there was the theater to look forward to tonight . . . and being with Drakefield once more.

By the time she began to ready herself for the evening, her spirits had begun to rise again. She had been considering only the worst of possibilities. Alan was undoubtedly unscathed. He had always prided himself on his luck, after all. And she herself had so much to be happy about.

She smiled at her reflection with pleasure. She had been just waiting for an occasion to try her frock upon society. It would be something in a new style for her, and she hoped it would create a sensation. A gold silk crepe frock worn over a satin slip, it was cut very simply. The only ornaments it boasted were the rich gilt spangles with which it was embroidered. She would shine this evening on Drakefield's arm. There were probably those who would say it was not suitable for an unmarried young lady, and others who would suggest that it was excessive for a trip to the theater, but as usual, she intended to ignore them.

She frowned at her reflection. No, something was not quite right. She discarded the pale yellow gloves she had chosen to accompany it. Only white could work with the gold. A little shiver ran through her as she removed them. Was it possible that she could be superstitious? Just because she always wore yellow gloves with the Black Dandy did not mean that they exerted any special power over him.

At any rate, when he arrived he did not seem to find anything wrong with her appearance. He complimented her upon her new dress with appreciative amusement. "Tonight you will live up to your soubriquet, La Colonne D'or."

Her dark brows drew together for a moment. "A soubriquet? I did not know of it. How annoying!"

"But far more annoying for all the unfortunate females you will outshine. Shall we go?"

She had for a moment considered changing her dress. The warm look in his eyes melted her. She would wear rags if it meant having a few extra moments with him. As she entered the carriage, the duchess nodded at her with approval as she greeted her and they set off.

It was to be a performance of one of Shakespeare's tragedies, to be followed by a farce.

"Have you visited the Royal Opera House before?" inquired the duchess.

"Oh yes, I saw Mrs. Siddon's farewell performance here last year."

"I remember her first appearance as Portia in the *Merchant of Venice* at Drury Lane. She was not a great success. She retired to the country for a time afterward. The theater just simply is not what it was used to be. I recall when Goldsmith premiered *She Stoops to Conquer* at Covent Garden, and just two years later was the first performance of Sheridan's *The Rivals*. I was in both of those audiences, and my dear, the response was electric. Of course, we had no idea that we should not have such playwrights with us forever."

"Sheridan might still be writing," commented Drakefield mildly.

"Sheridan, pshaw! Do not speak to me of him," said the duchess with a gesture of distaste quite out of keeping with her earlier tone. "You must agree that the theater is in a pitiable state. I do not know how much longer Drury Lane may continue, as poorly managed as it has been. And every new set of owners only seems to do worse. They will close within the year if things don't improve, mark my words. That is, they will if the theater does not burn down again. They are forever burning down, both of them."

"There is always Sadler's Wells," suggest Drakefield.

"Hmph. Aquatic spectacles indeed. I know what to think of such nonsense. It only goes to prove my point."

"My father took me to see Grimaldi there some years ago. I thought he was very funny," put in Sarah diffidently.

The duchess shook her head. "I suppose nothing will ever rival the great actors who abounded in my youth. Like me, they have seen better days now. Sometimes I have to wonder, though, why I bother keeping my box at all."

Sarah smiled at her. "Well, I for one am grateful for your invitation. I have not been to the theater this year."

The duchess patted her hand fondly. "Well, you should not have to listen to an old woman's complaints. Your last public appearance was rather a trial for you. I mean for you and my grandson to do nothing but enjoy yourselves tonight."

"And so we shall, your grace," contributed Drakefield, smiling at Sarah in a way that made her blush.

It was a pity that the words were not prophetic.

As they entered the theater, Sarah had the satisfaction of knowing that she had succeeded in her object. All eyes were upon them as they entered their box, and there were audible murmurings. She had assumed that unconsciousness which was becoming second nature to her, and appeared not to notice the sensation she was creating. Instead she smiled at her handsome escort as he seated her. He leaned over to whisper in her ear, "'I daresay that girl in the

first box over—on the bottom, there—see the one I mean—
is wishing you at the devil this very moment."

Sarah glanced discreetly in the direction he mentioned
and saw, glaring at her, a very fair blonde in a red net dress
trimmed with black, which had been embroidered with yellow roses. She barely repressed a gasp of laughter.

"Not a color she should wear either," added Drakefield
wryly.

Glancing around, she saw more than one young lady who
had chosen a similar motif, and several angry stares.

"They will all be in gold dresses in another week or
two."

She had extracted her fan from her reticule and was trying to hide her laughter behind it when it happened. There
was a commotion as one of the empty boxes directly opposite them began to fill.

Still laughing, she hardly noticed as the party began to
take their seats. It wasn't until she felt Drakefield stiffen
beside her that she knew something was wrong. She looked
up to see a pair of large brown eyes regarding them expres-
sively. It was Lady Fernsbury, though Sarah had no idea
who the handsome young man seating her was. Annabella
nodded at them deliberately, and Drakefield and Sarah had
little choice but to acknowledge her. Sarah looked at her fiancé's face. It was frozen in a stern mask, but his eyes did
not leave Annabella's face.

"Oh, finally they are about to begin," exclaimed the
duchess, unaware of these undercurrents.

Sarah obediently shifted her attention to the stage, but
she could not help giving one last peep at Annabella. The
brown eyes were still fixed upon Drakefield, and she was
mouthing some words at him, apparently confident that
they would not be noticed as the action was already beginning. Sarah became rigid. What on earth could Annabella
want? Sarah dreaded knowing the answer to that question.

The performance might have been a good one, but Sarah
could not be a judge. Her attention was distracted by the little drama being played out in the boxes. Annabella's eyes
did not leave Drakefield the entire time. Even the young

gentleman with her became visibly annoyed and seemingly
spoke to her about it, but she appeared to brush off his remarks. Drakefield, for the most part, seemed to have his attention fixed upon the stage, but every now and again Sarah
caught him glancing at Annabella. Well, she was hard to ignore.

Sarah's spirits did not rise when he excused himself during the interval, saying that he wished to procure refreshments for them. It did not surprise her that Annabella had
disappeared from her box also, though her handsome young
escort was still there, looking sulky. She tried to think optimistic thoughts, but it became harder and harder the longer
Drakefield was gone. She made her best attempt to respond
to the duchess's conversational gambits, but it was difficult.
Drakefield reappeared with glasses for them just as the cur-
tain was rising.

"I am sorry," he whispered. "there was a terrible crush,
since it is so warm tonight."

Sarah smiled and thanked him. There was no answering
smile, just the remote expression which she had almost forgotten to associate with him. She looked at the box opposite. It was empty.

The rest of the play passed just as before. Drakefield
fixed his gaze woodenly upon the stage, but Sarah was sure
that he did not see anything. His thoughts must be miles
away. It was a relief when the play ended and the duchess
confessed that she was too tired to remain for the farce.
Sarah's head was pounding. She had had enough of farces.
Hadn't she just starred in one herself this evening?

When they parted, there was none of the warmth she had
come to expect from Drakefield. He bowed over her hand
as if he were a puppet on strings. She looked desperately
for that spark to pass between them, but he was unreach-
able. His eyes did not see her, He did not mention when
they might meet again. Well, she was too proud to ask. She
smiled her farewell as if nothing were wrong, turned, and
went up the stairs to her bedroom.

It was a new subject upon which to brood. What could
have passed between Drakefield and Annabella? She was

certain that they had met during the interval. Why had he hidden the truth from her? And then why had he withdrawn from her in that manner?

Sarah was not one to fret unnecessarily, but she could not deny the cold fear that clutched at her heart. Her wedding was just a month away. Did she really know Drakefield at all? The man she knew was intelligent, humorous, kind, and courageous, but if he existed, how could he vanish so rapidly without a trace? She was still living with that great unspoken dread. Was he in love with Annabella? Was there something between them yet? And would there continue to be after her marriage?

Her experience in school had taught her that the nobility was different from her own class. Where marriages tended to be arranged for considerations of position, land, or money, it was commonly accepted that a married man would have a mistress. Her aristocratic friends had laughed at her naive horror at discovering this shocking truth. She loved Drakefield, but she did not know if she could marry him under those conditions.

The little sleep she received was restless and filled with unhappy dreams which she could not recall when she awakened. Her head was still pounding as it had been the previous night. Glancing at the clock, she saw that it was already past ten. She rang for her maid, who entered bearing a note. It was from the duchess, who asked if Sarah would call upon her today at her convenience. She must have risen early for Sarah to receive the note here by this hour. Sarah frowned a little as she considered what it meant. What could the duchess possibly have to say to her that might not have been said last night?

She heaved a sigh. Well, the only way to discover the answer would be to visit the duchess as she had requested. Sarah had no other plans for today, in any event. It was not as if Drakefield had promised to visit.

When she called upon the duchess in her home on Bruton Street later that afternoon, she thought that her hostess was looking more frail than usual, though the latter held out her hand and greeted her enthusiastically. Sarah took a seat as she was bidden but refused the duchess's offer of refreshments, coming right to the point instead.

"I understand that you wished to see me, your grace?"

"Yes. Will you get that box please?"

She indicated a large box of worn red velvet which lay upon a little piecrust table. Sarah rose and crossed to grasp the box before attempting to return it to the duchess. The latter waved her away. "No, no. It is for you."

Puzzled, Sarah opened it, then gasped. It was a beautiful set of diamond jewelry. There was a large diamond pendant suspended from a string of smaller ones. There were also two sizable diamond drop earrings, and another large diamond which looked as if it might be some sort of a hair ornament. "They are beautiful."

"They are my family jewels, my dear. I did not wish to present them to you the other night lest it cause some dissension among my son's family, but they are mine to do with as I choose. All the Wiltham jewels should be sufficient for them. I was not an heiress, but they are good pieces and quite old." She heaved a sigh and Sarah thought she had never seen the duchess look so tired. "I would have given them to my daughter, had she not married against our wishes."

Sarah's face must have expressed some shock, for now the duchess smiled, a sad, ironic smile. "I daresay it sounds cruel to you, but the gamester she married would have broken up the set and sold them. Nothing mattered to him beside his next gambling stake, not family, not honor, not love, and certainly not duty."

"I do not know what to say, your grace."

"You do not need to say anything, my dear. I hope that you will enjoy them, and someday perhaps you will have a daughter of your own to whom you may give them. Perhaps you will be more fortunate than I was."

"Oh, your grace—" Tears had started to Sarah's eyes.

The other shook her head. "It is nothing for you to upset yourself over. It all happened long ago." She sighed heavily once more. "I thought that perhaps it was time I told you

about my grandson." One corner of her mouth curved upward unhappily. "I daresay he has not told you anything
about his parents, has he?"

Sarah shook her head wordlessly.

"We had but the one daughter and one son. The late duke
unfortunately doted upon our daughter. She was a wild,
pretty thing, headstrong as he himself was, clever, charming when she chose to be, and humorous. In his eyes, she
could do no wrong. He was much more severe upon our
son. Poor Augustus, perhaps he'd be less of a cod's head
if . . ."

She expelled another long breath. "In her very first Season she promised to be a great success—she had scores of
offers from acceptable suitors. Unfortunately, she had developed a marked preference for a wastrel, the Earl of
Drakefield."

She pressed her lips together tightly, then continued. "I
have told you the sort of man he was. Very handsome, of
course, and he also could be quite charming, but he had already gamed away one fortune. She was deaf to everything
the duke and I had to say to her. I remember after one mas-
querade, where Wiltham had caught her in his company,
they had a furious argument. He told her that she must give
him up and she refused. She said that she intended to marry
him. Wiltham promised her that if she did, we would cut
her off without a penny and that none of the family would
have anything to do with her again. She stood there and
laughed. It was a terrible sound to hear. I still remember her
words: "Well, Father, you must do as you must, and I will
do as I must also.' Of course, he did not take her words seriously. She was given to tantrums and sulks when she did
not get her way; it came from being overindulged."

Her voice was trembling now. "When we awoke in the
morning, we found that she had fled in the night for Gretna
Green. It was too late to pursue her. Wiltham turned to me
and said, "Our daughter is dead to us now. We will never
mention her name again,' and we never did." She took in
another deep breath. "Of course, when I heard there was
a child, I would have dearly loved to have seen it, but

Wiltham was adamant. They should have no opportunity to dun us for money, although of course Drakefield tried often enough." She shook her head. "Our daughter never did attempt to contact us, though their situation I know was desperate . . . desperate. I cannot help but think that if they had been able to afford proper care, she might not have been claimed by illness at such an early age."

She lifted her chin to gaze directly at Sarah. "After she died, I would have taken the child in, but his father refused to surrender him to me. Well, he was in school by then, which somehow the fourth earl managed. Wiltham was gone also, so I had some contact with the boy, but not a great deal. I thought it all too likely that he would one day follow in his father's footsteps despite his publicly professed hatred for gambling. It is like those who are addicted to drink—it runs in the blood. And he is the very picture of his father at that age, and like him, fastidious in his dress. The Black Dandy!" She snorted her contempt.

"It wasn't until he came to me and told me he intended to repair the family fortunes by marrying you that I thought there was hope."

"Your grace—"

She held up a hand to silence her. "Wait, I have not told you all yet. At one time he had been near to being engaged to—well, you know her as Lady Fernsbury now—"

"I know." Sarah had to speak. It was one story she did not wish to hear again.

"You know?" The duchess was clearly surprised, but after a moment she went on. "Of course, at the time I thought that his judgment was proving to be just as poor as his mother's. Not a shred of character to her, though she was pretty enough, I grant you, and the creature would have run through every penny he had in a matter of days. Fortunately, the fourth earl died and Drakefield's situation was exposed. I have to give the gel credit. She at least knew it was not a suitable match."

Despite her best efforts, Sarah could not entirely keep the pain from her voice. "Your grace, why are you telling me this?"

"Because I was at the theater with you last night, that's why." She gave a sniff of outrage. "Think I didn't notice the creature making a spectacle of herself? She'd better have a care, or even old Fernsbury might divorce her."

"Then you also saw—" began Sarah uncomfortably.

"My grandson, as you may know by now, can be a great noddy at times."

"He still loves her." There was no question in it this time. It was a bitter truth. Perhaps it was better to face it now.

"That I do not know, and I doubt if he does himself. There is one thing that I can tell you, however, my dear." She leaned forward to emphasize her point. "I daresay you have wondered why I took such a great fancy to you, taking you to Almack's before you were even engaged and introducing you to society. Well, my dear, I thought you should have a glimpse of what you would be throwing away by not marrying Drakefield. I also wanted him to come to see the sort of gel you are." She was gazing directly into Sarah's eyes once again. "You are his only hope—no, not just to save his estates for him—but to save *him*. I saw at a glance that you were the sort of gel who could save him from being the sort of care-for-nobody who drifts through life as his father did. He needs to take his place in the House of Lords. He was given a fine mind as well as the power to make a difference in this world, and he needs to employ them for the good of others." She fell back in her chair; her exhaustion was obvious. "I suppose it sounds as if I've been talking pure gibberish," she commented ruefully.

"No," said Sarah slowly, still trying to assimilate these ideas, "but I do not know how—"

She smiled at her. "I have seen the change in him already, my dear." She paused for a moment, then added lightly, "As well as the change in you. Never underestimate love, my dear. It is the most powerful force in the world."

There was much to ponder in her words, and Sarah turned them over in her mind upon the drive home. Had she changed? Yes, she was certain that she had. And Drakefield, Drakefield himself had said that she had changed him. But was it love on his part? She wished she could know, particularly with the wedding so close at hand.

As she entered the vestibule, Fraley, the butler, stepped up to her. "You have a visitor, miss," he said, bowing and indicating the open drawing room door. She was half expecting to see Sheepnose again, but as she walked inside, she saw instead, leaning upon the mantelpiece, a tall gentleman clad all in black. As she closed the door behind her, Drakefield smiled at her and greeted her with a penitent expression.

"My dear, what a boor I've been! I am afraid that in my preoccupation I neglected you terribly last night, and I didn't even realize it until this morning. Please say that you'll forgive me. I've brought my carriage so that we might have a drive wherever you wish to go, in order to make amends."

Without a word she walked straight into his arms.

13

THE NEXT SEVERAL weeks should have been filled with days of unalloyed bliss. There were drives in Hyde Park, sometimes by themselves, sometimes followed by Bertie and Eglantyne in his new phaeton. It was amusing for Sarah to see how her bonnets and frocks and use of colors remained the fashion, any alteration on her part leading to slavish copies within a few days. Wedding presents arrived by the score daily and had to be opened and notes sent in acknowledgment.

There was the promised excursion to Kew Gardens on a Sunday afternoon, and a visit to the Argyll Rooms to hear a performance of the newly formed Philharmonic Society one evening. She recalled her vows to his friend Johnson, and they visited his laboratory one day, where Sarah was impressed by his progress. Another day was spent in examining the "Over Fifteen Thousand Natural and Foreign Curiosities" at Bullock's Museum at the Egyptian Hall in Piccadilly. There were pictures done in sand, miniature wax models of famous persons, and all manner of birds, beasts, and fish stuffed so as to preserve them forever. There was even a huge rhinoceros, which would have been as large as life except that the skin had become shriveled in the drying. Just as interesting were the live animals at the menagerie in Exeter Change. They saw lions, tigers, monkeys, a panther, a hyena, a camel, and even a hippopotamus. The elephant amused them all by courteously removing the Black Dandy's hat and then offering it back to him again.

They attended a grand fete held at Vauxhall Gardens to celebrate Wellington's victory at Vittoria. The event was honored by the presence of the Regent himself, as well as all the royal dukes, and Sarah experienced the thrill of seeing the Duke of York. The crush was so great that it took almost three hours for their carriage to cross Westminister Bridge.

Given that a young lady's social life was supposed to end from the moment of her engagement until that of her marriage, Sarah was enjoying an exceptional amount of entertainment, but then the length of her engagement made her circumstances exceptional too. Of course, she also enjoyed a remarkable amount of license not afforded to those young ladies unfortunate enough to be engaged to someone other than the Black Dandy. Drakefield was charming and attentive—in fact, he was everything that a young lady could wish. His friend Clavering had called more than once to take her to Gunther's for ices; it was becoming a tradition of theirs, and she could almost measure how her credit with the world rose with each trip.

The sole moments of discord were provided by the dejected visits of Sheepnose, who, although he managed to catch Bertie once by arriving early, had not yet worked out any arrangement with him to his satisfaction. Sarah was able to be particularly sympathetic, for she also was becoming quite disgusted with Bertie. He had adopted a peevish tone with her, blaming her for the postponement of his own engagement to Eglantyne. "Her parents would be most willing to give their consent, but they insist that it must wait until after you are married to Drakefield. Why on earth did you have to insist upon such a long engagement anyway? If you were less stubborn—"

She cut him off at that point, too impatient to hear any more. "I am sorry, Bertie, but I must leave. Mother and I are going to the dressmaker's today for a fitting of my wedding gown. There are but two weeks until my wedding, so I imagine that if you use all your resolve, you somehow will be able to survive them. Excuse me." She left without further discussion. She had enough to concern her without adding Bertie's problems to her own.

Of course, there were all the wedding arrangements to be

made, although fortunately her mother proved to be a tower of strength in that regard. Mrs. Baxter was delighted to plan all the details, and with her and the duchess working in concert, a great deal of work was accomplished. Sarah was particularly grateful for the latter's help, for she had a dread of doing something inappropriate, even though, as the duchess reminded her, she could to some extent write her own rules. She was busy enough that she hardly even noticed the times when Drakefield absented himself for his cricket games.

In all, she should have been gloriously happy. She might have been, except for two problems which refused to leave her mind. One was the curious absence of any letters from Alan. When in an optimistic mood, she had taken it as a good sign. Perhaps after his victory and promotion he was too occupied to even think of her—perhaps he was forgetting about her. Or possibly he had taken note of her lack of correspondence and had realized that matters between them had changed. At any rate, she would be married to Drakefield in slightly less than two weeks now, and there would be nothing that Alan could say to her then. He would realize that it had been only an infatuation on her part. These were the most hopeful of her thoughts, but the dark ones were dark indeed. She knew quite well that an absence of letters might mean that he was not able to write. She prayed that was not the case.

There was an even worse torment that she underwent daily. Despite all of Drakefield's attentiveness, he still had not told her that he loved her. She knew that he was attracted to her—that part was very clear—and he obviously held her in some sort of affection. Perhaps she was foolish for wanting more from an arranged marriage, for hoping that his feelings might equal her own. As matters stood, she might have borne it.

The uncomfortable part was that Lady Fernsbury had not left town. Though they did not encounter her regularly, they did so with enough frequency to distress Sarah. Most of the *ton* was not to be found in town in July and August. Why had Annabella persisted in remaining? There were no more pantomimed conversations, but whenever she saw her, Sarah was aware that Annabella's eyes always rested upon Drakefield. It was perhaps not enough to justify the dreadful suspicions that arose at three in the morning, but at the same time, even in her most rational moods she had to admit that there were reasons for concern. Once or twice she attempted to broach the conversation with Drakefield, but gave up before she started. What could she say, after all? Was it simply her nature to fall in love with gentlemen who did not return her affection? She had certainly been fond enough of Alan until his sentiments underwent a change.

At such times she felt very near to despair, but she scolded herself for such thoughts. She had never really known Alan, after all. She knew Drakefield much better—or at least she had spent more time with him. She gave her head a shake. Perhaps she was fortunate simply to be marrying a man she could love. He did not hate her, at least.

She had very little time to brood, however, for as the day of the wedding approached, it seemed that a thousand and one matters had to be settled. The trousseau was naturally a matter of great concern, and she had to ensure that there would be appropriate bonnets, caps, slippers, boots, stockings, petticoats, reticules, and gloves to accompany her new frocks.

She returned from one such shopping expedition the week before the wedding, and felt ready to collapse as she entered the hall. She found it in her heart to pity the poor footman who carried all her packages, though several more were to be sent from the stores. She had to consider it fortunate that Drakefield had begun a cricket match today. At least he would be busy for a few days while she devoted herself to this business.

It was just after noon, and she thought that after partaking of a light nuncheon, she might very well go up to her room to rest. The duchess had recommended it strongly. "Nothing is more unattractive than an exhausted bride," she had advised. Her maid approached her and, curtsying, handed her a note. She looked at the handwriting. It was unfamiliar. Her suspicions were not roused. Ever since the moment of her engagement she had been kept busy replying to notes, sincere or not, wishing her every happiness. This probably was just one more. She tucked it in her reticule. She could very well read it over nuncheon.

Later, as she was seated, enjoying some biscuits and cheese, the note recalled itself to her memory. She extracted it from her reticule and opened it. Her eyes widened in shocked disbelief. She leaped up from the table, knocking over the glass from which she had been drinking. She rushed into the hall.

"Mary," she called, "bring my pelisse and bonnet *now*."

Twenty minutes later, she stood before a large red brick two-story house and sounded the bell. The woman who came to the door in response to her query jerked her thumb upward and grunted, "Second floor, on the right." How odd to think that she had considered herself engaged to Alan and yet did not know where he lived. As she climbed the stairs, her maid close behind her, they passed a heavily veiled weeping girl descending. Perhaps there were other wounded soldiers here too.

The door was opened by a manservant who seemed surprised to see her. "Would you please tell Mr. Grenfell that Miss Baxter is here? I had a note which apparently a friend of his wrote, urging me to visit him." The room smelled pleasantly of lavender water. His nurse must be taking good care of him. The servant took her card wordlessly and disappeared into the other room for a moment before returning.

"Master will see you now."

She took a deep breath and stepped into the other room, half afraid of what she might see. Alan was lying propped on a divan, a coverlet over him, and he was wearing a dressing gown. He smiled and greeted her warmly.

"Sarah, my dear! How good of you to come so quickly."

His face was entirely different than her memory had pictured it to be. Of course he was thinner now, and paler too. She tried to smile.

"I was so sorry to hear the news. I had no idea that you had been wounded."

"Please, my dear, have a chair."

She took one, reluctantly. "How are you, then?"

His smile disappeared for a moment. "I took a ball in the shoulder. It hurts like the devil—beg pardon—but I shouldn't be invalided out for long." His smile returned. "The best part of it is that I have the chance to see you again, my sweet."

She tried to look as if the prospect pleased her. It was fortunate she had left the maid in the other room. "How long do they say it will take you to recover?"

"They do not know—weeks, months perhaps."

There were a few moments of silence as she tried to think of something to say. "It must have been a great battle."

"Yes." His face suddenly brightened. "And I've forgotten to tell you the best news of all. Before I was wounded, I received a promotion in the field. I am now a lieutenant!"

"How wonderful!" She hoped she sounded enthusiastic. Perhaps it was time to tell him now.

"Yes, so you see, my dearest, there is no obstacle before us. I cannot help but feel that when I return, there may be further promotions awaiting me. It has been an awkward time since my family cut me off, but now we need not worry about them, after all. We may be married whenever you wish, sweetheart."

Had anyone ever found herself in a more uncomfortable situation? She drew in a deep breath, trying to think of what to say. He looked at her concernedly.

"Are you thinking that your parents still will not approve, as you wrote me? We can have a runaway match, then, as soon as I am well. We'll go to Scotland—it will be an adventure. Come here, Sarah."

She did not know how to refuse, so she stood and crossed over to stand beside him. He took her hands in his and kissed them.

"I have missed you so much, you know. Why, I think I might well have died if I didn't have the thought of you to cling to." His voice was low and husky. "Your—your letters told me so much. I have kept every one of them."

His hands were warm. She drew hers away and felt his forehead. "Why, you have a fever," she exclaimed.

"Yes, but it doesn't matter. All that matters is that you are here."

"You should be resting. Have you had an apothecary come by?"

"You are all the medicine I need," he said, reaching for her hand and obtaining it again.

"I think I should call one for you."

"To be frank, I'm not in funds at the moment. I daresay I'll survive without one."

He was dreadfully thin and weak. "I'll pay for it," she said. "I think I had better go get one now."

"You cannot leave me yet, when I have waited so many months to see you." There was a note of panic in his voice.

"I will stay for a little while."

"Draw up a chair, so I can hold your hand, and tell me, Sarah, tell me all the things we will do after we are married."

What had she done now?

When she returned home, she went straight up to her room and sent down a message that she was too ill to eat, as indeed she was. She did not have the least idea what to do. She should have told him right at the first that she was marrying someone else—she could see her mistake now. If only he had been less pale and less weak. She felt like weeping at the sight of him. He had told her that his family had refused to have anything to do with him. Could she just abandon him to his fate? And he was so certain that she still wanted to marry him. Of course, anyone who had read her letters would have come to the same conclusion.

She might speak to her parents, but how could she confess the depth of her mistake to him? And if anyone else should ever read those letters . . . She shuddered at the thought. As innocent as her actions had been, her reputation would still be ruined. Drakefield would certainly have every reason to break off the engagement if he knew.

The more she thought about it, the more the conviction grew. She must get those letters back from Alan. She would simply have to march in there tomorrow and tell him that she was to marry another and that she wanted her letters back. She wished he were stronger. It had been somewhat pitiful, too, the way he had fallen asleep holding onto her hand.

It was raining when she awoke the next day, the climate seeming to have grasped her mood and acted upon it. It was a miserable day and a miserable ride in the downpour. Upon arriving at Alan's rooms, she was surprised to meet a clergyman coming out of them. He greeted her politely, though he gave her a searching stare. Heavens, could Alan have worsened so rapidly? She dared not even ask, but rushed into the room instead, calling his name. To her relief, he responded, once again requesting that she join him in his room. With scarcely a thought she abandoned her maid and discovered him in much the same condition as she had found him yesterday.

"Oh, heavens, I was so frightened. I met a clergyman coming out."

He smiled. "That should not frighten you. We—we were talking of marriage." He hesitated a moment, then added quickly, "I am hoping for the best, you see—that your family will accept this match."

It was finally time to tell him. "They will never accept it, Alan," she said, untying her bonnet and setting it on a table beside him.

He frowned. "But I am wounded, after all—in the service of our country. Perhaps they—"

She shook her head as she drew up a chair and sat. "I should have told you yesterday." She drew a deep breath. "I am engaged to be married to the Earl of Drakefield."

"No!" He sat upright for a moment, then with a groan of pain fell back upon the chaise. "No! You cannot—"

She tried to restrain him. "Alan, you must not excite yourself."

"Must not excite—my God! Do you think I am made of stone?"

Tears were running freely down her face by now. "No. Oh, Alan, I am so sorry."

"You are sorry! I don't suppose you have thought what this means to me! Why, all my dependence has been on you, and you certainly seemed—shall I tell you what you wrote?—'My own darling Alan,' you always began."

She was sobbing now. "Please—please don't, Alan. I know what I said."

"But of course he could offer you a title which I could not."

"It was not that at all."

"Sarah!" He took her hands in his and gazed intently at her face. "This engagement was not your idea, was it? It was your parents' ambition."

"Yes," she sniffed, "but—"

"Oh, my darling, forgive me." He kissed her hands again. "I am a jealous beast. For a moment I thought you had been willing to marry this Drakefield. You need not worry, my sweet. I will carry you off at the very altar if need be. I may not be able to afford a charger, but we will manage somehow."

She was crying too hard to be able to speak.

"My love, I promise you that I will take care of everything. No one shall force you into a marriage against your will, I promise you. And once we have wed, well, I know that there will be a scandal, of course, but I cannot imagine that your parents would cut their only child off without a penny."

"But I am not their only child," she managed to gasp. "I have a brother."

Why did she imagine that this news upset him more than the rest? "You have a brother?"

"Yes."

"But still, I—well, your parents dote on you, after all. I think they would not be unforgiving if you made a runaway match . . . even though it was contrary to their wishes." He was speaking very slowly now, as if trying to convince himself, and Sarah was not sure if he even remembered that she was there.

Sarah thought of the duchess's daughter. At least she had not been engaged to someone else when she had made a runaway match, but even so, *her* doting parents had never spoken to her again. She could imagine her own parents' horror if she ran off, leaving Drakefield at the altar, and shuddered. "I am not so certain."

He looked at her searchingly for a moment, and she had the feeling that he was troubled, but now he said more cheerfully, "Then perhaps we will just have to win them over. Come, has your engagement been announced yet?"

"Yes."

He frowned. "But—but surely you have not been affianced to this Drakefield for long. Surely we have a few weeks anyway."

"I have been affianced to him for two months, and we are to be married within the week."

He looked shocked. "Sarah, why did you not tell me of this?"

The tears started to her eyes afresh. "I did not know how." It sounded quite cowardly, so she added, "I thought there was nothing we could do, in any case. You were in Spain."

He laid his head back upon the pillow with an expression of anguish, and Sarah was filled with remorse. "Was—was the apothecary of help?" she inquired timidly.

"Yes, he prescribed a draught which has seemed to lessen the fever." He released her hand and laid his good arm across his forehead, closing his eyes with a grimace. "I think perhaps I had better have a rest and try to digest this news as best I may."

She was stricken with guilt. Here he was lying wounded and in great pain, and she had given him the worst news he could possibly have. It had probably been far too much of a strain for his weakened system. Without thinking, she leaned over to give him a chaste kiss on the cheek. His eyes flew open. With his good arm he caught her and pulled her down to an uncomfortably close distance.

"Do not worry, my darling," he breathed. "I will find a way out of this somehow. We will be married, never fear— even if we have to scandalize the world to do it. I will show your parents your letters. I will do whatever it takes to reconcile them to this match." His words were beginning to slur with his weariness.

Dear heavens, he still thought she wished to be married to him! And if he showed her parents those letters . . . She could not bear the thought of it. She pulled herself free. "Alan—" she began.

"No, my love, not another word. You leave it in my hands." His eyes were lined with weariness and pain. "I think I had better rest now."

"But Alan, I must tell you—"

"Ssssh." His eyelids were drooping.

"Alan—"

He did not respond.

She walked over to him. He had fallen asleep almost instantly. She noticed a bottle lying upon the table. She picked it up and examined it. Laudanum. He had probably taken a dose for the pain just before her arrival.

Well, there would be no sense in trying to rouse him now. Dear heavens, what was she to do? She did not wish to—in fact, she would not marry him. She realized that even if she had not fallen in love with Drakefield, Alan would still be an unattractive spouse. She had not liked to hear all his concern about her family's finances, for one thing. And even though he could be very charming, he was a little . . . well, a little superficial, after all. Of course, she felt sorry for him, but at the same time she was somewhat frightened.

It was then that the thought occurred. He was unconscious. What was to keep her from finding the letters and taking them with her? She walked over to the oxbow secretary, opened the top, and began to rifle through the papers in it.

The manservant stepped into the room. Sarah jumped

backward. He looked at Alan sleeping peacefully upon the divan and looked back at her curiously.

"Y-your master . . . he wanted to write a letter . . . I said I would do it, of course, and I was just looking for some writing paper—ah! He has fallen asleep! Well, it will just have to wait until my next visit, I suppose. She walked over to the side table, picked up her bonnet, and tied it on. "Mary," she called, "it is time for us to go."

She was in an inextricable predicament. The rain was still falling. Heavyhearted, she climbed into the carriage with the maid beside her, and they started upon their way home. She was gazing listlessly out of the window when she happened to spy a familiar-looking black phaeton drawn by a pair of black horses. Of course, it could not be, since Drakefield had his cricket match today.

It was a little hard to see, with the rain and with the phaeton's top up, but as it approached, she observed to her surprise that it indeed was Drakefield driving. Burdened with her guilty secret, she shrank back into the corner of the carriage so as not to be discovered, but she needn't have worried. All of his attention was focused upon the companion at his side. Sarah peered out of the corner of the window in an attempt to glimpse who it was. As his companion turned her face in Sarah's direction, she could not help but gasp. It was Annabella riding with Drakefield, and she was leaning upon his arm in a most familiar way.

Sarah felt as if she had been struck a violent blow. He had lied to her about the cricket match, then—and who knows how many other times he had concealed the truth? He and Lady Fernsbury were involved, just as she had suspected all along. The feeling of misery grew until it threatened to overwhelm her.

She could not cry with her maid beside her, so instead she just stared numbly into space. How ironic it was! She was engaged to two men—one of whom, though possibly in love with her, she did not wish to marry. The other, with whom she was in love, clearly was in love with someone else. She drew in a shuddering breath. She would not marry

Alan—and she could not marry Drakefield, given that it was to be nothing more than a marriage of convenience.

What was she to do? Various scenarios played themselves over in her mind, beginning with her parents' shock and disappointment when Alan showed them the letters. She'd have little choice but to marry him then. Her reputation would be ruined forever. And Drakefield—well, she did not want to think about him, after all. She could not face this—face the collapse of all her dreams and aspirations. It was as if a voice had spoken in her mind. "Leave," it urged.

It was an attractive idea. Neither one could marry her if she were absent. She started to laugh aloud bitterly at the thought, but ceased abruptly when she caught the startled expression upon her maid's face. But where could she go? Her good friends were all in London—there would be no escape here. She could not simply set off for points unknown by herself. She racked her brain for an idea. She had spent most of the pin money she had saved upon furbelows for the wedding and the apothecary for Alan. Where could she go with the little she had?

A childhood memory surfaced in her mind. Of laughing and playing happily with her cousins at Uxbridge. Her uncle and his family lived there. Of course! They had often invited her to come for a visit. No one would think of looking for her there immediately. She would flee to Uxbridge.

Another problem arose in her mind. How was she to get there? Even the coach would probably be too expensive, and she did not know which inn to go to. Besides, it would be easy enough to trace her movements if their carriage was to take her to the coaching inn. It was then that the great idea occurred. Her uncle had often recommended it, and had shared all the particulars with her. Her mother considered it a most vulgar way to travel, but that must mean that the fare was quite reasonable. It would suit her needs perfectly. But how was she to get to Paddington?

By the time she arrived home, her head ached from all the thinking. She meant to go straight to her room and excuse herself from dinner because of illness, but as she stepped into the hallway, there was a sound from the drawing room and a head peeped out of it. Despite the way she felt, she managed to force a smile. "Mr. Sheephouse, how are you today?"

"Well, thanks." Encouraged, he bowed as she approached. "Came to see if Bertie wished to go with me to the mill in Brentford tomorrow. Missed him, of course."

She smiled at him, hoping he would leave.

"I see you've just come in or I would offer to take you somewhere. How are you?"

"Quite all right," answered Sarah untruthfully but politely when the inspiration hit. She caught him by the sleeve and drew him into the drawing room, closing the door behind her.

"Mr. Sheephouse, you once said that you would be happy to do me a service."

"Most pleased," he said, bowing again to her.

"Well, have you any engagements for tomorrow—early in the morning?"

14

SARAH KNEW BETTER than to attempt to sleep that night, though she permitted her maid to dress her in her nightgown, so as not to awaken suspicions. She had a great deal of difficulty deciding what to wear and what to pack in the one bandbox that she thought she might be able to carry. She could scarcely bring any proper luggage. Her uncle and her aunt would have to understand. At least she hoped they would understand.

She settled upon the pale gray watered silk dress and a rather drab gray lustring pelisse. They were well made but should prove unmemorable for those persons she encountered. She selected a close bonnet of gray sarcenet to accompany her ensemble. It was old-fashioned, indeed it was rather dowdy, but anyone would have difficulty in seeing her face.

She was relieved when the rain ceased during the night. It had struck her that a rainy trip could prove most unpleasant.

A thousand reasons occurred to her as to why she should not go, but she could not imagine remaining. Perhaps she could be of some service to her aunt and uncle as a sort of nursemaid for the younger children—they had often praised her skill with them. Or perhaps she could find a position in a school. What her relatives would say when she arrived upon their doorstep with nothing but a bandbox, she dreaded to think. Well, she would not worry about that bridge until she crossed it.

She had thought to leave a note, but after crumpling several papers she abandoned the attempt. What was there to say, after all? She could not make them understand in a few short sentences why she had left, and perhaps it was better not to try.

The little Limoges clock chimed six, and she proceeded to tiptoe downstairs. Although the household staff would already be awake at this hour, they would not all be at their posts yet, and she hoped to escape detection. She was fortunate, for though she heard voices, there was no one in the hallway and she saw no one as she slipped through the door.

She found Sheepnose waiting outside for her. Really, it was most fortunate that his intellect was not great, for he had not thought to ask her why she needed a ride so early in the morning. He seemed a little surprised to see her bandbox and even more surprised to hear that her maid would not be accompanying her, but she explained glibly that she was going to visit relatives.

He accepted her words at face value and they set off for Paddington. She had not been abroad at this hour before, and she was surprised to see how busy the streets were. It was fortunate, for it obviated the necessity to make conversation. Her companion seemed perfectly happy just to drive. Their trip passed in harmonious silence.

It wasn't until they were approaching Paddington that he asked where she needed to be dropped. He was obviously startled when she told him that she needed to go to the Basin. More questions followed and she was forced to admit that she meant to travel on the canal boat. He looked at her with such apparent shock that she felt the need to embroider her tale a little.

"My uncle has always said what a jolly trip it is—and they will be meeting me in Uxbridge, of course."

"Travelling alone on a canal boat. Rather vulgar company. Seems cursed odd, if you don't mind my saying so. Your mother and father know about it?"

"Oh, yes."

They reached the Basin, and he pulled up the horses and simply stared at her in an unnerving, unblinking way. She blushed. "Well, the truth is that they do not know. It—it is a matter—well, I cannot explain. But I truly am going to my aunt and uncle's in Uxbridge, so I will be fine."

"Expecting you, are they?"

She could not quite meet his gaze. "No," she was forced to admit. "But they will be happy to see me, I know. They have invited me many times."

"Hmph."

He leaped down from the carriage, took her bandbox, and assisted her out, before turning to his groom to give him instructions.

After he had finished, she was thanking him prettily when she was surprised to see the groom climb up into the carriage and drive it off.

"What on earth?"

"Since you're determined, you need an escort. Fail in my duty to Bertie if I let you go off alone. Obligation and all that."

The last thing Sarah wished for was a companion. "You are very kind, but I am certain that I will manage by myself."

His jaw was set stubbornly. "Mean to go. Buy my own ticket. You can't stop me."

She realized reluctantly that he was right and heaved a sigh. "Very well," she said in an ungracious manner, "though I think it will be rather a dull trip for you."

He shook his head. "Something new," he offered gallantly. "Never been to Uxbridge."

She had had enough of men and the last thing she wanted was to be saddled with another one, but she tried to remain sanguine. It was not as if all her plans were overset. She was relieved to find that the fare was only a half crown, a substantial savings over what the coach fare undoubtedly would have been. Still, it left just one guinea, along with a few meager shillings and pence in her reticule, and she heaved another sigh. "It is really too ridiculous," she told her companion. "If I had known you would be with me, I would simply have had you drive us to Uxbridge."

His face brightened. "Happy to be of service." Then it fell. "Forgot," he said sadly. "No carriage."

It was not worth the trouble of making a reply. It was now nearly eight o'clock, when the boat would embark. She looked around them. There was not a great deal to see except for wharves and warehouses. "I suppose we can sit here and wait," she said, taking a seat on a nearby bench.

He followed her example. "Hope they serve breakfast on the boat. I'm cursed hungry."

When at last they were allowed to board and the horses were hitched and the boat set off, Sheepnose's wish was fulfilled. He stuffed himself happily with buns and fruit and could not seem to imagine why Sarah did not wish to do so.

"Better eat," he'd advised between mouthfuls of pear. "Get sick otherwise."

"You had better listen to your brother, young lady," an elderly woman advised her officiously. She had already become a thorn in Sarah's side by remarking loudly upon their boarding that Sarah and Sheepnose looked like a young couple who were "up to no good." She had elaborated upon her theory by supposing in carrying tones that they were probably embarked upon a runaway match. Sarah was ready to voice her annoyance when Sheepnose had surprised her by ingeniously informing the woman that they were brother and sister. The suspicious woman then had ventured to observe that there was no resemblance between them. He thrust his chin at her pugnaciously, all the while clenching his admirable fists, so that the woman hastily had retracted her statement and instead had appointed herself as their temporary guardian.

It was the most tragic moment in her life, and with Sheepnose beside her Sarah felt it dwindling rapidly into farce. If it had been anyone else, she would have felt like pouring out her soul to them. Clavering, for instance. Of course, Clavering was Drakefield's friend. He was hardly likely to be impartial. Unconsciously she heaved another sigh.

"Your sister seems to be in the dumps," commented another to Sheepnose.

"Well . . ." It took a moment for inspiration to strike him. "Her pet canary bird died. She was most attached to it.

Cheery little beggar. Sang like the devil all the day long," he improvised shrewdly.

Of course, she had to admit that she had to be grateful to Sheepnose also. The elderly lady had been one of the least serious of her immediate problems. Sarah had thought that she looked like a positive dowd in her gray ensemble, but she had realized too late that in comparison to most of the other passengers she looked a veritable fashion plate. She had attracted a great deal of male attention, but with Sheepnose beside her they had confined themselves to speaking looks and remarks muttered only among themselves. With the crowd jostling all about them, there was no telling what sort of personal insults she might have suffered.

It was impossible not to think black thoughts of her future. Her old schoolmistress had often traveled by canal boat, she recalled. If it was her destiny in life to take up that profession, this was the sort of company she would be keeping in the future. An old man sitting across from her belched loudly and winked at her. To think that she might have been a leader of society, that just weeks ago Lady Castlereagh had spoken to her at Almack's. How are the mighty fallen, she quoted disconsolately.

Sheepnose, though he had not planned upon making this trip, was apparently the sort to try to make the best of his situation. He had observed with interest and some expertise as the horses were hitched to pull the boat down the length of the canal, and had commented that they looked like sturdy beasts. His remarks seemed to please their drivers who, recognizing that he knew horseflesh, had taken an unaccountable liking to him. He seemed childishly happy to be informed of all the sights along the way—exclaimed when he saw Wormwood Scrubs, which apparently had something to do with pugilism, admired the spires of Streatham and Croydon, the foliage of Box Hill, and the commanding tower of Leith. He was fascinated by the work of the "leggers" who propelled the boat through the tunnels by lying on their backs and walking along the roof of it with their feet, and indeed waxed so enthusiastic that they offered to let him join them, which he promptly did. Sarah might have expired of embarrassment if her misery had been less all-consuming.

She was feeling more and more that this trip had been a mistake. She would have done better to have remained at home and told her parents the truth. They would have been shocked and wounded by the letters, but now she realized they would have accepted her word that despite being indiscreet, she had not actually done anything of which they should be ashamed. They would certainly not have forced her into marriage with Alan because of the letters. Nor, did she think, would they have insisted upon her marrying Drakefield once she had told them what she knew about him. At the thought of Drakefield, despite herself, her eyes filled with tears. All the rest might have been bearable without that. She might have contrived a way to obtain the letters, or at least she would have told Alan flatly that she would not marry him. She had been responsible for wrecking his life as well as her own, but she knew that marrying him would not repair matters. What a fool she had been. She extracted a handkerchief and wiped at her eyes.

"Odd how some ladies gets so attached to birds," commented one of Sheepnose's new friends to him.

"Well, it used to come at a whistle. Used to eat out of her hand too. Knowing little beggar."

"Do you mean that she used to let it fly about the house?" exclaimed the elderly lady, shocked.

"Oh, yes. Like one of the family. Came and sat at table with us when dinner was announced."

Sarah thought Sheepnose was carrying matters too far, but his credulous audience apparently accepted every word as true, though there were exclamations of surprise and amazement.

"How—" The elderly lady glanced at Sarah and lowered her voice. "How did it die?"

Sheepnose assumed an appropriately mournful expression. "Cat."

"Cat?"

"Cat." He nodded his head sorrowfully. "Came in the window when no one was looking. Poor little Dickey. One moment singing his little heart out, then the next . . . One pounce—and nothing but a few feathers to tell the tale. He'll never sing to us again, poor fellow."

He was becoming quite carried away with his account. There were some angry exclamations, and one plump lady sniffed audibly before extracting her pocket handkerchief.

It was true, thought Sarah blindly, that she would not be in this unbearable position if she hadn't taken it upon herself to run away. Why had she had such an idiotical notion? She took hold of Sheepnose's sleeve and pulled him down to her.

"I'm going back, do you hear? I'm not going to stay in Uxbridge."

"Excellent idea. Boat makes a round-trip passage."

She had to grit her teeth together to keep herself from screaming. "I am not going back on the boat—not if I can help it. It you have enough for coach fare for the both of us, I think we should take one back to London."

"Even better idea. I've plenty of the ready since I was going to Brentford today." A look of regret passed over Sheepnose's face. "Daresay it was a great mill."

If she had been inclined to offer him any comfort, she could not have done so, for now there were shrieks and exclamations from the other passengers. Her attention attracted by the gesturing hands, Sarah stared at the road behind them to see black horses drawing a black phaeton wildly along it. Except for his black top hat, the driver was garbed all in white, which dispelled a notion she had in her brain, and he appeared to be trying to signal the boat. He was shouting something at it, but was having trouble being heard over the answering halloos of the passengers. They were approaching a bridge, and he was forced to slow his horses as the gate approached. By the time they came out from under the bridge he was much nearer to them.

"Sarah!"

Was she dreaming, or was it her name she heard?

"Sarah! Sarah!"

She looked up, then rose, then rushed over to the side of the boat. It was. It was Drakefield, clad in his cricketing clothes. Apparently he did not feel the need to wear black for sporting contests. He had slowed his phaeton to the boat's pace now.

"Sarah!"

What did etiquette dictate in such a situation? She did not really want to speak to him, yet at the same time she did not want him driving his carriage alongside them, calling her name the rest of the way to Uxbridge. Compromising, she leaned out slightly and waved a handkerchief to let him know she was on board.

He must have seen it, for now he yelled a sentence at them.

"What?" Sarah cupped a hand to her ear to show that she did not hear.

He yelled again, but she was still having trouble hearing him over the chuckles and comments of the passengers. "He says he'll meet you in Uxbridge, deary," an appreciative woman, who had the appearance of a farmer's wife, informed her.

Sarah gave another wave to show that she had received his message, then sank slowly back onto her seat, keenly aware of all the pairs of interested eyes upon her. The questions and speculations were rising thick and fast, but Sheepnose made a last heroic effort.

"Well, of all the luck! That was our brother Robert. Daresay he's found Sally another canary bird."

His audience, older and wiser, greeted him with skepticism this time.

Sarah was fortunate in one respect. They had very nearly reached their destination, so she didn't have to endure their scrutiny for long.

When she disembarked at Uxbridge, thinking she had never been so glad to leave a company of people in her life, Drakefield was standing waiting for her. He was pale with fury, but he did not say a word, merely taking her none too gently by the arm. "Come with me," he said.

"But there is Mr. Sheephouse. He accompanied me to Uxbridge." She met the angry look in Drakefield's eyes and her own fell. "He is a friend of Bertie's and he would not let me go alone."

"Well, thank God he had enough sense for that, at least." He released her and strode over to where Sheepnose was being bidden affectionate farewells by the company.

"You'll have to take the groom's seat. Daresay it will be uncomfortable, but I will get you back to London."

Sheepnose followed docilely along behind him.

Drakefield helped Sarah in, then clambered in himself, and after making sure that Sheepnose was settled, he set off spankingly. Sheepnose leaned forward.

"Did you get a change in Uxbridge?"

"No, these are still my own. They had a breather there, and they'll last us back to town now."

Sarah had to feel sorry for Sheepnose. At best it was an uncomfortable seat, and with the way Drakefield was bowling down the road it must be well nigh unbearable. He did not complain, however, but sat placidly enough, though he held tight to his seat with both hands.

She had never seen Drakefield drive like this. In fact, she had never seen him in a temper before. It was obvious from the clenching and unclenching of a jaw muscle that he was having difficulty controlling his fury. It made him a little more human, she had to admit, though she still didn't know what he had to be angry about. She had not been the one carrying on a long-running affair with an old paramour— even though perhaps it might look like it. He would not know about that, in any case. At least she did not think he would know about it. She forced herself to turn her mind to her own anger. What right did he have to come take her home like a schoolgirl? Of course, he was her fiancé. But he would not be for long, after all—not when she got through with him. She would let him know exactly what she thought of him! Telling her he was at a cricket match when he actually was doing who-knows-what with Annabella! He had probably lied to her from the very first. Hmph! Much right he had to be angry.

She had worked herself into a proper rage, and it took all her powers of self-control to keep from venting it. It was

particularly hard when they reached the outskirts of London
and Drakefield had to slow the carriage, though she supposed she should have been glad of it for Sheepnose's sake.
Drakefield asked Sheepnose curtly if they might drop him
at home.

"No, prefer to go home with Miss Baxter. Since I took
her, I should return her, I think. Besides"—his eyes brightened—"might happen to see Bertie."

"I should think it very likely that you would," responded
Drakefield ominously.

Accordingly, they all drove to Tavistock Square. Sarah's
dread grew as Drakefield marched her up the stairs. In the
drawing room, she discovered her whole family, as well as
Eglantyne, anxiously waiting for her.

"Sarah!" Her mother was the first to rush over and hug
her, followed by Eglantyne, while the men contented themselves with patting her on the back. There were tearful
thanks offered to Drakefield, too, but when Bertie saw
Sheepnose his face grew stern.

"Fine friend you are. What do you mean by running off
with my sister?"

"Oh, Bertie!" Sarah caught his sleeve to attract his attention. "Mr. Sheephouse was my savior. He wouldn't abandon
me at the Basin, despite my urgings, and he accompanied
me on the canal boat in order to protect me from what I
must say was a crowd of very vulgar persons, even though
he planned to go to a mill in Brentford instead today. And
he had to ride on the groom's seat all the way back from
Uxbridge since he had sent his own carriage home at
Paddington."

The change in Bertie's expression was ludicrous to be-
hold. "I say!" he commented weakly, then thrusting out a
hand, his gripped Sheepnose's firmly. "I say. In your debt
and all that."

"It was nothing," said Sheepnose modestly.

Another thought occurred to Bertie. "Eglantyne, that is,
Miss Adstock, come here. You have waited far too long to
meet my oldest and dearest friend, Arthur Sheephouse.
Sheephouse, this is Miss Adstock."

"Most delighted, Miss Adstock," said Sheepnose, bowing gracefully. He straightened himself, grinning broadly with happiness.

"Mr. Sheepnose, would you care to remain for dinner with us? We will be informal tonight," said Mrs. Baxter. "The rest of us would like to offer you our thanks also."

"Delighted," said Sheepnose, bowing again.

"And Lord Drakefield, you will stay also?"

He shook his head slightly. "No, I appreciate your hospitality, but I am hardly dressed for it."

"Thank you." Her mother was holding Drakefield's hand in her own, and she looked ready to cry.

He nodded briefly and would have turned and left, but Sarah cried out after him, "Wait!"

He waited expressionlessly as she crossed the room.

"We must talk."

His countenance was wooden. "I will return tomorrow afternoon. We will talk then."

There was nothing else she could say. He gave one of his exquisite bows to the company, then turned on his heel and left. Tears started to Sarah's eyes, but she dashed them away hastily.

15

THE SLENDER GENTLEMAN carefully limped up the street, leaning hard upon his cane. Although it was well past three in the morning, his cravat was as spotless and unwrinkled as if he had risen just an hour before. He paused in front of a house to observe a candle burning within, and heaved a small sigh. He walked to the door, lifted his cane, and rapped sharply upon it.

"Open the door. It's me, Clavering."

There was no response, so he rapped all the harder. After a few moments he muttered a curse and tried the door. It swung open easily. He let himself in, shutting it behind him. A single candle guttered low in a sconce upon the wall.

"Drake!" There was no response, so he pushed open the dining room door. The Black Dandy, wearing soiled cricketing garb, was slouched in a chair, while on the table in front of him sat a bottle. Clavering's lips curled downward for a moment, but he did not say a word. He expelled a slow breath, and then began his halting way across the room.

"Your manservant left the door unlocked. Any ruffian might find his way in here."

Drakefield did not reply or indeed make any sign that he had heard.

Clavering lifted the bottle, shook it, and then gave it a sniff. "Nearly empty. Whisky too. Thought perhaps I'd convinced you to give it up." He walked over to the sideboard and helped himself to a glass, then poured a portion of what was left in the bottle into it. "I hate to see a man drink alone. They say it is good for pain—I will make the attempt."

He seated himself, took a sip and grimaced, then took another one. There were several moments of silence before he spoke again. "Very pretty night's work. How you will endear yourself to your bride. I daresay she would be overjoyed by this picture. You are to be married in two days, after all, aren't you?"

For the first time his words seemed to penetrate. "No." Drakefield roused himself enough to empty the remains of the bottle into his own glass. "Doesn't work for pain. I've tried."

"Was that negative the answer to my question about the wedding or not?"

"No wedding." His face bleak, Drakefield drained his glass at a swallow to his friend's rueful astonishment. He lifted up the bottle to pour another, realized it was empty, and threw it across the room, where it shattered noisily into fragments. "No wedding . . . not for me, that is."

Silence reigned again for several moments, and Clavering saw that no more confidences were to be forthcoming. "Hadn't you better tell me about it?" he suggested. "Not only am I your oldest friend, but you know I also have an insatiable curiosity about such things. What is more, I also count myself as a friend of Miss Baxter's. I should like very much to know what has occurred."

Drakefield's eyes were fixed broodingly upon the floor. "She's not going to marry me. Going to marry an oily fellow name of Grenfell—wounded war hero like yourself." He spat the words out contemptuously.

"Grenfell . . . now where I have I heard that name before?" Clavering frowned with a sudden thought. "Lancashire family?" he asked.

"Dashed if I know . . . or care."

"This all seems rather sudden. Did Miss Baxter tell you the news herself?"

He pulled in his lips as if he were trying to repress some deep-seated pain. "No," he said at length. "Oily fellow did."

"Then how—?"

"She ran away yesterday in order to avoid marrying me." He met his friend's eyes with bitterness in his own. "Is that proof enough for you?"

Despite himself, Clavering could not help giving an exclamation of surprise. "She went off to Gretna Green with this fellow?"

Drakefield shook his head. "No. With another. To Uxbridge."

In any other situation Clavering's bewilderment would have seemed comical. "Uxbridge?"

Drakefield heaved a sigh. "Yes, she had relatives there that she meant to shelter with or some such thing."

Clavering shook his head. "This all sounds most unlike Miss Baxter to me. And if she wished to marry this Grenfell, why didn't she run away with him?"

"I suppose because he's still recovering from his wound. Went with a fellow named Sheepface instead. Looks like a sheep, too. Thought I'd go mad until I saw that at least she did not wish to marry him instead of me."

"My dear fellow, I am afraid that you have lost me entirely. Perhaps you had better start with your cricket game."

Drakefield's eyes focused blearily on him again. "How did you know I had a cricket game?"

"I might have guessed it from your appearance, but I saw Fairfax at the club. He told me you left just as it was beginning. That was how I knew that something must be wrong."

"Very well." Drakefield heaved a sigh. "Her brother arrived at the match this—yesterday morning, asking if I knew anything about her whereabouts. Of course, I knew nothing. I returned with him to Tavistock Square and we questioned her maid. She knew no more than we did, except that Sarah had been visiting a young gentleman of late. I still did not suspect the truth. Bertie went to visit the Adstocks in case they'd had any word, and I drove to where the 'young gentleman' lived."

"Grenfell."

"Yes." He saw that Clavering was waiting for him to continue. "When I arrived there I found, as I said, this oily fellow—lying there with a hole in his shoulder—couldn't help but feel bad about that, of course, though I wish they had put the ball through his heart."

"Drake . . ."

"I cannot help how I feel. He is not the right man for her, no matter what she thinks. He will not make her happy. He's shallow—concerned with no one but himself, wants only her money—that much is clear."

"But Sarah herself did not say she wished to marry him."

"Here." He thrust a piece of paper at Clavering. "He gave me a letter to show her parents—'to win their consent to the match'—as he put it. I told him it would hardly ingratiate him with them."

Clavering read the letter carefully, then looked up. "Is it her hand?"

"Yes."

"But this was written in December, and she has not even written the year. Why, it is over half a year old at least and perhaps it dates from her schoolgirl days."

"He was shipped over in December. Says that is when their correspondence began."

"Well, does he have any recent letters from her?"

Drakefield frowned. "More recent. How recent, I can't say. Thing is, he told me he'd send them to the papers, do whatever necessary to make her parents approve the match. Told him from my reading of her parents it would be more likely to make them forbid him the house—if they haven't already."

"What a young scoundrel. And yet he hopes to win their approval—the money is the critical matter, then."

"That is my impression." Drakefield took the letter back and stuck it into his breast pocket. "On the other hand, if he's the one she wants to marry, her parents would do better to yield. Told them so. Told them they had no business trying to force her into marriage with me when her heart was given to another."

"Force her into marriage?"

Drakefield shrugged. "That's what the fellow said and I think he must be right."

"My dear fellow, I have never seen a single sign that Miss Baxter was *forced* to endure your company. In fact, I have it on very good authority that—"

Drakefield pulled out the letter again and waved it in his friend's face. "What could be better authority than this— her own words in her own hand?" He was struggling to get the words out now. "She says she loves him and wishes to marry him. She has never said either of those things to me."

There was a queer look upon Clavering's face. "I . . . have you ever said either of those phrases to her?"

His words clearly took Drakefield by surprise. "No." He frowned. "But she must have known."

"Do you love her? Do you wish to marry her?"

"Why—why . . ." He paused for a moment, then frowned again consideringly. "I suppose I do," he said softly as the realization began to dawn.

Clavering smiled. "Then why don't you try telling her so?"

Drakefield met his friend's eyes uncertainly. "But if she is in love with this Grenfell . . ."

"I cannot imagine anyone forcing Miss Baxter into a marriage against her will. She is a young lady of strong character."

"Her mother did say that she thought it was merely an infatuation that had run its course, but I dismissed it as wishful thinking."

"I think that if Miss Baxter truly had wished to marry Grenfell, she would not have run away. In fact, though I do not like to say it, it appears to me very much as if she were running away from you instead."

"Running away from me—why?"

"I think you had better ask her."

Sarah had been prepared for reproaches, reprimands, and tears, but to her surprise there was a complete absence of all but the latter. To her astonishment, not a single word of fault-finding was issued regarding her flight. Instead she found herself treated with the exquisite care due a much sought-after guest who has arrived unexpectedly and might decide to depart on a whim.

The excessive kindness with which she was welcomed was far more painful to her than the severest of scoldings would have been. They invited her to take dinner in her chamber if she felt tired. It had been Sarah's intention to do so, but at their suggestion she replied that she would be happy to join the company.

It was odd that her flight was not mentioned once during the course of the meal, though Sheepnose, seemingly oblivious to these undercurrents, entertained the company with an account of what it was like to travel upon a canal boat.

By the time dinner was over, Sarah could stand it no longer. It was a violation of convention, but as the ladies were preparing to rise, she addressed her parents. "Mother, Father, I must speak to you." In silent acquiescence the others withdrew.

She took a deep breath. "I am so sorry for the worry I caused you."

"My darling!" Her mother crossed over to her and gave her a quick hug. "We are so sorry also. It was all our fault. If only we had known! But you seemed so happy with Lord Drakefield."

Her father had risen and now stood beside her also. He cleared his throat. "We would not wish you to be unhappy, Sarah. If your heart is set upon marrying this Grenfell, then marry him you shall and hang the scandal."

She turned to him with puzzled blue eyes. "But I do not wish to marry him!"

It was their turn to be confused. "But Lord Drakefield said—" her mother began.

"He showed us the letter and told us about the others," added her father helpfully.

Sarah had to blush. "So you know about the letters."

"Yes."

She took a deep breath. "I am so sorry. It seems I have done so many things wrong that I cannot even keep count." She looked at both of their faces, more dear to her than ever, through full eyes. "I wrote those letters months ago, when I thought I was in love with Alan. Even though . . . even though I was indiscreet, I give you my word that I did not do anything of which I would be ashamed. I do not wish to marry him, but if you think it would be best for me to do so, I will."

Her parents broke into delighted smiles. "That's not what we think at all," said her father, patting her heartily upon the back. "So you do wish to marry Lord Drakefield, after all?" exclaimed her mother simultaneously.

Sarah was having trouble holding back the tears. "No, I do not wish to marry Lord Drakefield. In fact, I cannot marry him. I-I have my reasons." At the last minute, she was unable to share the truth about him. Was it just her foolish pride?

To her surprise, there were no questions and no admonitions, though their disappointment was obvious. Her father patted her gently once or twice more, before turning back to swallow the last of his wine. Her mother took one of her hands and squeezed it sympathetically. "This is all so very hard for you, isn't it? Do you wish for your father to go see Mr. Grenfell and Lord Drakefield for you?"

She smiled bitterly. She had wounded Grenfell, her parents, probably Drakefield's pride, and the resulting scandal would be even harder upon them all. Magnanimously, they still sought to soften the blow for her. "I think that perhaps I should have to deal with the consequences of my own actions," she said, her countenance bleak. "I will go call upon Alan tomorrow, taking a footman with me," she added quickly, "and I will tell him the truth. When Lord Drakefield calls tomorrow, I will inform him also."

Her mother frowned. "Do we need to send a notice to the papers? We will have to send notes to all those people we invited, and to package all those wedding gifts again so that they may be returned."

It would be a great deal of unpleasant work. It made Sarah's head ache just to think of it. "Let me speak to Lord Drakefield first. I would not like to do anything without his knowledge. Also, he will know best just what to do." She spoke with an almost childlike faith. If only she could trust him as absolutely in other matters.

If it had not been for her exhaustion, sleep would have been out of the question, but instead she fell into bed and did not awaken until sunlight was streaming through the window. Her stomach turned as she remembered the unpleasant tasks that awaited her today. Well, there was no point in postponing them. She rose, dressed, and forced herself to swallow some tea and toast even though she had never felt less like eating. Her parents stared at her anxiously across the breakfast table.

"Are you sure you don't wish me to go with you, Sarah?" inquired her father.

She shook her head with a tight smile. "You have your work today, Father."

"Are you sure you wouldn't like me to ride with you, at least, Sarah? I will wait in the carriage," offered her mother.

She shook her head again. "You are both too good to me, but no."

When she stood outside the door to Alan's chambers some forty-five minutes later, she wondered if she had been hasty. She badly wished for support of some kind. After her footman had knocked upon the door, the manservant opened it. In some surprise, she saw that a trunk and several valises stood packed in the outer chamber. Indeed, it appeared that Alan was planning to forsake the rooms shortly. To her further shock, when the manservant announced her, Alan came walking into the room. She gaped at him.

"Alan . . . you're walking!"

"Yes, um—well, when the fever left me, I became much better. Still rather weak, of course."

Had he been exaggerating the effects of his illness? She was certain he had not been lying about his wound. They would scarcely have sent him home if it had been only a scratch.

"Here, come into my chamber where we can talk," he said, eying the husky footman.

As he led her into his chamber and she took a chair, she began, "Alan, I have something to tell you."

"I saw that fiancé of yours yesterday," he commented, busily flinging cravats into a suitcase. "You don't mind if I continue to work, do you, my dear? I might make Smithers do this, but he has rather a full job packing up the household effects."

"Where are you going?"

He appeared embarrassed. "Ah . . . well, that is just what I was going to mention to you. You see, after meeting your fiancé yesterday and speaking with him, I could see that there would be no hope of reconciling your family to the match. I-I hope you understand."

A weight lifted from her heart. "I understand perfectly."

"Well, he seems like a good fellow. Make you a good husband, better than I would, I am sure." He paused to cough. "Going to be married myself, you see."

For a moment her mind was blank with shock. "You are? When? To whom?"

He coughed again. "This afternoon, as it so happens. To a neighbor of ours in Lancashire. Seems she had misinterpreted something I had said and had been considering herself as engaged to me all this time. M'parents cut up very stiff, said I'd ruined her reputation and was obliged to marry her—all that sort of balderdash. Of course, I'd said I wouldn't—considered myself engaged to you," he added hastily in a manner which made Sarah certain he was lying.

"In any case, that was when we had our great falling-out this spring, and they cut me off. Dashed if I could see what I was supposed to do about it. I was in Spain, after all."

That was when his letters had suddenly taken on a warm tone, Sarah realized.

"Then Cisley appeared here the other day, weeping on my doorstep and moaning about my promises—" he was continuing in a petulant tone when Sarah cut him off.

"Has she a fortune?" she inquired coolly.

He did not seem to think the question odd. "Not a great

one, but through an intermediary—oh, you saw the vicar here the other day—my parents did agree to make a large settlement upon us also if I did the deed. So I suppose it has all worked out for the best. Ooh." He grimaced, sat down upon the edge of the bed, and adjusted his bandage slightly. At least his wound had not been a false one too. Sarah realized that she now believed him capable of any villainy. What a narrow escape she had had!

She rose. "Well, then there is nothing to do except for me to wish you happy." She held out a hand.

He extended his good one and shook hers. "I must say, you're taking this admirably. I'll wish you happy also, then."

She had forgotten one thing. "Could I have my letters?"

He paled. "Forgot about them." He extracted a bundle from a drawer. "Wouldn't wish for Cisley to see them."

"Thank you. I'll destroy them—and yours also."

"Well . . ." He seemed at a loss as to what else to say. "Good luck, then."

"To you also. Goodbye."

"Goodbye."

She had never felt such relief in her life as when she stepped out that door. Except perhaps as an agreeable flirtation, he had never really had any interest in her. When his parents had cut him off, he had probably been thrown into a panic, and then he had remembered her letters. What a fool she had been! She had played right into his hands. He needed an income and here was an heiress, protesting her devotion to him. She was fortunate that he was not a complete villain, but instead merely the type to take advantage of an opportunity. He might easily have thought to blackmail her after her marriage to Drakefield. She had to shudder as she thought of it. Of course, she would not be marrying Drakefield now, she realized as she suddenly remembered the other unpleasant task awaiting her.

When she arrived home, she saw the black phaeton waiting. She would have to add lateness to her other offenses. She stepped inside, and without even waiting for Fraley to tell her, she strode into the drawing room and closed the door behind her.

The Black Dandy looked very much at his ease. He was reading a copy of *The Sporting Magazine*, and a glass of sherry rested beside him upon the table. He looked so handsome in his well-cut black morning suit that Sarah's heart gave a twinge of pain. He was not hers and never would be. Upon seeing her, he put down the magazine in a leisurely way, rose, and bowed.

There was dead silence for several moments as they regarded each other. The usual commonplaces seemed pointless. He was the first to break the quiet. He cleared his throat. "Your mother told me that you were calling upon Grenfell this morning."

"That is correct."

"I take it I am to wish you happy?" His mouth curled into a sardonic smile. "Even though the wish may perhaps seem odd coming from your current fiancé, I suppose."

She untied her bonnet and laid it upon a table. "You may wish me happy, but not with Lieutenant Grenfell. He is to marry someone else."

"Oh." His expression was unreadable. "Then, if you will forgive my effrontery, I should like to know the status of our own engagement—that is, if you do not mind telling me. Unless, perhaps Mr. Sheephouse is to be the lucky gentleman?"

"There is no need to be insulting." She sat upon a chair and gestured for him to take one also, which he did. "There undoubtedly will be many arrangements to take care of, and I would appreciate your help in knowing what to write and who to inform first and all that sort of thing."

"You overestimate my abilities," he said coolly. "I have never had to break an engagement before, you see. You decidedly have more experience than I."

He was deliberately trying to goad her. Sarah was having trouble keeping her temper, but she fought to maintain her calm. She must strive to remember that he must feel himself to have been wronged, and that his pride was consequently suffering. "I think that we may take care of this matter in a civilized manner without any undue display of bitter feelings toward each other."

He leaped to his feet. "Undue display—" He began to pace about the room, so as to relieve his feelings. "It was not I who leapt into the crudest form of transportation possible in order to flee from you. Can you even begin to imagine my feelings? Searching for you up one end of town and down the other." He halted for a moment, though he continued to speak. "And then there was that pleasant little interview with Grenfell. Yes, that was most entertaining. Not every young lady can boast of having two fiancés—particularly when neither has known of the other's existence."

"Drakefield—"

He took a menacing step toward her. "No, by gad, you will hear me out. And when that slimy fellow had finished with me and I realized I had come to another impasse, I was forced to go to your brother's friend's house and quiz his groom—and I shouldn't even have known to do that except that one of the footmen saw you leave with him."

"Are you finished?"

"No! And then I must make an idiot of myself by driving alongside the canal boat to Uxbridge, foolishly imagining that there was something wrong with you or that you might possibly wish to see me."

He took another step toward her, and she suddenly was frightened. "Drakefield, please—"

"My God! What were you about, Sarah?" His voice, filled with anger, abruptly softened. "Why couldn't you have simply come to me and told me that you wished to end the engagement? I shouldn't have liked it, but it would have been easier for both of us. Your reputation might have been ruined—or worse—by that mad flight." He shook his head painfully, not looking at her now. "I am sorry that you trusted me so little."

Her heart was breaking, but she could not let him see it. That earnest tone. How was he able to manufacture it with such ease? "I—I am sorry. There is nothing else I can say."

He rounded on her. "But why did you do it, Sarah? Can

you explain it to me? It seemed to me that we rubbed along extremely well. At first I thought Grenfell was the problem, but now it is clear that he was not. If you found me so repulsive, so loathsome, you might have had a hundred opportunities to tell me so earlier."

Startled, she stammered, "I-I do not find you loathsome."

"Why won't you marry me, Sarah?"

She shook her head. He leaned over, grasping her shoulders in his hands firmly. "I must have an answer, I will have one." His voice was hoarse with emotion. "Sarah! Sarah, listen to me. Can you say that you do not love me?"

It was a question she had been dreading. She lifted tear-filled blue eyes to his hard gray ones. She could not help but be honest with him. "I do love you . . . but I will not marry you."

The hope that had lit in his face abruptly died. "Why?"

She sighed. "I understand that you need funds—and it is true that we are good companions, but I wish for something more."

"Sarah, are you forgetting—?"

"No, I remember Greenwich and all those other times well, but the lesson I just learned with Grenfell was a hard one. One may be attracted to a gentleman, and it is still not enough upon which to build a life together."

"Sarah, I love you."

How often had she prayed to hear those words. Now it was too late. She shook her head violently and extracted a handkerchief from her reticule. She had certainly required a good supply of them lately.

"Sarah, I am telling you the truth. I love you and I want you to be my wife. Why won't you believe me?"

Oh, what a convincing liar he was. Alan was nothing to him. He had sunk to his knees now, and he gently lifted her chin with one hand, so that her eyes were forced to meet his. She could not postpone telling him any longer.

"I know, you see."

"What do you know?"

"I know about you and Lady Fernsbury."

The dark brows drew together in a frown. "Of course you know. I told you."

She gazed at him as steadily as she was able. "And your friend Clavering and your grandmother told me more. You had already told me enough from what you failed to say."

"Sarah—"

"No, it is your turn to hear me out now. I had my suspicions all along, but they were confirmed that night a few weeks ago at the theater. I knew that you met with her during the interval . . . and you did not mention a word of it to me."

He shook his head in some puzzlement. "She was making a nuisance of herself, and I told her I would not tolerate it any longer. I did not see any reason to tell you about it, and I am sorry that it bothered you." The gray eyes narrowed. "But it did not seem to trouble you such a great deal until now."

This was the moment that she had been dreading—the moment that would dislodge the last particle of hope, the particle that had ignored reality and clung to her, refusing to be dislodged. She felt that she had aged years in these last few days. However grim the truth was, though, she knew that she could not be happy with an illusion.

Sarah drew in a deep breath. "You see, I went to Alan's the day before yesterday to tell him that I did not wish to be engaged to him, though I could not seem to make him understand. As I was coming home, I saw your phaeton and saw you and Lady Fernsbury together inside it. You had told me you would be playing cricket that day."

"You little fool!"

She was unprepared for the burst of wrath, and she drew herself back instinctively. She did not care what he said now. He might call her old-fashioned or bourgeois. She knew that to share him with another would make life unendurable.

"You little fool!" To her surprise, he was laughing now. He pulled her into his arms. "What a terrible two days you have given me!"

She should have drawn back from his arms since they

were no longer engaged, but she was curious as to what amused him. "What is so humorous?"

He drew back and smiled into her eyes. "Little idiot. Did it not occur to you to look at the skies? You grew up with a brother who plays cricket. How were we to perform in that weather? The match was postponed until yesterday."

"But Lady Fernsbury—I saw her holding you—you cannot deny that you love her."

"I can and will. She showed me what she was the night of our engagement party, and never has any man been so thankful for an escape. I was deceived in her completely, which seems all the more strange considering how long I had known her."

"But she was in your carriage—"

"Her carriage had suffered a mishap, and you know how difficult it is to find a hackney in the rain. I took her in, though I found it to be a mistake, for she insisted that she was cold and *would* cling to me. In any case, we shall not have to worry about her anymore. Her husband's eyes were finally opened—by that disgruntled young gentleman that was at the theater that night, as it so happens. Lord Fernsbury was just leaving the house to go in search of Annabella as we drove up. Her behavior in my carriage—for she did not see him immediately—dispelled any doubts."

Here Drakefield paused and gave a little cough. "It was as public and vituperative a row as it has ever been my bad fortune to witness. Neither would listen to reason, though I urged them at least to go inside." He shook his head at the memory. "The long and short of it is that he packed her back to Yorkshire. They left yesterday."

Sarah gave a gasp as she belatedly realized the implication of his words. "He might have called you out!"

"Called out the Black Dandy? Not very likely. Don't you know anything, you dunce? Why he's been known to hit the wafer nineteen times out of twenty at Manton's."

The words were unintelligible to her, but they were irritating. Drakefield seemed similarly afflicted. "Bertie, what are you doing here?"

Her brother had entered her room precipitately, not bothering to knock. With her entire attention consumed by Drakefield's words, Sarah had not heard the door swing open nor the sound of his footsteps upon the Aubusson carpet.

"Just had to share the good news. Since it appears to be over with you two, the Adstocks went ahead and gave their consent for Eglantyne and I to become engaged."

"Congratulations." Drakefield turned to Sarah. "But it is not over between us, is it, my love?"

She shook her head shyly.

"So it's the wedding as planned, then. Good thing, for otherwise you'd look pretty silly on your knees, wouldn't you?" He paused to frown. "Do hope this doesn't mean the Adstocks will change their minds."

Drakefield now rose and took his future brother-in-law by the arm in an attempt to usher him from the room. "I do not think they will, but perhaps you should go speak to them immediately to make certain. If you will excuse us—"

Another figure, a tall, slender, disheveled one, bolted into the room, dragging a protesting footman behind him. "Drakefield! Thank God I've found you at last. I've been searching all over town for you. We've done it! With that last little bit of capital I managed to construct a working model!" He saw Sarah and nodded briefly at her. "Oh, hello, Miss Baxter."

"We'll be rich men, Drakefield, do you hear me? We shall never want for anything again!"

Drakefield, surrendering to the inevitable, pulled Sarah to her feet and placed an arm lightly about her.

"That's wonderful," she said, her eyes glowing. "Oh, Drake, now you may do whatever you wish." She suddenly realized that his newfound wealth might also possibly free him from the obligation of marrying an heiress, but before she could say anything, he held a finger to her lips.

"I am already as rich as any man could be, for I have you, my love."

"Hmph." Bertie was not one to be impressed by any romance but his own. He took the other arrival by his sleeve. "Tell you what—Johnson, isn't it? Why don't you step into the other room with me and have a spot of sherry? Daresay they wish to be alone, and I don't mean to endure it any longer myself."

"D'you have any whisky?" they heard the other asking plaintively as the two unlikely companions exited, followed by a relieved footman.

With the door safely closed, Sarah and Drakefield heard Johnson, out in the hall, exclaim "Clavering?" and heard the latter respond, "Well, is it on or not?" Bertie must have answered him, but all of Sarah's attention was upon Drakefield, who had crossed the room to turn the key in the lock.

"I hope you will forgive me, my love, but now that we finally have an opportunity to be alone together, I do not mean for us to be interrupted again."

As he returned to her, she sank into his welcoming arms and thought she had never experienced such bliss, all the dearer to her because it had been lost. Time would have vanished except that a minute later someone tried the door and then there was a pounding upon it. "Drake," she murmured.

"Shh, my love," he whispered in reply, and the pounding, though it continued, was lost to her ears.

"Hey! Sal . . . Drakefield . . . wedding's just two days away—don't forget." Bertie's voice, reproachful even at high volume, carried through the doors easily.

She could feel Drakefield's lips curl under her own, and now he raised his head and turned his face in the direction of the doorway. "Do not worry. It is occupying all of our attention at the moment. We are attempting to discover new ways to remind ourselves of it." He turned to Sarah, still smiling, and whispered, "Aren't we, my love?"

She said nothing, just closing her eyes and surrendering her lips to his once more.

New from the bestselling, award-winning author of
Silk and Secrets and *Silk and Shadows*

VEILS OF SILK
Mary Jo Putney

Golden-eyed Laura offers hope for a new life to Ian after years of captivity in Central Asia have shattered this army major's dreams. Ian, in turn, offers Laura a marriage proposal she dares to say yes to.

From India's lush plains to its wild mountain passes, they struggle to build a marriage unlike any other. Yet the danger and intrigue that surround them are less perilous than the veiled secrets of their own hearts—for only indomitable courage and unshakable love will free them to claim the fiery passion they both fear . . . and desire.